Girls

GIRLS

Bill James

Constable • London

Constable & Robinson Ltd
3 The Lanchesters
162 Fulham Palace Road
London W6 9ER
www.constablerobinson.com

First published in the UK by Constable,
an imprint of Constable & Robinson Ltd 2006

ISBN 13: 978-1-84529-332-1
ISBN 10: 1-84529-332-0

Printed and bound in the EU

Parts of Chapter 1 and Chapter 10 originally appeared in slightly different form in my short story collection, *The Sixth Man and other stories* (Severn House, 2006).

Chapter One

These days Mansel Shale drove the Jaguar himself owing to the quick death not long ago of his most recent chauffeur and bodyguard, Denzil Lake. Denz was found with the barrels of two Astra .38 pistols in his mouth. Both guns had been fired. Manse thought Denz deserved this. He did not replace him. Once you'd discovered a very trusted staff member secretly snuggling up to your enemies, you worried about giving somebody that kind of close job again. There had definitely been good aspects to Denz. Well, obviously, or would Manse have hired him and kept him on? All right, Denzil had sometimes refused to wear the special driver's navy blue peaked cap particularly bought for him by Manse, but Shale never went into a full rage over this. Denz probably thought the cap made him look like a flunkey subordinate. He *was* a fucking flunkey subordinate but Shale could understand why a man might not want this signposted. Manse put up with the bolshiness. Betrayal was different. Anyone trying it had to go.*

Afterwards, there'd been questions for Manse. Although the .38s belonged to Denz himself, not everybody thought suicide because squeezing both triggers at exactly the same moment would be a tricky one. And some said if he done it himself recoil should of jolted the Astras out of his mouth. However, by now inquiries were fading, luckily. Nobody beside his family would see Denz Lake as worth

---

* *Easy Streets.*

long-term fret, and possibly not them, neither. Now and then, Shale had looked back with quite a slice of longing to the days when Neville Greenage did the driving and so on for him. Nev had been reliable and brilliant. But he had gone off to somewhere in Yorkshire or Tasmania or Austria to start his own operation.

Shale drew up and took a good glance all ways before leaving the Jaguar. Since Lake passed on in that rather skull-wrecked style, Manse did his own look-arounds. The Agincourt hotel car park had a lot of shadows. It was a thing about car parks near buildings. You done some real eye work, especially at vehicles already standing here. Cars gave a lot of cover, above all cars in shadow. The point was, Denzil's dirty scheming and end had come during one of them all-out territory battles that often happened in high commerce – the kind Manse ran. And battles might continue. Always such heavy perils lay near. They could touch anyone in the trade, however major, not just slabs of shoddy like Denz.

Despite shadows, he did not mind the Agincourt too much. Every six months, or a bit less, Manse and Ralph Ember put on a great dinner in the hotel's restaurant for main people from their two firms. Business results and prospects could be talked over in quite a relaxed way. It was Ember who originally suggested these social meetings, but Shale would admit they could be useful. Tonight, there might be difficult moments. Manse knew this. Any bad difficulties – he would squash them, most probably without violence or gunfire, instead through personality. This was leadership. Manse believed in leadership – not frothing, Hitler-type leadership but sturdy. He climbed out of the Jag and moved towards the rear entrance of the hotel. The Agincourt's name was considerably historical, with what was known as overtones. Shale liked the historical item. It gave depth.

Following the meal and after the accounts had been presented, guests was entitled and even encouraged to raise queries. Shale or Ember or both would answer. Hotel employees withdrew. Tonight, as Manse expected, some ratty, scared questions came about the way immigrant dealers from old Soviet Bloc countries had moved in offering all commodities – ganja to crack to big H, plus girls if required – and stealing clients.

Although Manse recognized this was a tough problem, he would not discuss it now. Shale and Ralph always made sure they only spoke about convenient topics at these dinners. For instance, they would never disclose the firms' true profits, or plans by him and Ember to get rid of someone, or more than one, if a more widespread approach grew necessary, as could happen in this new millennium. They did always issue sets of figures for the previous months because it was expected. Shale understood that. But these only gave what Manse thought of as a *wise* or, say, *tactful* version of things, enough to take care of morale.

Shale and Ember had beautiful cooperation between their two companies, and the dinners were set up to help this happy arrangement. They took turns on a yearly basis to organize the meals, pick the wines and settle up. It was Manse's year as host. He loved it. In the two or three meetings he presided at, he could show he knew as much about grand fucking vintages as that loud smoothie, Ralph, with all his glossy wordage and grammar.

The firms' dinners always took place on a Monday night. Normally, the restaurant would be closed then but it could be booked for private parties. Manse thought the room more or less all right. Ancient weapons and other items hung on the walls such as swords, longbows, shields, suits of armour, boars' heads, and what Shale heard one lad call halberds, or like that – some pieces real, most mock. The hotel put on imitation medieval banquets at weekends, and these old war articles was supposed to give atmosphere then. In Mansel's view this wall stuff looked childish and naff and knocked dignity from the

Agincourt name. He thought of that famous song, 'Bring me my bow of burning gold, bring me my arrows of desire.' A bow and arrow of plastic did not fit this idea. But Manse believed in tolerance, up to quite a reasonable point. You could not expect refined taste from every bugger.

The firms asked for an ordinary menu and drink, with ordinary crockery and ordinary service, not waitresses putting too much on show up top, as in the banquet ads. Manse heard this used to be the rule in what was known as wenching times way back – such as the famed Nell Gwyn wearing sketchy garments to get the king going. But, for God's sake, the firms' Monday sessions was serious gatherings, where Manse and Ralph, chairmen of a pair of work-together companies, reported with total thoroughness and detail to their best personnel everything they could be allowed to know. Friendliness and some jollity seemed right in Shale's opinion, yes, but not a lot of boob skin.

Tonight, jollity was scarce because of them competition worries. As a sideline, some of the new, foreign dealers ran very young, smuggled-in, Eastern European girls, such as Albanian, who was fed drugs to hook them, and then put on the street. These girls sold the products, as well as themselves. This was a hellish tactic. Some Brits was starting to imitate these foreign dealers and mix a trade of commodities and whores. One name around that Shale heard was Adrian Cologne, from Hull or Preston or somewhere like that, although the second name sounded overseas.

'Ralph and myself personally, we definitely got the whole situation in mind,' Shale said, as the bleats piled up. These came from members of both firms.

'Unquestionably,' Ember said.

'Yes, Manse, Ralphy, you say that but these people are –'

'We definitely got it in mind,' Shale said. 'Ralph and self, we note all factors, you can believe it.'

'This goes without saying,' Ralph told them.

'But Manse, Ralph, if we don't –'

'This is an area known in boardrooms and such as "executive action", meaning leave it to Ralphy and me. You heard of executive action at all? A well-known, corporation term you might of missed. The topics you mention are not for open talk at a meat and potatoes do.'

'Manse is right,' Ember said.

'But Ralph, Manse, these guys are hard, usually tooled up and – the *Sun* did an article on the Albanians. I've got it here with me. They come in on stolen or forged Greek passports. I'll read a bit: "A police chief in the central European state" – that's Albania – "A police chief in the central European state told the *Sun* that the mobsters, many of them murderers, flee here because they see Britain as a gangster's paradise."'

'This is well known,' Shale said. 'We don't need the fucking *Sun* to tell us about Albs.'

'Listen, though, Manse: "Top Albanian cop Artan Bajraktari said: 'There are at least forty of them. Many are murderers. I am talking about really serious criminals involved in organized crime.'" See, Manse? This is a cop they can put a name to. This is authentic. He's head of Interpol in Albania. The paper says there's no extradition treaty with Albania, meaning these crooks can't be sent back for what they did over there.'

'OK, serious,' Shale said. 'OK, serious and duly noted. So, we leave it now. Right? Right?' He got really brickish brick wall into his voice. This was what he meant when he'd promised himself to squash nuisance people. This was what he meant by leadership. If you was host you made them know you was, and would run things the way you wanted to. And you let nobodies know they was nobodies.

Naturally, the Agincourt was not the only time Manse and Ralph Ember met. These dinners could be pleasant sessions, Shale would never deny that – what was referred to as 'bonding' – but they amounted only to extras, only to trimming. When he and Ralph saw each other alone, they would discuss large policy matters and decide their own rewards. It would be tactless to let folk at that hotel bean-feast know Manse and Ember each took pay of around £600,000 yearly from the firms. This might of led to unrest. Of course, anyone with deep experience of turnover would guess at the profits. Manse knew some believed it more – even a million. You could not control people's minds. But it was vital to take care nobody except himself and Ralph had the figures as actual, proved fucking fact. Guesses, rumours and gossip would never be enough to cause real bad envy and scheming, except in someone like Denzil, and Denzil was gone. Shale had made sure the cap sat on his coffin in the service, another victory.

In fact, there had been a dip in income for Manse and Ember lately. And Shale knew the Monday night questions strangled by him told why. In their routine, confidential pre-Agincourt pow-wow a week earlier, when proper topics could be truly discussed, Mansel had said: 'We got to do something, Ralph.'

'In respect of what, Manse?'

'In respect of overseas interests on the streets. We're sliding.'

The two were in Shale's den-study at his home for this private session. The house used to be St James's rectory, and it really pleased Manse to think clergymen might of prepared their sermons and written testimonials for parishioners here. Of course, clergymen being what they was, there might have been a bit of quiet wanking in here, too, but Shale did not think of this very much at all. Ember had brought a bottle of Kressmann Armagnac. Shale knew why. This sod probably thought it made up for the refusal ever to allow Shale into Ralph's own place, what he called 'a manor house', named Low Pastures. Ember's residence and family must be kept clean, and always separate from the substance game, mustn't they? Oh, yes, yes and yes some fucking more. The jerk was like that, hoping to seem gentry with paddocks.

'I see these disappointing figures as very much a temporary matter, Mansel,' Ember stated.

Always this bastard hated facing up.

'There's been unhelpful publicity lately about bad addiction cases,' Ember said. 'That kind of thing always squeezes sales for a while. Only a while, though.'

'We got to hit one of these people,' Shale replied. 'Urgent.'

'One of which people, Manse?'

'They think they can sneak in here and set theirselves up, like entitled. Remember Hitler in Czechoslovakia. It got to be stopped early, Ralph. We got to hit one of their high people. The one they call Tirana. It's the name of some town over there. Where he came from.'

'Albania,' Ember said. 'The capital.'

'Ah, the way they called George Washington after Washington.'

'Well, no, the –'

'If we hit him, this Tirana, the rest get to realize the situation – that they got no rights in this city. But they also get to realize that what they *have* got – got from us – you and me, Ralph – is big, smart opposition. Maybe then they'll all go back to their own country, or try it somewhere else – London, Manchester, Winnipeg.'

'This is extreme, Manse.'

Shale had tapped the genuine, For-Our-Eyes-Only accounts with a couple of fingers. 'This could get extreme. I mean the slide.'

'I don't say there's no threat, Manse, but as I see it we need a more gradual approach. A measured strategy.'

'People at the Agincourt next Monday night will want to be told how we're going to handle it, Ralph. They wonder about what's known as their career paths. They thought they had a brill future in the firms and now here comes this Tirana and such. There's Brit companies as well coming in, imitating them Albs and the other foreigners. You hear the name Adrian Cologne at all?'

'It's around, yes. But I'm confident you'll dispose of any unhelpful questions at the Agincourt, Manse.'

'Oh, I can close down their bother, but Tirana will still be a problem, and this Adrian Cologne and so on.'

'Perhaps we shouldn't exaggerate Tirana's impact, Manse.'

As Shale saw things, Ember was often like this – so dodgy about action. Many called him Panicking Ralph, or Panicking Ralphy, and he did get very severe hesitation now and then, the way other people got rheumatism. He had to be helped along. 'If we slay this Tirana in a nice spot, the crew who work with him or want to be like him will know what we're saying to them, Ralph. They'll know it exact.'

'What do you mean, "a nice spot"?'

'Like a sign.'

'In what way, a sign, Manse?'

'So that the way he been done and *where* he been done will show them they got business methods not at all suitable for here, not at all liked here. Well out of fucking order here.'

'I should think they already know that,' Ember said.

'But the slaughter of one of their generals – this would sort of clinch it for them, really light up the message. Like Goliath in the Bible. Or like with wolves.'

'With wolves, Manse? I don't –'

'Wolves. Shoot their pack leader and the rest are lost. Look, we got something lovely here, Ralph. Two busy firms in steady, careful agreement and the Assistant Chief Constable, Mr Iles, also happy as long as no violence from us where the public might get hurt. Yes, all right, there was the way Denzil got it, but something like Denzil and the .38s don't affect the main picture because it was out of sight and only Denzil, anyway. But now this Tirana and others arrive, and the whole thing, I mean the whole structure – the whole structure could be shook so bad it falls. *Our* whole structure.'

'These people, the Tiranas and so on, they fight among themselves, Manse, trying for supremacy, dominance. It has to be possible they'll wipe out one another. This is probably why Iles hasn't smashed them. He thinks they'll do it for him. That's policing, or it's Iles-type policing, anyway.'

'Takes too long. By then our firms could be finished. This Tirana, he got to be done, Ralph, and he got to be done by us and they got to know he been done by us. This got to be an execution and it got to be spectacular. You heard of that chopping the king's head off in history? That really signified something. Same with this Tirana.'

'Well, I –'

'Not an axe, I don't mean that. But like a show. Like a statement.'

'Manse, I –'

'Mr Iles – he would *expect* us to handle this. He would think it's part of the deal with him, not spoken of but like *understood*. Well, everything in the deal's understood. It's not going to be written down and signed like buying a TV, is it? Most probably Mr Iles is waiting to hear this Tirana been took out of the scene so the scene can get back to what it ought to be, meaning so sweet and peaceful and with our firms climbing so nice, not plunging.' Manse took a good mouthful of the Kressmann. It was great, no question, a prestige sup. Ember liked prestige. He owned a drinking club called the Monty, and got all his bottles cheap. He would not let Manse meet him there, either, though, because Ember hoped to turn the Monty into some high class joint one day like a grand, famous London club, for professors, judges, world-recognized hair-stylists, bishops, circus owners. Mad. The Monty was a sink. Half the members was in jail or come out last Wednesday, and the rest would be in there banged up *next* Wednesday.

Some called Ember 'Milord Monty', as well as Panicking Ralph. He talked as big as big.

'What you carrying?' Shale asked at their one-to-one.

'In what respect, Manse?'

'Armament. I don't mean what you got aboard now, tonight. I know you would not carry a gun into my home and not just because it was a rectory previous. You would have more respect – in general. You're sensitive, Ralph.'

'I –'

'But what I mean, when you *do* have to carry something what is it? You used to like a Walther, didn't you, but then a Beretta? Still the Beretta? Myself, I'm into Heckler and Koch, same as the police. They know what's the best stopper because they have stopped a lot, so why not copy? 9 mm Parabellum. But nice and lightweight even when the mag's full. Like you, Ralph, I hope I got some sensitivity about weapons and I would not bring them into this actual study where holy duties might of took place once such as prayer. But I expect you noticed a painting in the other room by what's known in art language as a Pre-Raphaelite called Arthur Hughes. I go for them Pre-Raphaelites. I don't know how it is, but they really get to me, Ralph. You heard of them at all – Pre-Raphaelites? Great on tresses, auburn tresses most of them, but other colours, also. There's a combo safe behind that with Mr Heckler and Koch in and some fat boxes of rounds. I got another safe in this room, but only for cash and our private accounts. The Pre-Raphaelite safe is what could be called the armoury safe.'

When the Agincourt function came in the week after, and them niggles kept jabbing from some troops, Shale would of liked to tell them about the Ralphy Beretta and the Heckler and Koch and the plentiful ammo, both lined up for the Tirana scheme, but not on, obviously. All Manse could say over and over was he and Ralph had matters in mind – true, but not satisfactory to staff. People wanted detail, but detail they could not have, not that detail, only untroublesome detail. Some information had to stay buttoned. At the Agincourt, he would not even mention the name Tirana, and definitely not the spot where Manse considered it best to do him – best because, as he had explained to Ralphy, it would speak a message.

During their meeting in Shale's house, working out the attack plans, he'd been afraid for a couple of minutes that Ember might go into one of his panics just at the fucking *thought* of a shoot-out, and get so he couldn't talk and hardly breathe. Manse would hate anything like that on his property. It was just not appropriate for somewhere that used to be a rectory. If Ralph wanted to go jabbery he ought to do it in his fucking manor house or at the priceless Monty. But although Ralph had one big tremble during their meeting, a lot of face twitch, plus a spurt of sweat on his top lip, things did not get worse and after a minute he seemed more or less all right.

And he seemed more or less all right when they drove out towards the Morton Cross area at around midnight on the Thursday after Agincourt to see off Tirana. Manse had picked this as the best location. To snuff him here would have a true meaning, and a meaning all invaders could read, even if their English was feeble. This was the point, wasn't it – until now, most of the town's drug dealing took place in bars and caffs around the Valencia Esplanade area, or, for richer users, on a dockside floating restaurant in an ancient ship that once carried tea from India but now called *The Eton Boating Song*, not far off. Shale's and Ember's people did their pushing there, a good and happy tradition.

But Tirana and other trespassers in their foreign, ignorant way had begun to work on the border of two different districts, Morton Cross and Inton, with Chilton Park in the middle. These were class areas, big properties and gardens. Some new Brit firms, like this Adrian Cologne, had started operations there, also. This was what caused most of them moans and snivels at the Agincourt. Some trade had already gone from the Valencia and moved to Morton and Inton. Although Manse tried to block and comfort them at the dinner, he knew the trouble was real. Clearly. And so that warning to Ralph in their rectory discussion. And so the need to turn rough.

Manse had ordered research on this Tirana. It showed he took a jaunt most nights to Morton and Inton and did a bit of dealing himself. But mainly he seemed there to scout around in the big BMW and make sure his people worked full out, pushers and girls, and that they got no peril from other crews aiming at takeover. Manse considered slaughter of Tirana in this high calibre district at a major trading hour would really let every outfit know – every outfit – Alb or Brit or Turk or wherever you could think of – it would tell them Morton and Inton was not proper places for pushing, and that Tirana and his friends and enemies could never be right for this kind of established local business, anyway. They did not know the decent, accepted rules, and would not fucking care about them if they did. That was what Manse meant about Hitler. People like that tried to make up their own rules. Mighty gratitude was certain from Assistant Chief Desmond Iles when he saw the Morton–Inton development rubbished by first class, point blank salvoes into Tirana at just the right location, and the selling once more nicely confined to its usual, dockland grounds, and to Manse Shale and Ralphy Ember.

Manse had watched Ralph check his armament before they set out from another join-up at the rectory to Morton Cross. 'So you *do* stick with the Beretta.'

'The same type. Not the same gun.'

Shale laughed gently for a while at this. 'Well, no, I didn't think so! Traceable. A switch every so often, or even oftener than every so often, but always you renew with a model that's familiar. Sensible. You can trust it. Myself, I'm getting to feel something similar about the Heckler. Sort of mates, sort of companions, aren't they, Ralph? Reliable comrades?' Important to make the poor sod feel calm and strong, save him from one of his guts-wreck spasms now the operation had really started.

They were in the Jaguar. Manse drove. Of course, he had put different plates on for tonight, although nobody in Iles's lot would look too hard for someone kind enough to take out Tirana in a smart coup. 'There he is,' Shale said. 'As almost ever.' The BMW stood on a small grass island where three roads converged. From here Tirana could watch dealers and girls near the Morton Cross shopping mall and two side streets leading away to Inton. Shale cut the Jaguar's engine. 'I drive alongside, pull up and we both fire. All right, Ralph? Both.' Shale took the Heckler from a shoulder holster and put it ready on his lap under the steering wheel. 'All right, Ralph? I mustn't wait here. He'll see and get clear or start gunnery hisself. It's a good moment. Not many folk about.'

Ember did not produce the Beretta. 'There's someone in the passenger seat with him,' he said.

'A girl. That happens sometimes. I heard of it. One of the imported kids they deal in, as well as the commodities. That's their disgusting way. He'll take her for the night. A perk. We can try not to blast her. Definitely. We'll be close and OK for accuracy. We got no fight with the girl. Just him. All right, Ralph? The Beretta?'

'What's the matter with her?' Ember replied.

'What?' Shale said. Oh, God, Ralphy breaking to bits after all – hanging back for ever? His legs spaghettied? Everything gone?

'Crying,' Ember said. 'Arms all around him, like life-saving in the sea. She's really weeping. Listen. The BMW driver's window's down.'

'They get excited, some of them kids. And they got to put on a passion act – especially she would for him, the master. This is devotion. They got to show it.'

'The way he's sitting,' Ember said.

'What?'

'Not right somehow.'

19

'Which way's he supposed to fucking sit, Ralph? Get the Beretta out.' Shale had some snarl going.

'She's holding him up. I think he's hit already,' Ember replied.

'He's *what*?'

'Hit. He's dead. No movement.'

'Christ,' Shale said.

'Dead or on the way.'

Shale stared. After a minute he said: 'Yes. Clever, Ralph. One of his own lot done him?'

'I told you. They fight. They snipe. They all want control.'

Shale did some thought. 'Yes, well we should vamoose, Ralph. Quit. Them others might be around still. This is peril. Or we could get hauled in for doing him, which would be sick when we didn't, only hoped to. We don't want to embarrass Mr Iles by getting caught here.' He reached to restart the Jaguar. Ember gripped his wrist and stopped him. Shale said: 'We can't do nothing now.'

'The girl,' Ember said. 'Wrong to leave her like that. A kid, a foreign kid, stuck in a car with a corpse. I've got a daughter about her age.'

'This kid's only a –'

Ember had already opened the door of the Jaguar and begun to run towards the BMW. Shale put the Heckler and Koch back into its holster and then followed him at a trot. Hell, was this Panicking Ralphy? He'd had a fucking backbone transplant? How? Pity for this teenage tart did it? Yet he couldn't be *all* panic, or he'd never have landed his club and his manor house.

They reached the BMW. Ember pulled open the passenger door. The girl was sobbing. She turned to them, foreign terror all through her, but Manse could still tell it was terror. The movement meant she released Tirana and he slumped to the side. As he did, Shale had time to see a tidy bullet wound in his forehead and a blood trickle.

20

'What happened, child?' Ralph said, his voice full of big caring and grease like a priest's.

'They came.'

'Who?'

'Yes, they came,' she replied. She made a pistol shape with one hand. The hand shook. It could be fright. It could be her coming down from a fix. She was plump-faced, pale-skinned, perhaps fifteen years old, her speech slow, her accent massive. 'But so quiet,' she said.

'A silenced gun,' Shale said.

She leaned across and put her cheek against the fat shoulder pad of Tirana's pinstripe jacket. 'He dead, oh, yes. But I love,' she said. 'I love him. And he love me. Much. Very much. He said this. He said love. Often he said love. Two times. Three.'

'Yes, I expect so. Leave here now,' Ember told her. 'At once. The police will come and you'll have problems. Problems. You know this word, "problems"? Trouble.' He took out a wedge of money and gave her what looked to Shale like five twenties. 'Get clear.' Shale searched his own pockets and found six tens and a twenty. He handed these to her. If Ember done it Manse had to or he'd look miserable and mean.

She folded the money, counting it. 'You pay. You want threesome?' she said. 'Sniff coke after?'

'Just go,' Ember replied.

'That your Jag? I been in Jags already. Many. And Mercs. Once a Roller – Roller Royce. You see, I know threesome.'

'This is talk and more talk,' Ember grunted at her. 'It's dangerous for you here. Disappear.'

'Ah, talk? You want talk? You want me talk dirty? Yes, me, I have many, many dirty English words. Prick. Clit.'

Chapter Two

'So, they're out there in our suburbs now, Col – Morton Cross and Inton,' Iles said. 'This death. Tirana, they call him?'

'Yes, sir,' Harpur replied.

'I'd bet you'll be back to those regions very soon again with more trouble.'

'I think so, sir.'

'Of course, Col, I'm very much a suburbs person myself.'

'Indeed, yes, sir: Rougemont Place.'

'I'm not ashamed of this,' Iles said.

'Hardly, sir.'

'But you, personally, Harpur, a Detective Chief Super, continue to live and bring up your daughters, Hazel, Jill, in that . . . continue to live and bring up Hazel and Jill where you do.'

'Well, I do, yes, sir.'

'I expect you think a house called Idylls in a street called Rougemont Place – except, obviously, not a street, a Place – I expect you think a house called Idylls in a street called Rougemont Place is somehow fruity.'

'Idylls I know comes from a poem you're fond of,' Harpur replied. 'I can't speak for Rougemont.'

'*Idylls* is Tennyson. He was quite well known in Victorian times, Col. Beard. A sequence of poems: *Idylls of the King*.'

'Right, sir.'

'I don't want shit like that Tirana dead on my front doorstep, Harpur.'

'We're doing all that we –'

'I have a wife and young child.'

'Certainly, I –'

'But I don't have to tell you I have a wife, do I?' Iles's voice began one of its quick, long ascents, like a balloon with the ballast ditched, as it often did when he mentioned Sarah to Harpur. 'You and she had quite a –'

'I'd be very aware, sir, that you'd object to gang violence near a Place called Rougemont. It's not just foreign firms. We think some new British outfits up there competing, adapting. Thomas Pyle – that's "Tommy the Strong", Adrian Cologne, Bobby Sprale.'

'There's all sorts live near me, you know,' Iles said.

'Well, I'm sure.'

'Distinguished folk, I mean.'

'Certainly.'

'Surgeons, the city's football manager, a judge, BBC people, stockbrokers.'

'It's quite a street. Place,' Harpur replied.

Iles became silent and thoughtful. Then he said: 'Tell me, Col, do I remember that Hazel's boyfriend, Scott, lives up that way?'

'Which way, sir?' Harpur prepared to become more obstructive. There were difficult, persistent topics between Iles and him: Iles's wife, Harpur's daughter.

'Of course, I've met the boy at your house,' Iles said. 'He lives near Morton Cross, I think.'

'I think he might.'

'About her age?' Iles replied.

'A little older. Seventeen. Hazel's only fifteen, sir. Yes, sir, only fifteen. A child of fifteen.'

'Scott Grant,' Iles said, as if recalling the full name from some back end of his mind. But he'd have it fairly foremost. He thought of Scott as a rival. 'His mother hates us, doesn't she?'

'Mrs Grant is not keen on the police, that's right, sir.'

'Quite a few like that about these days in luxury houses. It's because speed cameras do their four wheel drive jobs. They think it's persecution. They don't know what we're like when we *really* persecute, do they, Col? Does Hazel worry about things?'

'What? Being only fifteen? *I* worry about it, sir.'

'No, does she worry about a spread of the trading and atrocities to Morton Cross, where the lad lives?'

'Worry why, sir?'

'You haven't considered it, Harpur?'

'What, sir?'

'Might he get drawn in? Boys that age – the fascination with armament. There'll be more of these eruptions.'

'I expect so.'

'Which?' Iles said.

'Which what, sir?'

'When you say you expect so, do you mean you expect there'll be more incidents, or that you expect she worries in case he gets involved?'

'I've ordered a rapid response vehicle to be permanently around that area, sir,' Harpur replied.

And four days later, the rapid response vehicle called in and Harpur was out at Morton Cross again, this time to three deaths though, not one, and a wounding, in and near Chilton Park. God, a pattern starting? Iles had seemed to foresee that, and what Iles foresaw generally happened. Harpur went on television News as the clear-up at Morton Cross began and tried to sound confident that these horrifying crime outbursts in previously sedate areas could be contained and eliminated, but he wondered. His daughters saw his performance and next day Hazel told him he'd looked what she described as 'jumpy and useless'. This hurt. He craved the girls' approval. In fact, one of the main things about Harpur was that he longed for true success as a single parent. Of course, you never knew properly whether you'd been good at it until the children grew up and you could see if those early years made them confident and serene or caused bad twitches.

At fifteen and thirteen the girls could be tricky. For a start, they hated his job almost as much as Mrs Grant did, and when occasionally he drove them to school or judo they liked to get out of the car in a side street a few hundred metres away and walk the rest, in case kids recognized him from those TV News interviews he had to give occasionally, or could intuit cop by his haircut, eyes, shoes, suit and build. Both girls were infuriated when the News caption under his face after the Morton Cross outrage follow-up correctly spelled the surname. Hazel said: 'If they'd put Harper with an "e r" it could be all sorts. That's usual, the "e". There are two Harpers with "e r" in school. After all, we don't look like you. Oh, imagine! That *would* be a treat. But Harpur "u r" is us, just us. Where does it come from?'

'What?' Harpur said.

'The "u" in our "Harpur"?'

'Lineage,' Harpur said.

'Lineage, what lineage?' Hazel replied.

'There was a Harpur with a "u" in the Trojan horse with the Greeks. Bert Harpur, Bert with an "e".'

'We get remarks like, "Detective Chief Superintendent, my! Daddy is such a big, big lawman, isn't he? He'll save us all, see us right,"' Hazel said.

'I must have a word with you both about handguns,' Harpur replied. He had not wanted to discuss any of this with Iles. He did not like discussing much at all about Hazel with Iles, and this would be about Hazel, or at least about her boyfriend.

Hazel's voice took on frenzy: 'Didn't I tell you, Jill? Didn't I? I said he'd be on that again because of yesterday at Morton Cross. And when he says both of us he means me.'

'Were you, like, tooled up yourself for it, dad?' Jill asked.

'Should you be out there at your rank and age? Which weapon? Heckler and Koch? Smith and Wesson?'

'This was a street battle up at Chilton Park in Morton Cross,' Harpur said.

'Didn't I tell you he'd be on about that – where it was, Jill? Didn't I tell you, Jill?'

'We know where it was, dad – from the News programme. Floral tributes plastic-wrapped. The usual.'

'It's new,' Harpur said.

'What is?' Jill asked.

'A new location for this kind of thing,' Harpur said.

'Which?' Jill said.

'Gun battles. Turf battles: that's gang fights for what they call "territory".'

'Yes, we know what turf means, dad,' Jill said. 'Their ground – where they can sell their stuff.'

'There's been a change,' Harpur said.

Hazel said: 'Oh, dear! It all used to be in the docks area around Valencia Esplanade, the run-down streets, didn't it, nice and sealed off, so it never mattered? You could let them get on with it.'

'It mattered, but districts like Morton Cross were quiet and safe,' Harpur said.

'The burbs,' Hazel snarled.

'The suburbs, yes,' Harpur said. 'They can be very nice. It was my mother's top ambition to have a semi-detached house in the suburbs. They did make it, eventually.'

'So why don't *we*?' Jill said.

'What?' Harpur replied.

'Live in the suburbs,' Jill said.

'Mr Iles asked me that. *Your* mother didn't fancy it,' Harpur said. 'Different generation. The word "bourgeois" was big with her. And not favourable. Suburbs equalled bourgeois.'

'Meaning?' Jill said.

'Meaning all the things *my* mother prized and sought,'

Harpur said. 'People who kept themselves *to* themselves. Up and over door on the garage.'

'We're all right here,' Jill said.

'It's fine,' Harpur said. They were in the long sitting room at Arthur Street, Hazel pacing about, Jill on the settee with a copy of *The Sweet Science*, a boxing book, open near her. '*Were* you tooled up, dad?' she said. 'Waist holster or shoulder?'

'Do you know what was more or less my first thought when I got there yesterday?' Harpur replied.

'Oh, let me guess, let me guess, let me guess,' Hazel said. She put a hand on her forehead to help mental effort. It was satirical. 'You thought, "Hazel's boyfriend lives in Brant Road, near Chilton Park, Morton Cross." Bourgeoisville.'

'It's true I'd heard a youth or youths were involved, as well as the others,' Harpur said.

'Youths! Who calls them youths, except police?' Hazel said.

'Yes, I did wonder about Scott,' Harpur replied. He thought he would have wondered, anyway. But the chat with Iles sharpened things. So, was it a sick, automatic cop reaction, this suspicion? Did the speed with which it came help explain the hostility of people like Scott Grant's mother?

'You wondered about him,' Hazel said. 'Well, that's all right, isn't it, dad? You wondered, but he wasn't there, was he? And he's not dead. You've got the casualty names now, haven't you?'

'No, he's not dead or in hospital or nicked,' Harpur said. 'But these days – this part of the city, full of guns. Suddenly, thick with gangs. I don't say Scott is into all that but –'

'I thought that's what you *were* saying,' Hazel said. 'I knew, *knew*, you'd be saying it. Didn't you think that's what he *was* saying, Jill?'

Jill said: 'Well, I don't –'

27

'Oh, but you stick by him. It's hopeless.'

'Did you have to open fire yourself, dad?' Jill replied. 'Rapid? How many shots?'

'I don't know how easy it would be for Scott to stay out of it,' Harpur said.

'What does that mean?' Hazel said.

'Dad's worried about him, Haze,' Jill said. 'And he's worried about you, because of Scott. You care. You'd be so upset if . . .'

'If what?' Hazel said.

Jill said: 'If something . . .'

'If something happened to him,' Hazel said. 'Meaning killed. It won't happen. He's not into all that.'

Harpur liked this room now. There was space here and light. Quite a respectful while after his wife's death he took down all the loaded book shelves and redecorated without them. A lot of the hardback stuff she liked used to depress him and jut out from the walls too far, a sort of bullying – titles like *Beowulf, Wolf Solent, Untying the Text* and *Edwin Drood*. They seemed picked to get up people's noses. Harpur didn't know how anyone could read stuff with these names and similar, but he'd often seen her at it. Most of it was more than show. She'd run fortnightly literary chat meetings here. Jill had wanted to keep the boxing book and something called *Joe Orton's Diaries*, but the rest they got shot of.

To Harpur the room had come to seem habitable since the shelves went, at last OK for a home. When the girls were grown up he wanted them to look back on this room and think he'd made something friendly and relaxed of it, changed it from a library. He was not opposed to books, but he objected to books that seemed to badger you, by what they were called and/or by quantity. When the shelves were up and full of Megan's volumes, the room used to give him tightness in the chest like the start of suffocation, though he would never have told her that because she felt a sort of reverence for books. She might have got this from her parents who lived in Highgate. But *Mein Kampf* was a book. He'd never mentioned that to her, either. Harpur did admit that not all Megan's volumes sounded totally dismal, or Jill would never have saved these two.

'It's just like police,' Hazel replied, some rage spit flying.

'What is?' Harpur said.

'You, going on about Morton Cross, dad,' Hazel said. 'Called "guilt by association". It's famed. The Soviets. The Fascists. Senator Joseph McCarthy in America: "You lived next door to Alger Hiss, therefore must be a spy." We've done it in History. Political victimization, as when Zero Mostel throws himself from a skyscraper window in that film on the movie channel.'

'*The Front,*' Jill said.

'Dad, you think, Scott lives there in Morton Cross and there's trouble, so –'

'It's not about guilt. It's about safety,' Harpur said. 'And your happiness.'

'You want me to frisk him?' Hazel said. 'You want me to fink?'

'These lads' – Harpur almost said kids, but the lip-froth and wrath from Hazel were already enough – 'these lads compete, like all lads always, but for a lot of *these* lads competing means having a handgun, a rapid-fire handgun.'

'For "a lot" of them, maybe,' Hazel said.

'Yes, a lot,' Harpur said.

'"A lot" but not Scott. How do you know he's part of it?' Hazel said.

'I don't,' Harpur said.

'You said it would be hard for Scott to stay out of it,' Hazel said. 'Didn't he say it would be hard for Scott to stay out of it, Jill?'

'Dad's just scared for him, and you.'

'You always stick up for dad,' Hazel said.

'He can't help being a worrier,' Jill said. 'It's his age and the rank. They get like that. And the widowerhood. All right, he's got Denise, and she's lovely. But she's not here all the time, is she, and she's not our mother? Plus she's young and in the uni with plenty of student friends, men and girls, so maybe he won't be able to hold on to her. She'll have a degree. She can speak French. She even knows French poems. There's one about a pelican that tears open its own breast to feed its starving young. Denise could discuss things like that with them if she went to live in France. She might go anywhere. It's like he's on his own. In some ways. That causes fret because we're all he's got for sure. He doesn't want you to suffer.'

'Yes, it might be hard for Scott to keep clear of it,' Harpur replied.

'Of what?' Hazel said.

'Dad means the culture,' Jill said. 'Peer group pressures.'

'Oh, here comes Form Three Sociology-speak,' Hazel said.

'The gun fashion,' Harpur said. 'They get drawn in.'

'Who?' Hazel said.

'Youngsters,' Harpur said. 'Boys fourteen or fifteen up.'

'Into what?' Hazel said.

'The "this-is-my-patch-so-keep-out" wars. These are serious. They bring big excitement. They bring big money. Trafficking, mainly. Plus other activities.'

'Which other activities?' Hazel said.

'Other activities,' Harpur replied.

'You know, Haze,' Jill said.

'What?' Hazel asked.

'He means running girls,' Jill said.

'Pimping?' Hazel said. 'Is that what you mean, dad?'

'Crime patterns change. Villains slip in from abroad among genuine immigrants and asylum seekers. They don't think like home-grown crooks. They bring a different kind of trouble. More complicated. With them, things overlap – drugs, women, protection, menaces. A bit of everything. And they back it all with guns. Guns are natural to

30

them. Local gangs have to adjust, maybe copy in case they lose some of that precious *territory*. Some new British outfits are working Morton Cross. This gun fascination spreads down to youngsters who get little jobs in the firms – sometimes youngsters from ordinary, long-established, law-and-order families.'

'Like bourgeois?' Jill said.

'The geography shifts,' Harpur said.

'I enjoy these talks,' Jill said.

'Which?' Harpur said.

'Like police talk,' Jill said. 'Like the important side of it – not just shoplifting or graffiti. Like looking at things wide.'

'Widely,' Harpur replied. 'And you don't need all the "likes". We've discussed that before.'

'What?' Jill said.

'"Like",' Harpur replied.

'Everyone says it,' Jill said.

'I don't,' Harpur said.

'Probably you'll catch up, like,' Jill said.

'Why should the changes affect Scott?' Hazel said.

'I hope they don't. Just talk to him,' Harpur replied. 'It's dangerous.'

'What's dangerous?' Hazel said.

'To join up with these people.'

'Who says he does?' Hazel said.

'Nobody. But in case. In case he might. Ask him if –'

'No, I'm not going to talk to him about it,' Hazel said. 'I'd sound like somebody's granny or probation officer. And, please, dad, don't you say anything to him when he's here.'

'Dad wouldn't, if you don't want it. You ought to know that.'

'I *don't* want it,' Hazel replied.

'No, of course I wouldn't,' Harpur said. 'If anyone speaks to him it will have to be you.'

'Well, it won't be,' Hazel said. 'He'd know it came from

you. He'd think I was pathetic, a dirty little messenger girl.'

'Does he seem to have extra money these days?' Harpur asked. 'Better training shoes? Jewellery?'

'What extra money?' Hazel said.

'Does he?' Harpur replied.

'Is this an interrogation?' Hazel said.

And perhaps it was. He should ease up, try a scene-shift: 'I'd like you both to come out there with me.' He wanted to get instructional and effective: fatherly, not oppressive. Ten years, maybe less, his daughters would have flown.

'Out where?' Hazel said.

'Morton Cross, where it happened,' Harpur said. 'Chilton Park. I shouldn't but –'

'What for?' Hazel said.

'I just want you to see the streets,' Harpur replied. But that didn't quite say it, didn't at all say it. He wanted them to see the streets and feel the paving stones and road tarmac under their shoes and brush against walls and thick front hedges so that the place and the dangers there were real to them, not newsreel glimpses made dramatic and distant and tidy by voice-over.

'I know the streets already,' Hazel said. 'I've been to Scott's house, haven't I?' .

'Yes, but this would be different,' Harpur said: different because he'd give them a commentary on what he'd seen yesterday, seen and done yesterday, and describe the step-by-step awfulness of the fight. Although some of the step-by-steps then had been at a gallop, Harpur would take them over the ground more slowly, so he could do his tour-guide turn with good solemnity, and perhaps get some intelligent alarm going in Hazel about Scott. Harpur longed to make sure if he could that no more close contact with violent death came to the girls. They still had their mother's murder to recover from.* A trip around Morton

* *Roses, Roses.*

Cross would be graphic but not distressing. He reckoned that someone with a real talent for single-parenting could manage that kind of careful distinction. When they'd grown up and recalled these times, perhaps chatted them over, he'd like Hazel and Jill to feel he showed compassion and skill, as if both were natural to him.

'*I'll* come, dad,' Jill said.

'Oh, you *would*,' Hazel said. But Harpur knew it meant Hazel would come, as well. She could not let the younger girl have a special trip with him, even a trip Hazel didn't want.

As they drove towards Morton Cross, Jill said: 'Better not go too slow, dad, or they'll think you're a pimp yourself with two underagers on offer.' She was in the back but crouched forward to make sure all her contributions got heard properly by Harpur. She believed in herself. She always believed he needed her advice. Hazel had the passenger seat alongside Harpur. Sometimes, the girls' savvy appalled him. Possibly they meant it to. How old was he before he understood the word 'pimp'? And would he ever have used it as a joke to his father or mother? He had to hope this dire know-how kept his daughters alert to the dangers around. In a disintegrating world, perhaps only worldliness worked. The present trip was supposed to give them a stack more about these dangers.

Brightly, hungrily, Jill said: 'Now, dad, tell us how the whole thing goes. You're in your office and you get a call, right? "Shooting at Morton Cross, sir." Did they have details this soon? Number of guns? Injureds? Deads? Some of your people would be already on the scene, yes? This is like the armed rapid response vehicle etcetera. Volvo estate? You want to get out there fast, but, obviously, you wouldn't have a weapon aboard while you're dealing with reports and dossiers and such on your desk. Or you're in a meeting when the message comes? Something like that. You got to get to the armoury and draw something, have you? Or do they let you keep something plus ammo in your office safe? You wouldn't go with nothing, would you? What did you take? The H and K – "police preferred weapon" I read in one of the papers? Flak jacket? When you're driving in a flak jacket is it, like, all bulky and awkward, like Marlboro man? And you'd be driving fast – unmarked car but interior blue flashing light. This would be what's known as an "incident". Shooting is an incident, and you think you got to get there even though Detective Chief Super. Where's the weapon – waist or shoulder or just in your pocket? Navigation screen in the car telling you the route? Radio or phone to let you know all the time where the battle's moved to? Are you alone? Was Ilesy with you in the vehicle? Other cars and ambulances with you? Are you in charge once you get there, like taking over? You'd be what's called Gold, wouldn't you – Gold being top command? Or Mr Iles? Assistant Chief, so even Golder.'

'I'm embarrassed,' Hazel said.

'Well, yes, you would be, Haze,' Jill said. 'Embarrassed Scott or someone like that will see us around Morton Cross and think we're nosing and trying to nanny him? A trio of us, and one of us the police. We could be noticed.'

'"Someone like that" being his mother. You know what *she's* like. She'd want to know what we're doing here.'

'It might be an idea to tell her,' Harpur said.

'No thank you,' Hazel said. 'She'd make a fuss.'

'What *sort* of fuss?' Harpur said.

'*Her* sort. Loud – in the street.'

'But saying what?' Harpur replied. 'We're here to look after the safety of her son.'

'Are we?' Hazel said.

'She can't object to that,' Harpur said.

'This is just your say-so, your guesswork. But, in any case, I don't want her to know we're here to look after the safety of her son, if we really are. And I don't want her son to know.'

'Oh, I think you'd make a fine nanny, Haze,' Jill said.

34

'Keep out of it, will you?' Hazel said. 'Just stick with your stupid gun talk and Gold talk, off TV drama. Dad, I'm sorry I came. Can we turn around and go home, please?'

He ignored this. It took him some effort, but he ignored it. Perhaps when Hazel was grown up she'd look back on today and think him overbearing and heartless. Oh, well. He had to do what he could to save her from possible big pain now – this week, next, not when she reached thirty-five – big pain now if Scott remained unwarned, peer-grouped and sucked in by the culture, and as a result caught a bullet or two. Harpur found to his disgust that he could visualize an impressive cortège along these pleasantly wide, tree-edged, bonny streets, Scott's mother in the lead car after the hearse, maybe still loud, but loud with weeping.

Of course, what he feared above all was that the bullet or two caught by Scott in some future clash might be a police bullet or bullets. Hazel would never be able to forgive that, either now or later. There had been a few moments yesterday when Harpur, 9 mm Heckler and Koch automatic in his hand, safety catch off, saw a youngster of about Scott's size and frame, wearing some sort of khaki or beige track suit with the hood up, run from behind bushes in the park and out through the gate towards the main road. Although it was a hopelessly distant and imperfect sighting, Harpur's immediate thought was, Scott. But had Harpur brought that notion with him, that expectation, because the boy lived near? Had he made the facts fit a crazy premonition? Perhaps. The boy, also, carried a pistol, though Harpur was too far away to identify it. Training shoes. Expensive training shoes? Too far away to know that, either. Harpur had muttered, 'Thank God,' meaning 'Thank God he's not coming this way.' Harpur would have been forced to challenge him, maybe to drop him. Someone closer to this running figure did fire three rapid shots, and Harpur assumed that lad to be the target. He seemed

35

unhurt, though, and kept going until he reached the road, then turned left and away out of Harpur's sight. The poor shooting probably proved it didn't come from police, though one of the armed response crews had a spot close to that gate. And police wouldn't shoot someone running away, not threatening them.

He wondered now as they parked the car and he walked with his daughters into the park whether Hazel actually sensed he'd seen something to make him think Scott might have been here. She said she'd assumed he'd think of Scott just on account of the location, and had forecast to Jill he would. But the ferocity of her denials seemed to go beyond this. The defensiveness had grown shrill, intense. Perhaps because of what Harpur had seen, or thought he'd seen, his anxieties came over more strongly than he knew when talking to the girls. Hazel might pick up this special tone and guess something particular agitated him. Kids could be damn sharp on nuances – or *his* kids could, anyway. It was an eternal pest. 'There's dealing done in the park during daylight and then, when the gates are shut for the night, it moves just outside to Pater Street and Baron Square,' Harpur said.

'And girls,' Jill said.

'And girls,' Harpur said. Naturally, his daughters would know about the park. They had all the city's gossip from friends.

'These have suddenly become top-grade sites, and so they're fought over,' Harpur said. 'We've had problems before, but nothing as bad as yesterday's.'

'Right, I'm you! I'm you, dad!' Jill replied. 'OK? OK. You come into the park and draw your pistol.' She had on jeans and a T-shirt and reached down as if to pull a gun from her belt. Resolution spread across her face. She narrowed her eyes for aggression. 'You see, like, activity ahead – I mean, like real warring, sort of all-out, no messing about – and noise, obviously – gunfire, maybe some yelling – and you start to run towards it all.' She set off ahead of Hazel and

36

him, this slight-to-bony, long-headed, middle-height, light-footed child, masquerading as Harpur, who had been likened to 'a fair-haired Rocky Marciano', one-time undefeated heavyweight boxing champion of the world and with that kind of physique. No, as Hazel said, neither girl looked like Harpur. At least Jill did have the fair hair, though worn in a pony-tail. She held her right hand stiffly down at her side, as if she carried a pistol, pointed at the ground, so far, for safety. She began to yell in her thin, sharp, harmless voice: 'Armed police! Armed police! Put your weapon on the ground and your hands on your head.' She tried for a long stride, as an imitation of how Harpur might have run towards the shooting.

She didn't go very far but stopped alongside several of those 'floral tributes' as she'd called them: three bunches of carnations at the edge of the path, encased in transparent plastic against the weather. 'Look at that,' she said. 'Isn't it stupid?'

'Someone died there,' Harpur said.

'Yes, I could of guessed somebody died there, but who brings bought flowers into a park? The park's full of flowers.'

'Could *have* guessed,' Harpur replied.

'These days, it's just sort of mechanical – the flowers,' Jill said. 'Somebody's dead in an accident or a fight, so get down the service station and buy a few bouquets to stick on the spot. It's like . . . yes, like mechanical. Does it mean anything? They say it's all because of that Princess Diana killed in a car crash, and then a great sloppy pile-up of flowers where she lived from people who never knew her, enough plastic to parcel up a palace. But this, this would be some crook dead, anyway, wouldn't it, dad? Who'd care?' She bent to read a card. '"Rusty, Goodnight, Love, Marie." You know him, dad – Rusty? Hey, look, you didn't do him yourself, personal, did you? Wow? Did he have a piece himself and was going to knock you over?'

'"Personally",' Harpur said.

'You did? You did him personal?' Jill yelled.

'Personally,' Harpur replied. 'The word is "personally". No, I didn't do him myself, personally. He was dead when I arrived.' Yes, the man on the ground near the living flowers – and the only flowers there then – had been carrying a gun, but it must have spilled from his hand when he was shot and lay under him, hidden by the body except for about a centimetre of the barrel. 'We think it was a two-stage confrontation. Only a couple of people are concerned in the first part. They belong to different firms and argue about a drugs-dealing site. That's usual enough. But this time, one pulls a gun and pops the other. The word gets around, of course, and both firms smell apocalypse and send reinforcements, to hold the territory.' He pointed to the packaged flowers. 'This man was probably killed early. The rest of the fight and the other casualties happened at the opposite end of the park.'

Jill said: 'This is the first time you ever talked to us about a crime, dad, and largish words like "confrontation" and "acopal" . . .'

'Apocalypse,' Harpur said. 'Chaos.'

'I mean, *really* talked,' Jill replied.

'I shouldn't. But I want you to realize it's serious,' Harpur said.

Hazel stepped away from them and then suddenly came back and pushed her face against the sleeve of Harpur's jacket. He put his other palm gently on her head. In a moment, she pulled away: 'All right, it's serious,' she said. 'It's serious, it's serious. I don't need to see where anyone else was killed or hurt. I believe you. I don't want to hear about the second stage where they're all at it. I want to go home now.'

Jill said: 'OK, dad, you come into the park, you see he's dead, and you can't do anything for him so you leave him and go on towards the really dangerous set-to – shooting from all sides. That how it was? You, and the other police, all caught in the middle. You know, you could really of come unstuck.'

'*Have* come unstuck,' Harpur said.

'Listen, dad, did you see Scott here?' Hazel said. 'Is that why you brought us to the park?'

'I just want you to talk to him and tell him things are bad around here and will get worse,' Harpur replied.

'If he was in it, he'll know, won't he?' Jill said.

'He wasn't in it, he wasn't,' Hazel screamed.

'If he wasn't in it, how could dad have seen him?' Jill said.

'I didn't say he'd seen him,' Hazel said.

'You *asked* dad if he'd seen him,' Jill said.

'Asked is not said,' Hazel replied.

'Asked means you thought he might of been,' Jill said. 'Does Scott tell you things, Haze?'

'Listen, dad, did you see Scott here?' Hazel said.

'No, of course not,' Harpur said. 'Just talk to him, though. This is about the future, not yesterday.'

When they returned to Arthur Street, they found that Denise had let herself in and was waiting for them. Until a few months ago, she refused keys to the house, claiming she always lost her own and would be anxious all the time about an extra Yale and mortise. Of course, Harpur saw through this: she feared keys would commit her, make her part of the household. Harpur had kept on at her, though. He *wanted* her committed and part of the household. The girls would back him. Harpur was good at keeping on at people when after something. Keys did have overtones, symbolism, he recognized this. And so, he'd said: 'You're not scared of losing the keys. You see overtones, symbolism in them. That's nonsense. Keys are just keys, They're to *let* you in, not *lock* you in. Hazel and Jill would like you to have keys so you can surprise them sometimes, just by being here.' Eventually, she'd capitulated and to date had never lost either.

She surprised the girls and Harpur himself by arriving

today. It was a pleasure for them all, but especially good for Hazel in her present state. Denise had made herself a cup of tea and picked up Jill's boxing book from the settee while waiting. 'I've been reading about a title fight between Marciano and Walcott in 1952,' she said. 'Marciano's the one you're supposed to look like, isn't he, Col, except hair colour?'

'A lot thought him crude,' Jill said.

'Who?' Denise said.

'Marciano.'

'What do you mean, who?' Harpur said.

'But Marciano took Walcott with a beautiful short right in the thirteenth that wasn't crude at all,' Jill said. 'The only boxer ever to knock out Marciano died the other day. When he was an amateur, though. That other boxer played Joe Louis in a film.'

'There are no pictures of Marciano here', Denise said.

'Big jaw, big nose punched wonky, thick neck,' Jill replied.

'Right,' Denise said.

'Are you staying?' Jill asked her. The girls liked it when Denise was there to do breakfast. They said it felt like family. And Harpur, also, liked it when Denise could spend the night.

'Dad's kind, not crude,' Hazel said.

'Someone could be kind *and* crude,' Jill said.

'He took us out to the park, Denise,' Hazel said. 'The killing park. He thinks maybe Scott was there.'

'He said he *didn't* think Scott was there,' Jill said.

'That's what I mean – kind, not crude. He thinks Scott might have been there and wants me to know Scott might have been there, but he wouldn't just crudely say it. He'd say the opposite, from kindness,' Hazel replied. To Harpur, she sounded defeated by the kindness, if it *was* that.

'Yes, I can stay tonight,' Denise said. 'No early classes tomorrow, or none I wouldn't skip.'

'Oh, good, good,' Hazel said, and began to buck up.

In bed, Denise said: 'And *was* it the boyfriend at the park?'

'It might have been,' Harpur said. 'Only might. Very only. Very might.'

'But a worry.'

'Yes, a worry. At least he was smart enough to get clear.'

'This time. Should you speak to him?'

'Perhaps I should. Hazel will be furious – see it as meddling. Especially as I could be wrong with the identification. Well, it's not an identification. An impression. It can happen. And Iles had spoken about him.'

'Iles? That's weird, isn't it?'

'How?'

'Well, Iles, and the daft play he makes for Hazel.'

'Yes, daft. A game.'

'Might he want Scott caught up in something at Morton Cross, perhaps taken out of the reckoning?'

'Killed? That's ludicrous. Iles is not like that.'

'What *is* he like?'

'I've nothing that could be called evidence showing the boy there,' Harpur replied. 'I'd better think a while. There's an investigation still under way, of course. That might produce something.'

'I'm glad I came tonight. It seemed to help.'

'They need you, you see, Denise.'

'How about vou?'

'Oh, yes, they need *me* as well.'

'No,' she said, 'I meant the other way around.'

'What, this way?'

'You're so crude.'

'But also kind,' he said.

'Do *you* need me is what I meant – as you bloody well know I did?'

'Yes,' he said, 'I need you – as you bloody well know I do.'

41

Chapter Three

That latest violence at Morton Cross really troubled Ralph Ember. For one thing, his daughters' big-fee school, Corton College, stood in this district. Obviously, he did not want his children in some fucking uncultured, catch-as-catch-can comprehensive, although he thought the *idea* of equal-chance comprehensives for all youngsters great. There were quite a few people about who thought the *idea* of comprehensives for all youngsters great, but not for their own youngsters. Some of these people were in the Government.

One reason he'd picked Corton was its decent surroundings. But then came the Tirana death nearby and now warfare. Although he'd guessed something would follow Tirana's execution, the scale of this latest fighting and the number of killings definitely got to Ralph and depressed him badly. Often Ember thought about the decline of Britain and to date didn't know how he could stop it. He had power in his firms and the Monty, but something wider than this would be necessary to turn the country around.

He'd seen that lout cop, Harpur, afterwards on TV describing things and trying to reassure, but, in fact, Ember had heard of the shootings hours before this, and while they were still under way. The news flashed about as soon as the battle started. People telephoned him at home in Low Pastures, including Mansel Shale. He had apparently been informed by someone he knew living right alongside Chilton Park, who obviously had a gift for casualty reports.

'Ralph, what we said would come *has* come.' That's how Shale opened the call. It sounded almost like something from the New Testament referring to the prophets. Shale liked a bit of resonance now and then.

'What, Manse?'

'Up Morton Cross and Chilton Park.'

'What, a further incident thereabouts?' Of course, he meant further following Tirana's death, but Ralph had built this habit of smart phone vagueness for sensitive matters. He never liked being too exact and knowledgeable. All right, this was a landline call, his end at least, and maybe more secure than on two mobiles, but dicey just the same. Although police were supposed to follow special procedures for authority to phone tap, Iles would most likely say, 'Fuck procedures,' and do it.

Ember must show no link to the Tirana business. Ralph liked ample distance between himself and such episodes. True, he had certainly not been implicated in killing Tirana. Could he prove that, though, suppose someone like Iles, or someone like Harpur, decided it would be convenient if Ralph *was* implicated: that is, made to *look* implicated by adjusting evidence? *But you were actually seen running towards the BMW, Ralph, then pausing there.* Those two knew plenty about making people *look* implicated. Naturally Ember realized he could have been noted spending time near Tirana's car, telling the pathetic babe floozy to scram. Dangerous. Later, Ember felt puzzled by his behaviour that night. He acknowledged Shale probably had it right and they should have withdrawn immediately they discovered Tirana was dead. Ralph knew many would actually expect this from him. Behind his back, didn't they call him Panicking Ralph? He'd found out about that. On the quiet, even Shale might refer to him as Panicking and must have been shocked when Ember went to help the child, regardless. Looking back, Ember eventually decided he'd acted as he did because, as he'd told Manse, one of his own daughters, Venetia, would be around the age of this lost, exploited kid. That touched him and brought a kind of duty: he'd found he could not leave someone so young alongside a degenerate, extremely foreign deado, the girl almost certainly without papers and in a mess if the police found her.

'You call it "a further incident thereabouts",' Shale had said on the phone. He went chuckly for a while, some high merriment, definitely of a mocking type at Ember's code talk. Manse could be like that occasionally. 'Yes, you could call it a further incident thereabouts. In fact, a lot of fucking further incidents thereabouts. It's brilliant, Ralph. It's all we ever prayed for. There's two finished for definite and another *en* fucking *route*, with what looks like most of his nose and top jaw gone from something heavy calibre, even a .45. That's my info at this moment in time, and ongoing a treat. A real, beautiful, fucking outbreak, Ralph. In daylight. Lunch time. They don't care. You remember that town in Iraq?'

'Which, Manse?'

'The one onslaughted and onslaughted by planes and the US Marines.'

'Fallujah?'

'It's like that up Chilton Park current. I mean, as we're talking now. I'm bringing it to you Live, like the BBC say, meaning some deads. That's the picture I get. They'll all destroy one another. This is barrages. Fire-power barrages. It's a blessing to us, Ralph. Competition finished. My source – he don't know who's who and can't identify, only do descriptions. He's not in our kind of enterprise, so don't know personnel no matter how major, but he says some big, thuggy-looking lad, terrible suit, H and K, arrives a bit late, on a call-out, that's obvious, and does a bend over one of the deads, then gets on fast through the park. I'd say Harpur. Not Iles. Iles is not thuggy-looking, only thuggy, plus his gorgeous garments, always handmade by some

44

possibly unpissed tailor. And my source says a kid around the scene.'

'What kid?'

'He's part of it.'

'Of the fighting?' Ember said.

'This is a kid, male, maybe sixteen or seventeen. Trainers. He got a piece. He might of started it all, blasting off. You know what they're like for armament, kids that age. If God asked what they wanted, a big cock or a big gun, they'd pick the gun.'

One of the drawbacks with Manse was he could get thrilled and start mouthing, on the phone and in a group. He'd forget about caution. He believed in optimism. He spoke optimism. Ralph understood and even sympathized to some extent: if such an uneducated cunt managed to get to where he was, and to what he had, he would naturally feel born to triumph. Optimism could be great. It could also be stupid. For instance, he would take these women such as Lowri or Patricia or Carmel into his rectory and then kick them out with some piffling gift after a spell, never thinking one might turn rough at this coolness and start selling tales about his private commercial matters to the newspapers. They were bound to see where his money came from and, with proper art hanging in his place, not prints, they'd guess he brought in bucketfuls. Ralph liked quite a lot about the Press, and the local daily often printed letters from him as Ralph Ember and Ralph W. Ember on crucial environmental topics, the need to stop pollution, and the slide in social and education standards. But the Press could also be damaging. Nixon. People still talked of how those Washington journos wrecked a President of the United States.

'You was right, Ralph. I got to admit it.'

'In which regard, Manse?'

'When you said no need to get involved because they'll look after the self-extermination *for* us, and so we're soon back to the old happy peace and trade harmony. Plus there'll be them armed response wagons up there, Volvos, meaning that what the gangs don't do to theirselves the police will do *for* them. They got some lovely marksmen. It's training, including night vision, although not needed this time. There's this boy, Callinicos.'

'Who?'

'Vic. Armed response. He can hit anything, running, jumping, standing still at 300 metres. Only a sergeant so far but he'll do bullet clusters like inspired. I heard this about him : "Holes are where the heart is." Get it, Ralph? It's like a well-known old saying my mother used to tell us, "*Home* is where the heart is," but they change it to "*Holes* are where the heart is," owing to the gunnery of Callinicos and where he's aiming, the heart. That's what they're taught. No wounding or winging, kill.'

The thing about Manse was he could really enjoy tales of this jolly park carnage at Morton Cross because he did not have skill at long-term strategy and visualizing of a situation, and he had no children in a school near there. Manse's son and daughter did get private education, naturally, but at the other end of the city. Ralph had considered that school for Venetia and Fay. But, despite the fact that there'd never been even one stabbing or rape there, this school offered nothing on the Classics, not even English language versions of such tales as *Atalanta and the Golden Apples*, so he'd been forced to tell the head it would regrettably not do, though no hard feelings. Ralph considered that in a very unsettled world scene, such as Iraq, Bin Laden and shag-around MPs, the Classics provided quite a comfort and a glimpse of enduring quality.

Manse's phone message had come at just before 2 p.m. on the battle of Chilton Park day. Ember was due to pick his daughters up at 3.45 when classes ended, but he decided he would go earlier. Hostilities could spill to anywhere. All right, that ace, Vic Callinicos, mentioned by Shale, might be able to put bullets only where he wanted them, but others would bang off, lacking finesse, and anyone might catch one of the strays. Kids generally waited outside the school as the queue of parents' cars edged forward picking up, and this might leave the last few very open.

Although Ember had the Beretta in a floor safe under bedroom boards at his country house, Low Pastures – plus a couple of other pistols, also locked up, in his private office at the Monty – he decided not to go armed. The tone would be so wrong, for God's sake. He often considered tone as far as guns were concerned. Schools and firearms should be kept very separate, unless, of course, matters became really uneducational. Another point: police were sure to be swarming and he might get stopped, even given the once-over. A beautiful weapon, the Beretta, but he'd hate one to get fished from his pocket by some officer in front of Venetia and Fay. That would not suit the usual image of a father with children at private school – that is, getting the best possible done for them. Ralph valued this image of himself as parent. He longed for the girls to esteem him. Possibly they already had some notion of a roughish side to Ember's career, but he did not want this given a big, unmistakable display in their presence, plus the arrest that would go with it for carrying a gun.

Previously, when Iles more or less – well, more – when Iles more or less ran the patch, nobody would have had the gall to stop and search Ralph Ember. But Iles's control of the scene had slipped, and might slip more. The new, easier laws on substance dealing weakened him, because his wise and constructive protection in the trade context wasn't so vital any longer. Plus, so much stuff came from Afghanistan now the Talibans didn't rule – opium production up seventeen per cent there for H. All sorts here could have a go trading and didn't need Iles's help. He would fight to get his sway back, naturally, and Manse and Ember would try to give him aid, but there had to be some uncertainties. Also, a new Chief had taken over from Mr Mark Lane, and Iles was forced to kowtow to some extent, could not ignore and/or browbeat his boss. In some ways it might be seen as progress if Iles became normal and close to human, but that brought harmful effects to trade and profits. And, in any case, Ralph felt a sort of regret: Iles was not made to be normal, or even near. This would be part of the general national decline Ember grieved over.

Although he had taken a route that touched only the rim of Morton Cross and the Park region, he saw plenty of police vehicles full of officers in bullet-proof gear making for the trouble, or for the aftermath. Some streets were closed to normal traffic. He reached the school at about 3.25 and took first place at the waiting spot. That pleased him, obviously, but he did wonder whether there'd be questions about why he arrived so early. No other parent would have received an as-it-happens battle briefing from Manse Shale. Ah, well, this was a minor worry. The important aim must be to get Venetia and Fay safely to Low Pastures.

On the way back, Venetia said: 'So you made it to the head of the queue today, dad. The buzz says some pop-gun bother not far off. That why?'

'What buzz?' Ember replied.

'Around the school,' Venetia said.

'Morton Cross and the Park,' Fay said.

'These new foreign guys on the block giving heat?' Venetia said.

Ember hated the way kids seemed to know everything faster than himself. And he hated the way they talked. You'd think if they were studying *Atalanta and the Golden Apples* and Zeus, even in English, they'd have a nicer way of expression. This place, Corton, was fucking thick costs in duplicate three terms a year. He'd like to see some polish. 'Heat' – slang.

Very late in the evening of the day following that park warfare, Ralph received another call from Shale. Ralph was at the Monty now, making sure things went all right there. He spoke to Manse from his office. A disturbance like

48

Morton Cross could unsettle the city in general for anything up to ninety-six hours, and he needed to keep an eye. Tranquillity had to be worked for, nursed. It did not just come. He thought of the Monty as like a thermometer. If some part of the city turned feverish, the Monty would register it at once. In a way, Ember felt proud of this. Didn't it show lovely, sensitive linkage with the community, or at least part of? But hazards came, too. Some Monty members could be nervy about any kind of increased police activity, especially people out on bail conditions, or well into setting up something that might have been grassed, or both. Shale said: 'You seen Harpur on TV about it, did you?' He put on an unrough, serious voice, imitating: '"Unacceptable violence", "affront to the majority of peaceable householders in the area" – that kind of fucking nothing, Ralph. Iles low profiling, of course. I laughed right through the Harpur bleat. He should switch to vicardom when he retires.'

'Manse, I don't want to leave the bar area unattended too long because –'

'Why I'm ringing, Ralph, is he was up there again today. This got some meaning. This got what's known as "overtones". You heard of them at all? Yes, overtones – meaning . . . well . . . meaning meaning. This needs discussion.'

'Who was up there?'

'Harpur.'

'Where?'

'Morton Cross. The Park.'

'Well, that would be routine, wouldn't it, Manse? A fresh look at the scene in calm conditions. Clue-seeking.'

'Yeah, but listen, Ralph, he's with his kids. Not with Ilesy or other cops. His kids! He got two girls, right – like yourself?'

'His daughters with him?' Real amazement hit Ember.

'Showing them the details. There's still a lot of his people around, measuring up, looking for spents, doing

49

photographs – the usual plod detective carry-on, but he's with his kids. They hang about the flowers.'

'The flowers?'

'A big conversation, Ralph, specially with the older girl.'

'You mean, he seemed to talk to them about flowers growing in the park?' Ember said. He thought he spotted a reason for the visit. 'Oh, I see why, Manse. It's to show his children Nature goes on despite the turmoil. This is what's known as "an eternal verity" and people can take solace from it.' During the general subjects foundation year for his mature degree at university – in suspension at present because of these special business difficulties – during that year, Ember had studied a poem where the very famous Irishman, William Butler Yeats, moans about getting old, although fifty-nine swans he's watched arriving at a certain time every autumn for nineteen years in some park over there stay always young and strut about, no trouble, in the water.

It's shit, of course, because the swans he's looking at now are different ones from the flock he first saw nineteen years ago, but the tradition of going to this park at this time for a strut about in the water has been passed down from swan generation to generation. However, poets don't have to be logical, only egomaniac, and he wants to say Nature is timeless, full of renewal – though, somehow, not the bit of Nature that W.B. Yeats is. Such an idea could be what Harpur was trying to get over in his flower lecture to the girls, and Ralph gave Shale a quick account of the poem. This might not be up Manse's street exactly, but it seemed right to show him the wider aspect. 'Harpur's children have heard of the violence and are upset, maybe. He's trying to soothe. It's good parenthood, Manse.' Ember sometimes felt a link with Harpur – both with a pair of schoolgirl daughters, and keen to lead them into a happy life. He would bet Harpur was as determined as himself to show his daughters a good, fatherly image.

Of course, Harpur had to do it by himself since his wife went like that. On the other hand, Ember's wife, Margaret, definitely gave him some help with the children. 'These flowers growing imperturbably, fearlessly, in the park despite all the bullets were intended as reassurance to his kids, Manse.'

'Fucking bunches,' Shale replied.

'What?'

'The flowers – they're not growing. They're not for ever, not even like the blarney poet's fifty-nine swans. They been cut, Ralph. These was RIP carnations. They say, "Rest in peace now you been downed in war." You know the palaver. Cards with messages on. That sort of flowers. They're where Harpur stopped and inspected a corpse on the day. My source knew him now because he been on TV as mentioned previous. The cards might give the police some names to follow up, unless they're just signed "Sugar" or "Thongy". That will be a thing about identity cards when the Government gets them going. Women could call theirselves Thongy but what's known as a data bank would come up with the truth. We'll all be in it. What used to be called "Blunkett coverage" until he went, on account of *Spectator* sex, meaning not voyeuring but banging a bird from the *Spectator* magazine. Yes, a real name could be discovered, as long as police could find Thongy and ask her for her identity card. Obviously, Ralph, Thongy's not a pet name a woman should use when elderly and getting cumbersome, so this would reduce the possibles.'

'Harpur talked to his daughters about the deaths? Is that what you're saying, Manse?'

'The young one started galloping down the path like armed and shouting "Police." It's panto, Ralph. And the other kid – Hazel? – the one they say Iles gets inappropriate about – she's weeping, and Harpur's stroking the top of her head, those fucking hands like horse hooves.

That's my source said that – like horse hooves, Harpur's hands. He can do phrases, my source.'

'He's a plus, Manse.'

'He got a property up there, by the Park. I don't hear of no swans in this Park. But all this activity, it's under his bedroom window. Maybe he was guessing a bit about the nose and top jaw getting shot away, but he can see quite good from there. He's in what's often termed the media, which you've heard of, I'm sure, Ralph, working from home a lot with a modem. They got no end of modems in media. Being in media is how he can do phrasing and report the conflict, and how he got a property in Chilton Park, which is quite an area. Was.'

I'm surprised you know people like that, Manse. But Ember did not actually say this. It would sound insulting, as if Shale could have no contacts accomplished enough, literate enough, to do all right in the media. Mind, it *was* more or less impossible to understand how Manse *could* have friends accomplished enough, literate enough, to do all right in the media, but some of those women he let into the rectory during his mating seasons might have all sorts of connections and would introduce him. It was also more or less impossible to understand why any unbraindead woman *would* introduce him around, but they might. After all, if you thought of Manse in an ex-rectory, with possible genuine art, apparently not thieved, and his children doing pay-for education also – if you thought of him like that, which is how he wanted to be thought of, he did possess a sort of social status.

What sort? Ember had often wondered about this. Manse's children were called Laurent and Matilda, which showed he aimed at prominence. Quite a time ago his wife went off to live in Wales with a surveyor or broker. Women could be like that these days. They felt entitled. She didn't care about the rectory or the paintings or the social status. She just left. So, Manse, also, was a bit like Harpur, as they both had to bring up children alone. Manse and the kids stayed on their own in that big house, except when one of the stand-by women came in for a fondness stint. Manse had told Ralph very strongly that, to keep things wholesome and not upset Laurent and Matilda, he would never have more than one girl at a time cohabiting. Although there was no order from the court, Shale gave his wife access to the children. He could turn generous quite often, as a matter of fact, although he'd been slow shelling to Tirana's tart.

'Don't ask me what they do with the bodies, Ralphy.'

'Which?'

'Tirana. People like that. There could of been some local firms fighting as well up at the Park, but mainly this is people from Albania way.'

'Yes, Albania.'

'Some of them countries, they make a fuss about the body. In a religious style. You know the kind of fuss they kick up in places like that, all wailing and chucking theirselves about to prove they do classier mourning than anyone else. It's a competition. They want the body back for a proper funeral. This Albania will be getting coffins every day or two from Morton Cross. Their mothers and fathers over there, they'll think Morton Cross is like that massacre place in the First War.'

'Passchendaele.'

'These was quite nice streets. And the Park. It makes me feel ashamed, Ralph.'

'Well, yes, it's bad.'

'If there was water in that park with fifty-nine swans on it the swans might get to look really worried and haggard because of all the shooting, not young at all. Fifty-nine is a big spread of swans, Ralph, and long necks. One or two might easily get hit by loose bullets.'

'I see this kind of thing as symptom of –'

'But in another way it's good,' Shale replied. 'It's just clearing them fucking Albanians and maybe some others out of the way, Adrian Cologne, to name one. Don't tell me we're going to let them Alb lot into the EU as well as the fucking Turks, Ralph.'

If Harpur had made a big thing with his children of the memorial bouquets, not the park's own flowers, Ember realized he should change his interpretation of the visit. This must be some kind of warning to them, mustn't it? The flowers they talked about meant wipe-out, not ever-lastingness. Of course, Manse had seen that, too. All right, he could not put words together but he had moments when he grew aware of things. You didn't get an ex-rectory and art from a different century without these. 'Them kids of Harpur – they connected, Ralph?' he said.

'With what?'

'It's all right to put his paw on the girl's head to make her feel better, but then you got to ask what's he taking them up there at all for and showing them horror scenes. This kid is upset, scared. Is that good what you call it – parenthood? Unless something behind. This is why I said "overtones".'

'What kind of overtones, Manse?'

'This could give a kid nightmares. All right, one of them is enjoying it, chasing about like Dirty Harry, but she's younger, she don't see the total scenario. You heard of that at all, Ralph – "scenario"? Meaning the general picture.'

'What *is* the total scenario, Manse?'

'Why I'm ringing. This is to try and sort things. There are what's called "insights", Ralph. You could have some insights. I could have others. Then, when we put them together, we got a real portrait of things.'

'I don't know if we should talk about this kind of topic on the phone, Manse. And, in any case, I need to get down to the bar and –'

'When I say connected, Ralph – this older girl. You know what they can be like at that age. What is she, fourteen, fifteen? They're like full women a lot of them. Oh, they're well into the world. Think of your own daughter, Ralph, if you don't mind me saying. Venetia? Lovely name. Lovely kid, I'm sure. But didn't you have to send her to a sort of convent school in France to quell some of her ways before they got too much grip? I wouldn't want to speak out of turn, Ralph. I see it as more the men's fault than your daughter's.'

'Her mother and I had always planned a European element in the girls' education, Manse. Venetia's time abroad was simply part of that scheme, believe me.' Ember considered this might easily have been true. Some schooling abroad could undoubtedly bring a child extra poise. He thought the nuns did keep her from more trouble over there, without trying any carry-ons with her themselves: grim things about convents appeared in the newspapers. It had been a successful gamble, as far as he could tell.

'Anway, she's back now and I should think really glad to have seen the French side of matters, Ralph. But that's Venetia. We got to think about Harpur's kid. What we got to ask is, when noting this trip to the Park with them, what we got to ask is, does Harpur think she's tied up somehow with the disgraceful ding-dong there? And he takes her there to see them "with deepest sympathy" tokens on the so-called fucking "floral tributes" so she can get an idea of what it's really like and decide to be a home-girl again, because she's afraid.'

Ember had been thinking like this, too. 'It's very speculative, Manse,' he said.

'She into boyfriends, that sort of thing? I know about Iles and the leering and the red scarf with tassels he wears, but boys her own age? You see the way I'm thinking, Ralph? You see what I mean when I say "connected".'

Yes, Ember saw.

'This kid up there – I mean the boy my source saw. The kid with the armament. Trainers. She know him? If there's some local firm at it as well as the Albs, this kid, the boy kid, he could of been pulled into it. This could be Adrian Cologne, Tommy the Strong, Sprale. One of them promise him a gun and he'd do anything. That's how a lot of them are. Fight the Albs, fight anyone, as long as he got a piece for his own self. Harpur wonders about this? He gives the girls a lesson – not just talking to them, but the scene, the clingfilm carnations, what schools call "visual aids", like cocoa beans to show agriculture abroad.'

'This is an interesting thesis, Manse, but –'

'I see a couple of very rosy possibilities here, Ralph. From our trade point of view, I mean.'

'In what respect?'

'I see a way of doing Harpur some good here, Ralph. That got to be useful from a commercial aspect, for sure. He's going to think of this favour we done him and he'll be grateful. He's an ape, yes, but he's also the kind who would know about gratitude and want to repay. How do he repay? Obvious. By being friendly to our firms, Ralph. This is a valuable matter at a time of very high commercial uncertainty, meaning you even had to give up your university studies.'

'On hold. What favour, Manse?'

'As I regard it, he can't speak about all this to the boy hisself. Not on. It would be like accusing him. The daughter would hate Harpur for this. To her it would be nosing. It would be bringing heavy cop things into her love life. That's why he got the girl up the Park, so *she'll* do it.'

'We don't know it *is* the boy, Manse. Your source can't identify. This is a kid of sixteen, seventeen, with trainers and a pistol. That's as much as we have.'

'Plus we have Harpur up the fucking Park, Ralph. That's to say, a big crime scene with his daughters, and giving one of them daughters pain and also some comforting after the pain, but it's the pain he wants to give most. Now, all right, Harpur's an ape, but I wouldn't say he's the sort who would plan to hurt his kid, or even any kid, unless he thought this was the best way to get somewhere. He got an objective at that Park, Ralph. We can help him. We back up the warning for him – the warning he wants his daughter to give this lad.'

'But how would we reach the lad, Manse? This is a kid who was in the Park, but where is he now? How do we find him?'

'Maybe you're going at it the wrong way, Ralph.'

'Which other way is there? We have to identify him.'

'If it's the girl's boyfriend we can find out who her boyfriend is, can't we? That's just a bit of research, no problem at all. We do a little watch and there's her boyfriend coming to Harpur's house, or meeting her somewhere at a disco or some other club or that crowd always around the bus station, skateboarding and ganja and so on. So, we got him. We tail him home. We ask some youngsters playing hopscotch in the street, Who lives in that house? We get his name. So, we can arrange to introduce ourselves and have a little word with him about the perils. This boy's going to listen better to some giant of the game, such as yourself, Ralph, nor he would to his girlfriend, even if the girlfriend's talking Harpur at him.

'Or maybe we could both chat to him. Plus, this would give him a bit of terror, if he thought we had him identified. He'll know you don't like no rivalry in the trade, up Morton Cross or anywhere else in the town, and he'll know I don't like it neither. People have been seen off for trying competition. I don't want to speak much about that, but they have been, haven't they? That's just an ordinary part of the company scene. This is just dog eat dog. You can look a bit worrying when you're angry, Ralph, or acting angry. Yes, yes, I know it's famed you could be mistook for Charlton Heston when young – that's when *he* was young – but sometimes it's like Charlton Heston when young but in a rage, say because of cruel overseers in *Ben Hur*. So we tell him, Just get out of it, sonny, drop the gun in the river, and mention to your girlfriend that you had a chat with Mr Ralph Ember and Mr Mansel Shale and they persuaded you to give it up. Then the girlfriend tells daddy, and Harpur has big warmth to us and shows it the best way possible. I mean, we get looked after in the trade, Ralph. All right, you'll say, Have they got the power now to look after us, him and Iles, in view of all the developments? Well, maybe they can't do it the way Iles used to, but they could still do the opposite, that is, they could fuck us up if they wanted to. These shootings – all right, they're not in our trading area, but you got to think of the Government.'

'Think of the Government in which respect, Manse?'

'The Government won't like street shootings – not so many. This is a Government that believes in law and order. All right, they don't *get* law and order, obviously, not here and not in Iraq. But they *believe* in it. When they hear about three deads in a Park battle here and some injured, they're going to tell the police in this town to make sure it stops. They're going to tell police in this town to hit the drugs firms. *All* the drugs firms. The Government won't know the difference between dealing up Morton Cross way and dealing nice and orderly and very traditional around Valencia Esplanade. The Government can't come out and say, Hit them fucking Albanian bastards and the ones imitating them for fucking up the trade arrangements, can they, because that's going to sound racist and they got to be so careful on that? Plus, they can't talk about the previous trade arrangements as if they was great, because officially there shouldn't be no trade arrangements at all. So, they're going to give orders, Smash *every* fucking drugs firm and stop this warring – like equal treatment for each drug firm, Alb or not. They got an election coming soon. They got to make this country look safe, even if they can't do it in Iraq. But if Harpur knows we been looking after his daughter, by looking after his daughter's boyfriend, he'll keep us low on the priority list for targeting. The other firms will get done and we'll be back to sweet monopoly and fine peace, Ralph. That will satisfy every-one -- the Government, everyone.

'All right, you'll say, Harpur might be like this because of thankfulness to us, but Iles won't be. You'll say Iles would not want to *save* this boy, he'd want him taken out, so there's an open way to Harpur's daughter who Iles been trying glam and lech approaches to for months or longer regardless of underage.'

'Oh, I don't think Iles would be like that, Manse.'

'Like what? Like fancying underage?'

'Wishing harm to the boy.'

'He's a mystery, that Iles.'

'Yes, he *is* a mystery. But just the same I don't –'

'I see this as two dads,' Shale said – 'you and me – wanting to help another dad – Harpur – even though he's not in no way a colleague, and could even be said to be the opposite of a colleague. But there's like a bond through that fatherliness. This I reckon got much nobility to it. We terrify the shit out of this kid and get the silly little fucker back to safety.'

God, perhaps Manse could do strategy after all. Ember heard voices getting untoward in the bar. He needed to be amongst them quickly. 'I'm going to think about all this, Manse.'

'Yes, think about it, Ralph. Give it urgency, all right?'

Chapter Four

Harpur awoke alongside Denise and for a minute or two, eyes still shut, wondered if tailing Scott and/or taking a look on the quiet through his parents' house might prove whether he'd been drawn into working for a drugs firm, and whether he possessed a gun. 'On the quiet' meant breaking in when the place was empty. Or not actually breaking. He hoped a bit of plastic would do a lock for him. Harpur always enjoyed having these looks on the quiet through other people's property. It could tell you a lot about them that you would never otherwise get to. He likened it in some ways to psychiatry. A psychiatrist was interested in the furniture of a patient's mind. Harpur was interested in furniture as furniture.

They had a routine at Harpur's house when Denise slept over. Hazel and Jill came into the bedroom with a cup of tea for both of them quite early, and then, having chatted with the girls and/or Harpur for a while, Denise would go downstairs and make breakfast while he pushbiked to the newspaper shop. Except for the shop trip, each segment of this ritual had big importance, beginning with the cups of tea. These days, the children opened the door and walked in without warning though each had a hand tea-less and free to knock. Harpur understood their thinking. They wanted to show they saw his relationship with Denise as normal, open, wholesome and, in fact, to Harpur's credit. For them to be in bed together was part of this normal arrangement: Hazel and Jill knew something of the world.

Tact from the girls would have been a kind of squeamish reproach. They regarded themselves as well above all that – on condition the woman alongside him was Denise, and invariably Denise.

Although they entirely approved of *her*, the girls – and Hazel, especially – mistrusted Harpur and could turn on him if they thought he might be looking about elsewhere. When he came home late, Hazel often queried his claims to have been working, although frequently, in fact, Harpur *had* been working. Often, he had explained that police duties could not be governed by the clock. The girls would nod and doubt. They considered that, when youngsters, Harpur and his wife, Megan, dead now, inhaled too much relaxed morality from the 1960s and '70s. This needed correction whenever it showed itself. They believed that Harpur's feelings for Denise might keep him reasonably spruce, though their own liking for her was not based only on this. She guided, amused, encouraged them. Mothered them? The girls might say so. Possibly Denise would dislike the word. She was a student at the local university up the road, only a few years older than Hazel, and generally talked to the girls as she might have done to contemporaries.

She did cook these magnificent, long-lasting, meaningful breakfasts, though – the kind of thing good mothers offered, to sustain the family for the day. Hazel and Jill enjoyed being sustained as parts of a family, a full family, or as near to that as possible now. They thought Denise helped them get nearer. Harpur could cook fine breakfasts and so could his daughters themselves, but these excellent meals amounted to no more than excellent meals. They lacked the happy, bonding symbolism of a Denise breakfast. When she was not around and Harpur gave his daughters a large breakfast – including black pudding, sausage, mushrooms and beans, as well as bacon, egg and fried bread, of course – yes, when he really went for it, he hoped this would stick in their memories: as adults they might then recall a grand provider and altogether brilliant single parent, not just someone to be regarded as dissolute and in danger of getting poxed when out late. But he recognized that, for the present, the Denise breakfasts ranked much higher than his and had a resonance beyond the actual piled-up greasy chow and choice of coffee or tea and red or brown sauce. He not only recognized it, he shared the enthusiasm his daughters had for a Denise-concocted meal.

'The way we see it, you got some big, but I mean *big*, trouble coming, dad,' Jill said. She stood at the head of the bed on Harpur's side, ready to offer the cup of tea when he awoke a bit more. Hazel waited on the other side, close to Denise. The girls wore school uniform. And, looking at Hazel in this classroom gear, Harpur found it almost absurd to imagine she might get touched, destroyed, as the result of a drugs war. But that thought was suddenly squashed by a brain-rush he could not control. It proposed – insisted on – three certainties: (i) the lad in the park had been Scott, (ii) if Scott stayed in the game he'd get hit, (iii) if he was hit, Hazel would never recover from the distress. Harpur did not often cave in to intuition, and he tried to resist these emphatic, badgering notions now. He switched on some matter-of-fact heartiness. 'So, who's got big trouble coming?' he said.

'You,' Jill said. 'You being you and you also being the police. We're worried.'

'Oh, we've got enough big trouble already,' Harpur said. 'Always have.'

'Haze and I both take Sociology at school, you know, Denise,' Jill said. 'That's where we're coming from.'

'Yes, it's true we've done some Sociology on the situation,' Hazel said.

'Ah, learned stuff,' Harpur replied.

'Look, dad, here's the question we've been thinking about – what's going to happen now at Morton Cross and

62

Chilton Park?' Jill said. Harpur sat up in bed and took his cup of tea from her.

Denise, on her stomach and still three quarters asleep, waved a nicotined hand slackly once. It might mean that Hazel should put her cup of tea on the floor, please. It might mean, 'For God's sake, stuff your theories, kids, shut up and go away.' She grunted but said nothing intelligible. He couldn't tell whether she'd registered the children's remarks about Sociology, or whether this would interest her, suppose she had. But he forced himself to keep his mind on Denise, and on his unwavering delight in her, rather than listen to those harsh, internal self-briefings. Harpur loved the way Denise could relax here, as if she belonged. Her unconsciousness spells were classics of blottoness. He'd never seen a head dig deeper into the pillow, like really fixtured, the way woodworms got at planks.

'What we thought is, you'll fill the streets and the Park with officers now,' Jill said. 'You'll have to.'

'There'll be a visible police presence, yes,' Harpur said.

'That's what it's called, like officially, is it? "A visible police presence".'

'Not "*like* officially",' Harpur said. 'Officially.'

'Like a cop-swarm, anyway,' Jill replied.

'Yes, you'll have to,' Hazel said.

'There's big houses, a lot of rich people with big, brassy voices up there,' Jill said. 'They're going to make a fuss. The thing is, dad, people like that know how to make a fuss. Ever come across the word "articulate" at all? Meaning they can mouth. That's what they are, articulate. This is how they get on so fast. Articulate. Think of Clinton. Or that big thinks woman who died, also U.S.'

'Susan Sontag,' Hazel said.

'But some British are articulate, also. These people up there at Chilton Park are going to blame you, dad, for what happened. I mean you, the police. A girl at judo lives up there. Her father's in what's known as the media. It's sure he knows about influence. He's in touch with all sorts – editors, MPs, business people. He can modem everywhere and get replies, known as "working from home", and very common these days. Most likely he'll do some real big complaining because World War Three was nearly into his front garden chipping the bird bath. Down goes the value of his house, or his *property*, as he'd call it, I expect.

'People in properties like that think they shouldn't have gunfire banging off close like Iraq when they paid so much for the property and also big council tax. Yes, it would be *properties* up there at Chilton Park. They'll all be double-glazed to keep noise out, admitted, but the people still won't fancy that sort of carry-on near. These are the sort of people the Government want to keep sweet so they'll vote for them at the next election. This is what's known as Middle England and they're the ones whose votes make all the difference. New Labour was cooked up just for them. John Prescott is there to get the *old* Labour lot in, so he doesn't have to be articulate. But *New* Labour with all the bright smiles and full stops just right is for Chilton Park and that sort.

'So, anyway, you got to clean up there and put in this whatyoucall . . . this visible police presence and you got to keep it there a time. Well, then we got to ask what happens to the firms who been working in the Park and around? There's survivors. They don't give up, do they? They got to live. Morton Cross, Inton, the Park – these are what's called their "career path". But, now, they look around and see it's too dangerous in these nice areas with properties, and they got to think quick and very quick of somewhere else. So, *which* somewhere else? They take another look around and find there been dealing going on for more or less eternity very lovely and peaceful down Valencia Esplanade way. All right, there's no *properties* there but there's houses and streets. They decide they better move there. That's why we said Sociology. These firms who been working in the smart areas up Inton, Morton Cross and

Chilton Park realize it's not no go no longer, or not for the moment, anyway, because police everywhere and punters are scared to come because of that or more bullets although it used to be a ducky area, but in a scruffier place, like the Valencia, it will be all right because that's what's *usual* in scruffy areas – that's what scruffy areas are *for*, and the Government don't have to worry about looking after scruffy areas because the people there would never vote Tory, through habit.'

'Or even Lib Dem,' Hazel said.

'Called "Labour heartland", due to docks and steel in the old days,' Jill said. 'But, of course, there's already druggy firms down the Valencia and on that floating restaurant near, in the docks, *The Eton Boating Song*. Some say Mr Iles looks after them as long as they keep off of violence. That's the tale around in school, anyway. It's Ralphy Ember from the crummy Monty club and Manse Shale, mostly, isn't it, dad?'

'You should be careful with names,' Harpur said.

'But if these other firms, some foreign, such as Albanian, come down from Morton Cross and wanting to take over the Valencia because Morton Cross is dead useless because of a visible police presence, then there'll be big war down the Valencia,' Jill replied. 'In Sociology lessons we also heard about what's known as "the territorial imperative". I don't know if you ever heard of that, dad. I expect Denise heard of it in the university, though. There's books re this. It means animals and people will always fight to keep their own ground, even if they are not usually fighters. Such as hen sparrows. This means you got big trouble in the Valencia and it could be *so* big you won't be able to pretend it's not there, known as blind-eyeing, even if it *is* only in the scruffy old Valencia.'

'We don't pretend,' Harpur said, 'or discriminate because of wealth and social class. That would be very poor policing indeed. One district is like another to us.'

'Yeah?' Jill replied. 'Hark at him, Denise.'

'Is that what will happen, dad?' Hazel asked.

'What?' Harpur said.

'Just the trouble shifts and gets worse – more danger-ous?' Hazel said.

'In school the tale is that Ralphy Ember and Manse Shale are very nice and no bloodshed if things are going sweet for them, but if someone gets out of line they know how to hit. Well, obviously. Would they still be around and coin-ing it if not? They don't like invaders. That's what I said – big trouble.'

'Is that right, dad – more dangerous?'

Harpur said: 'This is all simply –'

But Hazel didn't wait for his answer. She put Denise's cup and saucer down on the floor, slopping the tea a bit, and went quickly from the room. Harpur thought she was near weeping again. Perhaps she shared his bad intu-itions. But possibly she couldn't suppress them, the way he tried to.

Jill said: 'She's worried. She's scared for Scott, isn't she? All right, you'll say, Just a kid romance. But think of Romeo and Juliet. William Shakespeare. Many plays. This is also something I get at school. Don't tell me they was old, Romeo and Juliet. And yet this was real love, bringing death. That's why the play is what's known as a tragedy, although they were young. The comedies of William Shakespeare are not comedies. They don't make you laugh, only groan. But the tragedies are tragic and plenty of deads.'

Denise turned slowly on to her back in bed and opened her eyes. She had brought a short-sleeved nightdress with her because of the way the girls barged in first thing. 'What's it all about?'

'It's about what if it's Scott,' Jill said. 'Dad's frightened her. I don't say he should not of frightened her, it might be right, even kind. But all this has what is called "impacted" on Haze. I don't know if you've heard that word around.'

'*Have* frightened her,' Harpur replied.

Denise propped herself on an elbow and reached down for the tea. She had no tattoos on her arms, only the couple of entwined green and gold leaves, maybe Olympic laurel type, just above her arse, for low-slung trousers, and naturally not on show now. She took a few sips. '"If it's Scott." Is it? Was it?' she said. 'Is she afraid that if these firms move to the Valencia, Scott will go, too? That's supposing it *was* Scott. Do we suppose it *was* Scott, Col?'

Without being asked Jill passed Denise her cigarettes and lighter from the dressing table. The girls knew her procedures. Surprisingly, they had no policy on smoking. Denise did it, so it must be OK. Also, they thought that if there was a campaign against something it must be totally fine to do it. For instance, Harpur didn't know how to make them observe the warnings against unprotected sex and sex too young. 'All that just now – it was Hazel who really thought it out,' Jill replied.

'What?' Harpur said. Denise lit up and gave herself a vast invasion of fume.

'But she said it must be me who said it because she'd get too upset, so I learned it off. Like *the territorial imperative*, and *the Third World War* and the modem and Middle England up Morton Cross making a fuss because their *properties* get to be worth less,' Jill said. 'Haze knows about that kind of thing from Sociology. I know *some* from Sociology but she's two years ahead so she knows more about it on the political side and she finds books about it in the library. And it was Hazel who knew about Susan Whatyoucall. But she didn't say the thing about Iles. She wouldn't never say anything to hurt Iles, such as letting them forget the law, and trade drugs for the sake of peace. That was me said that. Some say Iles can't run things like that now, anyway, because of the new Chief and other things in the law. It was Hazel who said about the brassy voices and the bird bath getting chipped nearly. Hazel said Scott's mother calls their house a *property*. His mother

67

thinks people who got vans up there for work shouldn't park them on their drive because they're not right for the *properties*. And I expect she doesn't like police vans up there, either. She doesn't like police at all, really.'

'A visible presence will remain necessary for a while,' Harpur said.

'Anyway,' Jill said, 'how Hazel sees it is this – if these dealers move down to the Valencia, it's going to mean, most probably, more shooting, more people dead – but she knew if she said it it would make her cry – being scared for Scott. Well, she's crying just the same, most probably, which is why she went like that just now. And she asked me to say it to you instead, but I do agree it could be right what she worked out, so I didn't mind saying it and adding the bit about Iles, which people at school say, anyway, it's not a secret. She did not mind if I said her stuff in front of Denise because Denise is part of things here – you, Denise, Haze, me.'

'Of course,' Harpur said.

'Thanks, Jill,' Denise said.

But sometimes Harpur wondered whether Denise totally liked this kind of favour. She might feel the girls aimed to tie her into the family. The girls *did* aim to tie her into the family. So did Harpur, though he tried to be less blatant, worried she'd get frightened off. Denise was young and perhaps edgy about too much commitment. And maybe she had to consider what her parents would say about involvement with a widower and two children. He could sympathize. 'You'd better go to Hazel, Jill,' Harpur said. 'She shouldn't be by herself.'

'OK.' Jill sat down on the side of the bed. 'Is it right, dad?'

'What?'

'What she said. Worse trouble.'

'We're alert to any developments,' Harpur said.

'Oh, you sound like a spokesperson. And is it true – Mr Iles, his power's gone?'

68

'Mr Iles is still Assistant Chief (Operations).'

'But he used to be *the* Chief (Operations), didn't he? Under Mr Lane, Iles did what he liked. Will they all have to fight for themselves now – Ralphy Ember, Manse Shale?'

'It's our job to prevent fighting of any sort,' Harpur replied. 'The main duty of police is "to keep the peace". Haven't you done that in Sociology or History?'

'But you can't, can you? Look at Chilton Park.'

'We contained it.'

'What's that mean?'

'Kept it within limits.'

'What limits?' Jill said. 'Inside the park railings? Three dead, some hurt. It's funny in a way, isn't it, dad?'

'What?'

'All of this being about Scott and Mr Iles – the two of them around Hazel, like sexual,' Jill said.

'Oh, I don't like that word much,' Harpur said.

'Which?' Jill said. '"Sexual"?'

'"Around".'

'Why?' Jill replied.

'I don't know. It's off-colour,' Harpur said.

'Like flies around a honey pot,' Denise said.

'Well, yes,' Jill said.

'Cheapening,' Harpur said. 'And not true. Mr Iles clowns about and wears his vermilion, tasselled scarf but it's all a joke.'

'You think,' Jill replied.

'And nobody has said the trouble at Morton Cross involves Scott,' Harpur said. And he never *had* said it to them, as a certainty. Occasionally, and more than occasionally, he did say it to himself as a certainty, but he was attempting to deal with that.

'It *could* be Scott, though,' Jill said.

'Nobody has said it involves Scott,' Harpur said.

Jill pointed at him with the index fingers of both hands. 'Oh, that's what he does when he doesn't want to talk about something, Denise. He keeps saying the same thing. He's the way politicians are in TV interviews – keep on spouting what they've been told to spout regardless of the question. "On message" they call it. I think dad hopes people will get tired of it before he does. Or it could be he doesn't want to say something is true in case that makes it turn out true. Do you know what I mean? I expect he does it with you sometimes, if you ask him something he wants to keep to himself. I expect there's a lot of things he wants to keep to himself. He's like that. It's not just police things. All sorts. It's like him saying, "Get lost" but more polite. Or he'll start this heavy, big-time talk, like "We're alert to any developments," meaning "We know how to shut a stable door after the horse has gone." It *could* be about Scott, couldn't it, dad?'

'Nobody has said it's about Scott.'

'We can like *feel* things sometimes,' Jill said.

'Who?'

'Haze and me.'

'"Haze and I",' Harpur said.

'No, not Haze and you. Haze and me.'

'It should be "I". Grammar. What things?' Harpur replied.

'Like in the air. Things that nobody's said at all but that are there in people's heads – like in *your* head, dad. Sometimes we get a message from inside people's heads.'

Intuition. 'You do telepathy? I didn't know,' Harpur said. 'Telepathy *and* Sociology.'

'Well, I suppose everyone can do it – guess what's in someone's head,' Jill replied. 'Like when they say, "I know what you're thinking." But the Chinese are what's known as "inscrutable" because they don't let you see anything in their face. *Is* it in your head?'

'Am *I* inscrutable, although not Chinese?'

'You're police. That's even more inscrutable than the Chinese. *Is* it in your head?'

'What?'

'About Scott.'

'Nobody has said it involves Scott,' Harpur said.

Jill went into an enraged, cold whisper. Sometimes she seemed to have dumped childhood and behaved like someone twice her age. 'I know nobody has *said* it involves Scott, but is it in your head it *might* involve Scott? And is that idea coming through to Haze and I?'

'Me,' Harpur said.

'You?' Jill said. 'It can't come through to you if it's in you already – in your head.'

'I meant you should say "coming through to Haze and me" not "Haze and I". Grammar,' Harpur replied. He liked a chance to correct her. It helped bring her back to kid status. 'Go and see she's all right, will you, Jill, please? Calm her down.'

'No good anyone asking him, is it?' Jill said. 'Scott himself.'

'I don't think so,' Harpur said. It might happen, if Harpur collected some real evidence, enough to convince not a court but Hazel. Yes, he must consider how to get it.

'Most likely Scott would say, "No," nothing to do with him,' Jill said.

'Yes, most likely he would,' Harpur said.

'And then maybe Scott would get nasty with Hazel, or even finish it, because he'd think dad – dad, the police – has been sniffing.'

'Which is right, isn't it?' Denise said.

'Even if it was only Haze who asked him, not dad, Scott would think that and he wouldn't like it. He'd hate it and might even hate Hazel,' Jill said.

'I'm not going to ask him,' Harpur replied. 'I've promised Hazel, haven't I?'

'It's not just because Scott and Haze are . . . are like a relationship,' Jill said. 'But it's like about peer group loyalties, isn't it? That's another saying from Sociology, "peer group". That's peer with two "e"s not the other one, in the sea. I don't know if you heard of them, them loyalties. They're strong. It means kids don't just listen to what their mothers and fathers say – or just their father, here – but also they got to fit in to how other kids think and what they do, such as Haze got to fit in with Scott. It's natural. Kids who only listen to their parents and not to their peer group – well, their peer group would think kids like that were against the peer group and goody-goody.'

'Thanks for this briefing, Jill,' Harpur replied.

Cycling for the papers, he felt all his fears reassemble. Again he wondered whether he could tail Scott for a while unspotted and discover what contacts he had. Harpur was trained to gumshoe, of course, but hadn't tried it for years and might have forgotten the skills. In any case, as he remembered it, most of the training assumed a *team* of plain clothes officers replacing one another at fairly frequent intervals, so the target didn't notice a constant face and physique behind him/her. As to physique, Harpur had always been bulky for this work, too wide for cover from a lamp post. He looked cop. But he could not enlist a team now, and he couldn't order someone else to dog Scott. This had to be confidential. The object was not to build a prosecution case against someone, the normal reason for surveillance. He wanted to know as a certainty whether Scott had been sucked into crookedness and hazard. If Harpur did know that as a certainty he would reclaim the boy from both. There'd be no more hesitation or tact or anxiety about offending peer group values. He didn't want his daughter devastated by another death. Scott running around with a drugs firm and carrying a gun might any day become another death. Might? Now and then, Harpur thought this didn't do. *Would* any day become another death. But, with something to go on, Harpur could pressure and scare Scott into a change. Harpur knew how to pressure and scare. Of course, tailing Scott might sometimes mean tailing Hazel. She would regard that as the dirty depths of snoopery if she found out, and this might bring eternal damage to her view of him. But, to ignore the possible risk to Scott, and the shock and hurt that might hit Hazel, could damage Harpur's view of himself more.

And on his way back with the newspapers he allowed himself some thoughts about that other option. Now and then, in comparably difficult situations, he had broken into a place – house, flat, rooms, though, possibly, never a *property* – and done, for special reasons, a private, illicit and illegal search. Yes, these intrusions always thrilled him. He felt he could read people from a quiet look at the arrangement of their living quarters. But perhaps the comparison with a psychiatrist was high-falutin and bombastic. So, try someone else. He kept a saying in his head from a novel he'd once looked at: 'The mind and the instincts of a burglar are the same as the mind and instincts of a police officer.' Occasionally, when Megan's books still lined the sitting room, he'd pull a volume out and scan it if the title sounded interesting – *Scoop, Treasure Island, Portnoy's Complaint* – and he'd found those couple of lines, or something like, in a novel called *The Secret Agent*. They stuck. Naturally they did.

But the police officer's motives should be different from the burglar's. If Scott had a handgun it might be hidden somewhere in his parents' property when unneeded. Suppose on his visit Harpur found the weapon, he would certainly take it and any ammunition, as a burglar might take something. Harpur would take them and ditch them, though: a safety drill, not gain. And he'd be ready, then, to believe all his other suppositions were right, and start the pressure-and-scare programme on Scott. Harpur didn't allow himself to consider how he would deal with it if he were caught doing a prowl inside Scott's parents' house – property. Iles, the Chief, the Home Office, the Press and broadcasters would all find that startling. No, perhaps not Iles. On the whole, Iles did not believe in getting startled, especially by anything Harpur did. Furious, yes, contemptuous, yes, desperate, yes, startled, no.

The tailing and break-in ideas took on sharp, urgent, unrelenting form. For a couple of seconds he found himself trying to blur them, in case the children's famed antennae reacted, discerning – intuiting – what was in his head. But the breakfast passed comfortably, with a deal more Sociology chat about class, and discussion of some music Jill liked, Hazel claimed to despise, Denise had heard of, and Harpur hadn't. Then, after the girls left for school, Denise said: 'I get one of those messages.'

'Which?'

'From inside your head.'

'Oh, like the kids? My, my.' He would give her the performance – amusement, mockery, blandness.

'The message I get from inside your head, Col, is that you worry over Scott so much, and worry so much about the shock of a possible disaster on Hazel, that you could easily do something really stupid.'

'Like?'

'*You* tell *me*.'

'Like?'

'Ah, the brick wall repetition again.'

Obviously, Denise had things right and what he intended really was potentially stupid. So best not tell her, or at least not yet. She had read the message but luckily the message didn't go the distance, provided no details. He almost always listened to Denise. She had a brain. And, even though so young, she had judgement. He regarded her as an advertisement for higher education and its analytical training. However, he did not want the brain or the judgement applied destructively to these particular schemes. He tried to imagine what she would say in her damned highly educated, analytical tones about them if he did tell her.

This effort sharpened his own brain and judgement. He saw now that possibly the most stupid part was the plan to tail Scott, and therefore, almost certainly at some stage, to tail Hazel, who'd be with him then. And, also almost certainly, she would notice him, even if Scott did not. Harpur's way of moving and of standing still and of giving attention to what he saw would be printed on her subconscious, and similarly his height, weight, clothes, retreating hair. A father trailing his daughter! Snooping, as she'd certainly call it. God, contemptible. He was inviting catastrophe – permanent catastrophe in his relations with Hazel. Jill might not think much of him, either, when she heard about the spying. Probably, they'd fail to understand that his only aim was to protect Scott, and so protect Hazel. He would never recover his status as a fine, above-board single parent. This prospect terrified Harpur. He loathed the thought that he might get categorized in their recollections as a professional nose and not much more. Although his life could not allow a lot of above-boardness, he did often try to maintain it with the children. He decided to forget the tailing, just do the break-in. The objective was the same: nail Scott before someone else did. Of course, he saw a freighterload of difficulties around a break-in. Of course, he saw he could fail and saw that, if he did, someone else might nail Scott before he did, but nail him in a different way from what Harpur hoped.

Denise and Harpur washed the breakfast things and then went into the sitting room. He'd like a little escapism, a little selfishness, before he had to face up. But, at first, Denise did not allow that. 'And she's right, of course.' With another ciggie going, she was on one of the new settees Harpur had bought when changing the decor and ambience, legs folded under her.

'Who?' Harpur said.

'Jill.'

'About?'

'Romeo and Juliet.'

'Just kids were they?' Harpur said.

'Absolutely. So, you're right, too, Col.'

'About?'

'To worry. The feelings are real. They're young, Hazel and Scott – school kids – but the feelings are real. From her, anyway. I don't know him properly.'

'Oh, yes, they're real. They might not last. But for the moment they're real. She'd be poleaxed, if he was. I can't have that.'

He sensed her put the questing, undergrad brain on to this: 'No, you can't. No parent could. So, as I've said, you *might* do something stupid?' she asked.

'Yes, there's a bit of that in it.'

'Would it be doing something just for the sake of doing something?'

'Yes, there's a bit of that in it.'

'What I thought originally was you were scared that if Hazel lost Scott she'd be so off balance that . . .'

'She might turn to Iles in distress? Yes, there's a bit of that in it. You should be doing Psychology, not Literature and French.'

But Denise had grown fed up with the chatter. 'You know, Col, I look around this lovely room and feel that as a priority we should make love in it.' She pointed her cigarette at a selection of walls.

Thank God. She could turn him away momentarily from Scott, Hazel, guns, the war. 'Well, yes,' he said.

'This would have a fairly terrific significance.'

'*Will* have,' Harpur said.

'I see this room as the most important and significant part of the house. Its fulcrum.' She did an imitation of the words Jill used when she thought she might be going too fast for Harpur: 'You heard of "fulcrums" at all? It's quite a common word. Like crucial points or areas. This is the fulcrum.'

'I think so.'

'It used to have all those significant books belonging to your wife, didn't it?'

'Significant, yes.'

76

'Books do tarnish a room. But *nous avous changé tout çela.*'

'Sorry?'

'French. A famous line in literature.'

'Yes?'

'Meaning, "We've changed all that."'

'That's literature?'

'This would clinch it,' Denise replied.

'What?'

'Having it off here.'

'It will, it will. A priority, as you say.'

'Did you ever make love in this room surrounded by books just after breakfast with *her*? But is that a degraded, prying, unforgivable curiosity?'

'Yes.'

'Which?'

'Which what?'

'Which is the "Yes" for? Are you saying you *did* make love in here surrounded with books just after breakfast with her? Or, are you saying this is a degraded, prying, unforgivable curiosity?'

'If the "Yes" is for the second question, the first collapses,' Harpur said. The smart-arse waggishness could divert him for a while. Thanks, Denise. He'd keep it going, if he could.

'Don't dodge. *Was* the "Yes" for the second question?' she said.

'I bought these big settees in case you got to feel like this one day just after breakfast during the school term, when the children had left,' Harpur replied. 'They're part of the changes you mentioned in French.'

'Got to feel like what?' she said.

'Wanting a terrifically significant bonk in this previously book-bland room.'

'You thought I might get to feel like that, did you?'

'Oh, yes.'

77

'Usually I have to nip away pretty soon after breakfast for a lecture or seminar.'

'Yes, I know.'

'But there've been some emergency cancellations of teaching this week because of staff illness.'

'Yes.'

'When you bought the settees – what was it, months ago, a year ago? – anyway, when you bought them you guessed, did you, that there'd be some emergency cancellations of teaching today?'

'I felt you had certain plans for this room, it being what's known as a fulcrum,' Harpur said. 'You heard of that word at all?'

She ran a hand over the upholstery. 'Col, I feel honoured by the purchase of these settees.' It was as though she knew he needed to stay playful, silly, for as long as it could be made to last.

'It's true that not many girl undergraduates have settees bought with them naked specifically in mind, or men undergraduates, either, I shouldn't think.'

'Did you have me naked specifically in mind?'

'Oh, look, Denise, it would be crude, juvenile, to have you in mind naked all the time, but I do now and then. There's more to you than flesh. Oh dear, yes. After all, you know *Romeo and Juliet* and sayings in French.'

'Me *specifically* naked? Only me?'

'True,' Harpur replied.

'I don't mind you having me in mind like that as long as it's me specifically you have in mind.'

'What do you think – should I close the curtains?'

'This settee has a high back so we'd be concealed from the street and neighbours. And there's no newspaper boy to come up gawping close to the window and then putting a tale around about the Detective Chief Superintendent at it a.m., because you've already been for the papers.'

'Agreed,' Harpur said.

'Did you also have that in mind when you bought the settees?'

'What?'

'The high back.'

'I think there would be something base and furtive about closing the curtains,' Harpur replied. 'It would dim the . . . well, the significance.'

'Yes, I felt that. We're very much *en rapport* you know, Col, despite the age difference and so on.'

'Which "and so on"?'

'I'd say I've never felt so *en rapport* with any other man,' she replied.

'Well, don't keep searching for someone to match it,' he said. Her words solaced him. All of this after-breakfast situation solaced him, for now. He prized this *rapport*. He'd never experienced such a closeness with her, and, despite his previous intention to keep her in the dark, he now decided this would be disgracefully sly. It would mean he treated her as a helpful digression and that only. He must not endanger the brilliant, instinctive harmony.

And, so, afterwards, as they got their clothes on again behind the settee's high back, he told her his plans to do a search of Scott's parents' house. 'I knew it would be something like that,' she said.

'What do you think?' Suddenly, he felt he needed her fresh, dauntless, trained analytical mind after all.

'No choice,' she said.

Yes, she had it right straight off. But he'd like more clarity, more explanation from her. 'Well, there *is* a choice,' he said. 'I could do it or not do it.'

'No choice you being you,' she said.

Yes, she had it right again. That would do. They could go back to knockabout. 'Me being me,' he said. 'But what if I wasn't?'

''Well, I wouldn't have made love to you on this new settee in your own sitting room right after breakfast if you weren't you, would I?'

'You can always beat me on logic. It's your university tuition.'

'There'll be a lot of police around his parents' house,' she replied.

'This is a plus.'

'Is it?'

'*I'm* police.'

'Ah, true,' she said.

'I could be conducting inquiries. I *will* be conducting inquiries. A daytime call on someone who might have witnessed the action or part of it. However, there'll be nobody in. A plastic-card-on-the-front-door entry.'

'Alarms?'

'I hope none. And, in any case, sometimes the plastic doesn't set them off because it's acting almost like a legitimate key. Burglary is less than a science but does have some scientific aspects.'

'This will be a really fatherly thing, Col.'

'That's important.'

'I'd say crucial to you. Why openly in daylight?'

'I told you. It would have seemed inglorious and stealthy to make love behind the curtains.'

'No, I meant why do you have to break in up there during daylight?' she replied.

Naturally, he'd known that's what she meant, but he'd wanted a break from the listing of problems. 'The only time the house is liable to be empty. Mr, at work. Mrs, shopping or having her hair done. The children in school. I'll watch for a chance. A lot of waiting around.'

'Listen, if you're caught and they demote you to inspector I'll stick by you, Col. Women do that kind of thing. All the women stick by Phineas Finn when he's wrongly accused of murder in Anthony Trollope – though, mind you, he *is* handsome.'

'They'd demote me to constable.'

'Oh.'

'Possibly charge me.'

'Oh.'

He couldn't work out whether her shock was part of the jokey playacting or part of the occasional intrusions of the actual and the bloody sombre. 'Maybe I should be in the street to cell-phone warn if someone comes back early,' Denise said.

'Cell-phones are insecure, especially on a crime site. Plus, you'd be noticed up there. They'll notice everyone. And there's all the seminars and lectures you might miss.'

'Down to constable?' she said.

'It's possible.'

'I'd find that a challenge.'

Jokey? 'So would I,' he said.

'In uniform?'

'Possibly.'

'Hazel and Jill would hate that.'

'They would,' he said. 'And there'd be no point telling them it was all on account of trying to look after Scott and Hazel.'

'Kids can be cruel and narrow-minded.'

'It's all –'

'Oh, God, you're sure Scott's going to get killed, aren't you, Col?' For a bad, ungovernable moment, the badinage was dead. She looked as Hazel had looked – very close to weeping.

'Perhaps my mind's gone dodgy,' he said.

'I don't think so.'

'I hope so,' Harpur replied.

'Iles wouldn't let them take away your rank, would he?'

'Iles isn't the power he was. Besides, he likes a jape.'

'That would be a jape?'

'An Iles-type jape.'

'If you went to jail I'd be outside waiting on your release day,' she said, and smiled, to show things were back to whimsy.

'Good.'

Denise said: 'There's a Somerset Maugham story about a man sent to jail just after getting married and he wanks so often, thinking about his pretty wife, that when he comes out he's exhausted all his feelings for her.'

Jokey? Very darkly jokey? 'Sometimes I think you read too much,' he said. 'I wouldn't be surprised if you'd like a sitting room with book shelves all round.'

In the Grants' sitting room Harpur stood for a few minutes, well back from the windows, and did a quick survey. He felt that old excitement and that old annexed entitlement: the excitement and wholly unfounded entitlement of the invader. Mrs Grant would probably argue him out of that if she suddenly turned up. Perhaps this room, also, had fulcrum status, but it could not keep Harpur's attention for long. It was hardly the place where Scott would hide a gun, if Scott had a gun, and if Scott ran with traffickers and had been part of the Chilton Park inter-gang *Come Dancing*. The room conveyed to Harpur a family flavour, a high-flyer family. Most of the furniture looked as if it came from the Leather Paradise store, not too much shine on the surface, but a gentle glow saying wearability, as well as chic comfort. Harpur had looked at settees there when rescheming at home and greatly liked several, but found them too dear. At Leather Paradise they were called sofas, not settees.

The room had no fitted carpet but an oak board floor, varnished to a grand gold tint, and a couple of bright rugs with Picasso-style designs on in mostly red, cream, blue and yellow. Harpur thought they more or less got away with it as to taste, but realized he might be short of that. A boy brought up in this kind of setting should be aware of style. But he might decide that style required money. An oak floor would be an expensive extra and conceivably the rugs also cost. Had Scott decided to look for income early? Hazel visited the house now and then and, as far as

Harpur could recall, never mentioned the rugs, so possibly she found them a hoot and didn't want Harpur to regard her friend's parents as gross, awkward, jumped-up. But, examining this room, Harpur, in fact, considered these were people ready to work industriously at image, and made quite a job of it. They earned their postcode, and what this postcode previously represented, before folk like Tommy the Strong, Adrian Cologne, the Albs and Bobby Sprale did some colonizing. Hazel could be hard on bad taste. Of course, Scott, in the dogmatic way of youngsters, might detest this property – not just the rugs and oak floor and sofas, but the entire sweet nest for nestlings and their elders, and so he acquired a handgun, and the kind of life that kind of gun was part of.

Harpur thought the pictures hanging here good. The art took its theme from the rugs: surreal and diagrammatic prints in narrow, silver, metal-look frames, on temperate striped wallpaper. The prints – more Picasso? You wouldn't meet sailing boats or tame rural scenes nor that very popular singing butler here. It seemed to Harpur that Scott's parents might be regarded as avant garde, for Morton Cross. Harpur had not decided yet on art for the sitting room at Arthur Street, following removal of the book shelves. He had put up a couple of framed certificates won by the girls at judo. Plenty of blank wall remained. Although he, personally, quite liked the singing butler, Harpur couldn't be sure what his daughters and/or Denise would make of that. Denise's view was very important now they had given the sitting room extra significance on the settee. Although the singing butler had definition and panache, Harpur would not bet it was the kind of definition and panache Denise might like, even though she spoke of the splendid *rapport* between her and him.

Scott had a younger brother but Harpur easily found the right bedroom. Two framed photographs of Hazel stood on the pine dressing table. In both she smiled cheerily.

They looked like back garden shots, perhaps here, definitely not Arthur Street. It seemed to be summer. Hazel wore jeans and a white blouse in one and denim shorts and string vest in the other. The rest of the photographs in the room were publicity pictures of local ice hockey stars. Three vivid posters for recent games had been Blu-Tacked to the walls. Gingerly, Harpur started his search. This could not be a customary police rummage. If possible, he must quit the room and the house without leaving evidence he'd been here – unless, that is, he found a gun, in which case the sign of his intrusion must obviously be its absence. Only Scott would know about that, when he came looking, checking, ready to adore, and he wouldn't mention the loss.

Harpur didn't find a gun, and nothing else that would tie Scott to drugs, using or dealing. He came across no big cash store nor any clothes or footwear or jewellery or technology above the norm for a boy living in Chilton Park, Morton Cross, and whose parents laid out enough for an oak board floor in a five-bedroom, triple-garage property, with a sturdy little front garden wall to give separation from the street, and top hotel quality stair carpet in russet. This was either a boy clever at establishing a standard teenage profile, or a boy with a standard teenage profile. Harpur discovered no condoms either, and wondered whether he should be pleased or anxious.

Chapter Five

Mansel Shale hung about in a car not far from Detective Chief Superintendent Colin Harpur's house in Arthur Street waiting for Harpur's older daughter to come out. He would tail her. He thought it shouldn't be difficult. Although she most probably had heard of Mansel – or Manse – Shale through kid gossip at school, or on the streets, or in clubs . . . yes, heard of him as undoubtedly one of the city's main commercial figures over quite a period, she would not know what he looked like, and he intended to keep well back. Of course he didn't know what *she* looked like, either, except she was under consent age, which would not bother Iles, being an Assistant Chief. Shale never minded when people shortened his name to Manse. It was a bit familiar, but to object would be raw pomp, and not like him. However Ember could go very unpleasant if people called him Ralphy, instead of Ralph or Ember, saying it made him sound like someone's retarded cousin.

Shale had the basics on Harpur's family from Ralphy. There was two daughters at John Locke Comprehensive – Jill, thirteen, boyfriend, Darren Cope. And Hazel, fifteen, boyfriend, Scott Grant, but also given approaches and a lot of breathiness by Iles. The girls' mother had been murdered on a train, maybe after something on the extra-marital side in London, supposed to be shopping – *Oh, do look what I got at Harrods, girls!* The intelligence was that what she got at Harrods wasn't all she got. Then, also, according to Ember, Harpur's more or less regular girl-friend, Denise Prior, aged about twenty, was often around the Arthur Street house since his wife's death. Shale wondered whether she'd arrive or come out now, maybe eye-balling the street in that brassy, awkward way youngsters did. He had to keep alert. She went to the same university down the road where Ember started his mature student course, a gap year at the moment, and most likely for fucking ever, though Manse would not say that to him because Ralphy needed hopes and display, and if they failed he could get crumbly and next to useless.

Ember said that sometimes Denise stayed in Harpur's place all night, a true cohabit thing with breakfast, although she had a room at a student hostel. Ralphy believed in research. Manse wondered what the girl's parents would think if they knew she was snuggling up in a serious way to someone as old and unfinancial as Harpur, with a house down such a rough quarter as this, dog shit and cans everywhere, girls' arse pages from the *Daily Sport* blowing about, and daughters not in a private school. Shale would not like his children brought up in a street like this. It was not quite what they called 'disadvantaged' meaning low, but it was not advantaged. It could affect them right into when they was adults. Denise Prior's parents lived a long way off, Stafford or Southampton, that kind of spot, Ralph said, and when Shale thought about his own daughter, Matilda, only a child for now, he wondered was it a good idea to send girls to college in a different town if they was going to get on deep bodily terms with someone local and crude like Harpur. Ralph told him this girl learned French at the college, but what was the use of that if you half lived in a place such as Arthur Street? He didn't mind France as a foreign place, but Albania he could not take because of them new merchants up Morton Cross bringing so many unnecessary, non-British problems.

Recognition of the older daughter, Hazel – that's why this ploy must start with the watch on Harpur's place.

Manse needed to identify the girl and then see where she would lead him. Obviously, where he expected she would lead him to was her boyfriend. And this boyfriend he thought – in fact, he expected – would be right in age and frame for the lad around Chilton Park on pot-shot day. There might be other ways of finding the boyfriend. Mansel could of put one of his research people on to it, and he would soon come up with the data to a T. But he didn't want one of his research people on it. This had to be Manse acting solo. This would be a special, personal message from him to Harpur and would require a gesture in return. So, the waiting and the tailing seemed simplest. Shale occupied a Residents Only space for now but might agree to shift if a householder arrived in a vehicle and asked him politely, no road rage or property-owner bollocks, which might turn Manse uncaring.

He had noticed a middle-aged-to-older woman staring towards his car from the front room of a house a little way along from Harpur's, but she didn't seem set on giving trouble, or not yet. But would she pick up the phone and do some alerting soon? She might fancy herself as a sentry. Householders these days became jumpy about a loiterer in a car, even down a crap street like this. Maybe especially down a crap street like this. Poor areas often did worst for burglaries. She'd dial 999? He wondered if he should offer a happy smile to signify harmlessness. The trouble was, she might not read it that way. Women who spent their time peering from windows into the street could have mighty kinks. Manse liked all contact with women to be nicely controlled. Occasionally, he failed to fix this, of course. His wife would not of gone off like that if he really had things tied up. Just the same, he *aimed* for mastery, such as the carefully timed harbouring of companions like Lowri or Carmel or Patricia at the rectory. Manse thought it wise to be very choosy about which woman/women you opened up to, so he did not try charm from the Ford Focus on this old bit of pry in Arthur Street. He concentrated on Harpur's place.

When Shale found the boy, he and Ember could perhaps have a tender yet illustrated conversation with him and persuade the lad to get out of it fast and final. And the lad would tell Harpur direct, or through Harpur's daughter, that he was getting out of it fast and final after considerable insights given on a kindly, individual basis by Mr Mansel Shale and Mr Ralph Ember, established business colleagues of each other, famed and full of mature commercial knowledge. They could warn this lad he might get killed or wheelchaired or unattractively scarred, such as his nose mashed by a straight-on 9 mm hit or ricochet, in another Chilton Park-type clash. And tell him he was very fortunate not to of got killed or wheelchaired or unattractively scarred last time, don't strain his luck.

On account of police rules, this would be the kind of funeral Harpur could not attend if it was found the boy had a gang job and got killed in it. Sometimes police went to crime victims' funerals, but not if the crime victim had been well into crime hisself. Maybe Harpur would even stop the girl going to the service. This lad should think about that. Being alive was one thing, but being dead different. That seemed obvious, but not everyone cottoned. This boy might be the sort who'd really like his girlfriend at his funeral if shot, giving noticeable grief in token. Probably he had never thought that Harpur might block the funeral off for her, because of what was known as protocol, the daughter of an officer mourning a gun-kid pusher. This could be explained to the lad by Manse or Ember. Ralphy fancied himself as a talker, as long as he wasn't so scared of something he could only gibber.

Shale saw no movement yet at Harpur's house. He had not brought the Jaguar because Harpur might recognize it. Shale was in this silver Focus. Image did not matter now. Secrecy did. He had realized there might be plenty of waiting. Patience – an element Manse knew he had vats of, and which Ember did not, or would he be called Panicking? But Ember could usually do the heavy chat, perhaps owing to some education. Shale thought that when the two of them had a good parley with the lad about quitting, they might find out what outfit he belonged to. Everyone knew the Albanians was edging in with substances and girls. But this boy would not be with them. Albs stuck to Albs, like an Alb network. There was these new Brit firms up there now at Morton Cross. The names was around – Sprale, Adrian Cologne, Tommy the Strong.

Shale knew Ralph Ember and him should of done more inquiries about them before this. Sloppy. It would be this two-way, three-way, even four-way competition that started the bullets flying among cared-for flower beds in such a damned disgraceful fashion, and made the deads die there. One tale said Adrian Cologne had tried to take over a tart favoured by Iles. This girl called Honorée was ethnic, but not a recent arrival – here a real while, and with Iles a real while, off and on in the way of things with a tart. He would not like it if Cologne grew brutal with Honorée.

Shale had moved into the back of the Focus and observed from its rear window, a trick he often used on a watch like this, being much less obvious. US cop drama on TV made everyone expect surveillance to be head on, the detectives very evident through the windscreen drinking coffee from flasks, taking radio calls, talking pussy and checking their guns. Alone, Manse just sat still and crouched as low as he could.

Even if the lad didn't get hurt by warfare, he might get killed and worse as a likely grass, suppose someone discovered his girlfriend's father was Harpur, and someone would. Ember said the girl did not look like Harpur, which was great and a blessing for her, but information re him as her dad could be around. There might be people who thought the police arrived too fucking prompt and full of fire-power at Chilton Park, the way police arrived *too* fucking prompt at the jewel robbery in that film, *Reservoir Dogs*. People might start wondering about a rat – a rat who talked to his girlfriend who talked to her father. It did not matter whether this was true. If someone believed it they'd act. The boy had to be warned. Manse's mother used to tell him that 'a word is enough to the wise', a well-known saying from Latin or her uncle Les who worked in London for the BBC or W.H. Smith. Manse and Ember would give this lad more than *a* word, though – that is, more than *one* word – because he did not seem to Mansel wise at all if he worked with a gang at his age. The frighteners had to be put on him good *for* his good.

A fair-haired girl of about thirteen in a long beigish coat over jeans walked past the Focus and went into Harpur's house. This would not be the right child, though – too young. Jill. She had passed quite close to the Focus but he hoped she did not spot him. She did not stare back once she'd gone on towards the house, or anything like that, but you could not tell with the kid of a cop, they might of been taught deadpan by Harpur who had a lot of deadpan hisself. It would most probably be on his record card at police Personnel – 'Oxfam suits but excellent deadpanness.' The way the girl walked – it was a saunter, like relaxed. That could be an act, too, though.

Shale admitted to hisself his whole project now could seem far-fetched, even crazy. That's why, at this first stage, he would handle it unsupported. Ember? Manse could tell Ralph had big doubts. But Ember almost always had big doubts, which could sometimes nearly strangle him, and change him into Panicking Ralphy, often dangerous for people he worked with.

Shale watched the house windows for a while now, instead of the door, in case that young girl gave an alert and someone had a gape into the street from behind curtains, wondering about the Focus, maybe Harpur, possibly getting binoculars going. It could be tricky if he came out and asked Manse why the loiter. Perhaps Manse would have to give the true tale, explain his peace programme. But would Harpur understand? People could be dim. For instance, when he had described to Ralph the little scene where Harpur comforted the daughter on their Park visit, Manse saw immediate it didn't mean the same to Ralph as it did to him. To Manse it showed she had some tie-up with the shootings, maybe through a boyfriend. Of course, Manse would admit an amount of guesswork came into the way he read these things. Or that's how our super knowall, Mr Higher Education (suspended), Ralphy W. Ember, would consider it: just guesswork, speculation. Shale preferred another word, a word with dignity and scope in it. Vision.

Someone tapped the side rear window of the Ford. Shale was concentrating on Harpur's house since seeing the girl go in and had not noticed the approach of Mrs Sentry. She was older than he'd thought. Whatever her age, he didn't want her near the car, making him more conspicuous than he would be anyway. How, how, to get rid of her fast? He rolled down the window. 'Can I help you in any way, madam?' he said. Manse reckoned it was a voice of terrific sweetness, not at all the kind of tone she would be expecting from a parked Focus.

'You Vice?' she replied.

'What?'

'You police? Vice Squad? You watching 126 for vice? Unmarked vehicle as cover-up?'

'Vice?'

'That's what I said to myself when I noticed this car just waiting, and someone in it, and the gaze down towards 126. I thought, Brilliant! About time!'

'A certain mission in this street,' Shale replied.

'Well, obviously. I expect you hear what I hear.'

'That's possible.'

'I hear from someone in a house opposite to 126 of vice in there, no curtains drawn. And this is supposed to be a police officer. The address of a police officer, and not just

91

an ordinary police officer. This is a top man. That's what I understand. He's in the phone book. Or an *on*-top man. So, you are police hunting one of your own? That 126 – a disgrace. This was the full act, that's what I hear, not just oral or a hand job, and before ten o'clock. I mean ten o'clock in the *morning*.'

'We keep an eye,' Shale replied. A different sort of vision.

'I knew you must be Vice because of watching from the back. That's always a cop trick – to pretend you're not there.'

'We like to be discreet.'

'That's more than that one is in 126. This was defiant and flagrant, as I'm told it. Arse absolutely in view for minutes and not inactive. And there are children in that house, you know. Young girls. What will they make of it?'

'We got it all in mind,' Shale said.

'Grand.'

'Thanks for your guidance, madam.'

She turned and went back to her house, but remained watching from the porch. He did let her have a smile now, as he put the window back up and got his eyes on to 126 again – the kick-off point for his real vision. Yes, 'vision' was the term he would set above Ember's 'guesswork' and 'speculation'. Manse honoured vision. Naturally, Ember thought *he* supplied all the vision in their arrangement and did not believe Manse had much of it at all. But Ralphy often got things wrong, especially about Manse.

Shale saw no curtain movement after the girl, Jill, went into 126 Arthur Street. Of course, he realized something might have happened there while he was preoccupied with the neighbour. But Manse believed that probably when Jill strolled past the Focus it had been only an incident, with no results. She had been out somewhere. She came home. Simple. Manse could not allow time to get anxious re that. He had to think in a more global way – this being what he regarded as his role. Shale thought that word, 'vision', had a sort of high-class religious feel to it.

The woman came out in the street again from her porch. This time, though, she did not approach the Focus but stood on the pavement giving Harpur's house a stare. She would be able to see it better from there. Perhaps she hoped for an encore. It pained Manse – the way her busybodiness might cut across his large, humane, visionary project and possibly put it in peril. No true leader operated without vision, and Manse did see himself as quite a leader. Napoleon, Churchill, Walt Disney, Florence Nightingale, Mao – one gift they all had by the palletload: vision. Manse would bet that if you read what the papers said about any one of these when they died you would find vision mentioned often because it drove them. In fact, if they didn't have vision they would not of done what they did do when alive and so the papers would not be writing about them at all when they was dead.

The woman went back into her porch, thank God, and glanced towards the Focus. Shale allowed her a brief wave with his hand just above the window frame to show he appreciated her cooperation and signal she should fucking stay there. So, Harpur had it off in his front room with the student, did he? And made a morning show of it. Rotten, really. Shale agreed with the neighbours. He detested unkempt behaviour. He tried to keep a proper, clean outlook on the future – yes, to keep a *vision* of it – and then he meets ugly information like this, something so jarring and rude and back-street. Whereas, Mao with his *Little Red Book* of thoughts: these were worldwide vision in Chinese. The language did not matter. Anyone could have a vision. The book was not called little because the thoughts in it were little but because it was small and could go into a Chinese smock pocket and be there when someone wanted a read of Mao's ideas and visions for morale. All right, lately Ralph Ember had a class or two down the university so he now believed everything had to be calculated and proved like arithmetic before you made a move. Fine at the fucking   look-each-way-before-you-cross-the-road   level. But the real, creative business giant had to use absolutely different qualities in himself/herself now and then. These could be summed up in another quite well-known term. Intuition.

Wasn't it Florence Nightingale's intuition that told her soldiers needed hospitals with antiseptic when they got a leg shot off in Russia, so she became 'the lady with the lamp'? Vision and intuition, they mixed with each other, was part of each other. Manse's feeling that somehow Harpur, and perhaps even Iles, must be kept in a good alliance with himself and Ralphy was one bit vision another bit intuition. This vision, this intuition, said, Look after Hazel Harpur's boyfriend, save him, and her father will be into very helpful gratitude.

Luckily, that kind of big thinking was easy for Manse. Periodically these days, he would do a survey of the skills he found most powerful in himself as a company figure-head, and always at the summit came what was referred to in business manuals as 'strategic awareness', sometimes also called 'over-view ability'. His mind went that way now as he resumed watching Harpur's front door, not the windows. The door looked like phoney wood, just veneer with packing. Pathetic: all Manse's doors at home had true, genuine weight, being real old timber from quality times when the house was St James's rectory and wood meant wood, a rector having quite a rank, higher than a vicar. Anyway, Shale thought that, in trade, if you had built something of grand scale and good earnings, you must plan beyond the day-to-day. Yes, vision. Yes, listen to your intuition and feel glad you got some.

Of course, he'd admit that now and then urgent, immediate decisions might be needed on a day-to-day or night-to-night basis, for instance the emergency scheme to see off that top Albanian, Tirana, although, obviously, this turned out inappropriate once they found him already done. No question, short-term actions could become vital from time to time, but, never mind how sudden, even rushed, these had to be, they should also fit a company's general policy and aims – its strategy. This would mean agendaring not just for the day-to-day, or even week-to-week, but for the widest future.

He noticed some cramp and possible seize-up coming on and changed position in the Focus to get more relaxed and able to continue his thoughts. Although Manse despised all vanity, he knew he had a brain that could cater for months ahead, several months – three, four, no trouble. And he realized he must do some of that now, following the Chilton Park tussle. Manse felt sure the people running, say, ICI or Coca Cola had a similar grip on times to come. They tried to estimate what sales possibilities would be then in Argentina and the Yukon, for instance. Manse had to think of sales possibilities far ahead, also. Vision. Over-view. That's why he waited here now, watching Harpur's home, an address – as the woman said – that anyone could find in the fucking phone book, which Shale considered mad for a police officer. That front door – useless. It wouldn't keep out a bullet, it wouldn't keep out someone who gave a bit of shoulder.

He wondered whether what made him value a long view so much was the Pre-Raphaelites. Surely, if you had paintings of that brilliance and era hanging in your drawing room, you must realize life amounted to more than now, now, now and grab, grab, grab. You had to build a firm that would last, even though the fucking Albs, plus some others, stole punters, and even though cocaine had suddenly gone so give-away cheap. *What'll you take, squire, a cappuccino or a line of coke? Same price.* Bad market tumbles like this was bound to shake a company. But auburn tresses on girls in Pre-Raphaelite pictures showed a beauty that had lasted a century-plus, and he reckoned would probably go on. Good art often did. Naturally, he saw an example for his business in this. Stability. Endurance. Some

95

paintings went even further back than the Pre-Raphaelites. He often thought of Leonardo da Vinci twisting his body all ways up ladders before metal scaffolding to paint ceilings that you could still see on culture tours. One thing about ceilings, they would not decay like ancient canvas could if it was not looked after right.

The young girl, the one he thought must be Jill Harpur, came out of the house. She still had on that long coat. It seemed to Shale like she had not took it off when she went in. It had that look – that it had not been took off. She began walking up towards the Focus. He wondered if she had noticed him, or half noticed him, when she went past earlier and had decided to give it a few minutes and then come back out and take another squint to be certain. Quickly, he got off the seat and lay across the drive shaft on the floor of the car, his face down. Manse reckoned it would be very hard to make him out unless she stopped and stuck her eyes against the window. Maybe if she thought she had seen someone earlier she would change her mind and decide it had been a mistake. Or she might imagine whoever had been in there had left the car and was in one of the houses now, so it would be an ordinary visiting or resident's car, not a snoop. As well as keeping his face nice and unflinching against the rubber mat on the carpet down there, Shale also got his breathing quiet, in case while she stared through the window she also done some listening from close.

Many would say this was not the kind of position that someone of his commercial rank should be in, but Manse would never consider himself too refined and eminent for any work that had to be done, and this had to be done now. He did not want news about this Focus and himself blurted by the girl in Harpur's house, or it would be hard to stay unnoticed if he got behind the girl's older sister on the way to Scott. After about five minutes he raised his head and turned it slightly, so he could look up and see whether Jill Harpur had her face against the side window noting him. That would be awkward if he stared at her while she stared at him. But the window was clear. He stayed down there another thirty seconds then lifted himself and took a place on the rear seat again. Through the windscreen he could see the back of Jill up towards the end of the street. She seemed to have continued walking and had not lurked around the Focus or gone back to the house to report. He felt more or less all right again and brushed the floor muck from his clothes with the back of his hand. He resumed his watch through the rear window.

The point was that although, definitely, the Pre-Raphaelites would never be called 'a flash in the pan', Manse thought *he* might be a flash in the pan, regardless of his boardroom flair and ability to wipe out all fucking opposition, until now, anyway. Obviously, he knew his work marketing substances would never give him the kind of permanent glory da Vinci gained and deserved because of them ceilings, nor even the kind of fame the Pre-Raphaelites had – which covered a shorter time. But he did want his firm to carry on, get quality, reliability, for a grand while. A lasting presence – that's what he planned for his company.

Lasting but not eternal, though. Obviously, this was hardly the sort of firm he as a parent would like to hand over to his children, Laurent and Matilda, the way, say, Mr Rupert Murdoch would hand over TV stations and newspapers to *his* kids, or Mr McDonald with the eateries for his nephews and nieces. Manse aimed to set the children up through big profits he made during many good years of – let's be fucking frank, he thought – many good years of dirty commerce, but so they could start a different kind of organization, not drugs. He wanted them out of that business sector. This was why he felt it crucial to stick some kind of clever leverage on Harpur, to prevent the firms – his and Ralphy's – getting squeezed now, and

perhaps snuffed too soon. Them words – stability, endurance. Vital. Manse needed stability and endurance to stack
capital so that when Laurent and Matilda grew up and
thought about what enterprises to try they'd have enough
backing for, say, a chain of fashion shops or a bubble-wrap
factory, and wouldn't get flattened by some enemy or
bank, which could be the same, of course. Manse thought
girls should have identical chances with boys in a career.
He definitely believed in equality for women, even though
his wife, Sybil, had gone off like that with some surveyor
or pool table salesman to live in Wales.

One thing that was a plus was, if Jill *had* seen him and
spoke of it, and, as a result, Harpur approached the Focus,
he would be able to tell right off from total absence of coat
bulge that Manse carried no armament. Well, of course not.
Was he likely to bring a gun for this kind of duty – tagging
a school kid? Manse would regard that as out of propor-
tion and sick. It was a mission – the word he used to the
woman – not a –

Another girl appeared from Harpur's house and the
sight of her cut into Manse's thoughts, putting a pause on
them due to urgency. This could be the right girl, Hazel –
fair-haired, taller, a couple of years older. She wore a
denim jacket over a cream blouse or shirt, jeans and trainers. She began to walk quite fast, approaching the Focus.
Of course, Shale watched to see whether she took a sly,
special look towards him and the Focus, in case she'd had
a mobile call from her sister. Being nose down into a
fucking mat so there'd be no skin shine off of him as a
give-away, only the back of his jacket, Shale did not know
whether the younger kid, Jill, had looked in – a *real* look in
on the second walk past to make sure she had seen what
she *thought* she might of seen like casual on the first walk
past. That woman would probably know whether Jill had
stopped and looked into the Focus, but this could not help
Shale now. If Jill *had* seen him stretched out down there she
would be sure to think it was unusual and she would

guess he was hiding or dead and she might mention to the house on her phone what she'd observed. This would clearly make the other girl, Hazel, curious and she would take an eyeful of the Focus now. Oh, God, would he have to get down to the floor again? But what use was that? She might be coming this way especially for a gaze at someone on the floor.

Manse stayed where he was, watching the older girl's face, her eyes. It did not seem to him that she was what you could call focused on the Focus but, again, you had to remember this was Harpur's daughter and he could of taught her all kinds of fucking sly procedures, such as pretending you was not interested in something when you really could not be *more* interested in it. She had the jauntiness and freshness of skin that girls around this age generally had, and he could see why Iles would want to cling to something like this just before he went into his scrap-heap time. It was well known Iles worried about what people thought of his Adam's apple, but he might think a girl as young as this would not of paid attention to all that many Adam's apples in the general population and so wouldn't see his was a such a giggle.

Shale wondered whether he should just sit up normal in the back of the car and if she looked in he would look out at her with true politeness and give a smile or a nod, like he was waiting for the driver to come back from a call at one of the houses, which was why he, Manse, was in the back not the front. Of course, she might remember him from this, and it would make things dodgy if he wanted to follow her later, looking for Scott. Shale could not see what else to do, though. He would just have to wish she was *really* not interested in the Focus and would not even notice him. So, that was the strategy. He got himself into a proper sitting situation, looking ahead, not squinting out of the back, and became like someone just sitting in the rear of a car while the driver did an errand. It might of been better after all if he had been in the Jaguar because then it might of looked like it was the chauffeur who had gone somewhere, and Manse being in the back would not be unusual, being the boss. Not many with a Focus would have a chauffeur.

But the girl, Hazel, did not reach Manse and the car. Of course, because he was looking towards the windscreen and ahead, not watching through the back, he could not see her, and just had to wait until she drew alongside. She failed to come though. He thought she should of been there after about a couple of minutes. When that did not happen, he swivelled a bit for a quick look through the back window again and saw she had returned to the house and was just letting herself in with a key. He thought she must of forgotten something and would appear again very soon, but she did not. He felt almost sure she had not been close enough to see him in the Focus, so he felt really puzzled, and stayed puzzled. What did it mean, them two girls in and out like that? Did they think it was a bit of a joke to mess him about? This angered Shale. After five minutes, though, he decided he had no chance of sorting out these things and he let his mind go back to how he had been thinking before she appeared.

Guns were the topic in his mind then, and Manse had been accounting to himself why he would not carry a weapon on what was a mission, not a hunt, for God's sake. He believed Harpur would most likely appreciate this tact in him. But Harpur had *not* come out of the house, might not even be at home. It had been the girl who came out, and as far as Manse could see, this did not really alter things at all, whatever they was up to, the pair. He settled himself to watch from the rear window again, and considered them wider matters once more, such as the art and so on, where he felt more comfortable. The point was them two girls might think they could fool with him, but he was still Mansel, or Manse, Shale with his own rectory and pictures. And when he studied them painted tresses at home he dwelt with wonder and joy on such an unfading glow in the colours, and he knew it would of been the same if he looked at the da Vinci church ceilings, although he would not be able to get so close. From them tresses, his mind naturally went to the big need for his organization, and possibly Panicking Ralphy's, to live on in their own unfading glow, though, yes, a different sort. And, also naturally, he then sketched in his head how Harpur and Iles could help get this happy steadiness for him and Ralphy, despite all the law shit certain to fly after that Chilton Park outrage, plus the fucking worldwide coke slump because them greedy, we-want-it-now Colombians was doing too much bloody supply, a fucking glut, short-sighted, no restraint.

Restraint – so vital, so worthwhile. Manse definitely believed in restraint. And so, all his weaponry stayed properly locked up in the rectory wall safe behind an Arthur Hughes painting unless a situation came which could not be handled right without guns. Exceptional. Rare. *Very* rare. Now and then Manse did worry that it might show a crude opinion of art to use it to cover Heckler and Koch 9 mms instead of just having the picture up to be delighted by, like in a gallery. Decorum. Manse had an enormous belief in that also, and from way back – he thought his mother might of spoken of this, as well as the word to the wise. A year or two ago, Patricia, one of the girls he'd allow longish guest terms at the rectory, mentioned in a light way what she called the 'distinguished, diabolical deviousness' of this fine picture placed over an armament safe as mask. All right, all right. Manse would never hit any woman for a dim joke in big words starting with the same letter. And he certainly did not even consider getting back at the cow by cutting the standard outlay on Patricia's fashion garments and skin moisteners while she remained at the rectory for her spell. That would of been weak and spiteful. One point was, he did often have a true and special fondness for Patricia, who had absolutely never tried to talk to him about marriage or getting into the rectory permanent. But for an unusually long while after her coarse remark about the painting he did not invite her to stay again, although he heard she hadn't moved in with someone else on anything more than one-nighters. He thought she'd understand how she'd angered him. Patricia had a mind, no question. Naturally. Almost never would Manse shag a dumbo woman even if a looker, and he would definitely not invite any absolutely stupid bird into the rectory for a spell of up to quite a few weeks, like Patricia and the others. Oh, undoubted Patricia would realize her mouth should go more careful. If she was so fucking jokey she better see how much she could make as a stand-up.

Shale shifted again on the Focus back seat but did not break his observation on the door of 126. He thought he'd keep his watch here for another half-hour. It obviously could not be non-stop. He had to look after other aspects of the firm. Since Denzil went like that, Mansel had been forced to handle a lot more tasks himself, minor, Denzil-type things, but they took time. He must have a drift around the Valencia district, for example, in case of signs that people who'd been working the Morton Cross turf had already begun a switch to there because of the police swarm up the Park. This could be bad. This could mean more battling eventually, more gunfire, though on different ground. Manse and Ember might get involved in that. Well, definitely. If people started elbowing into your territory you had to resist. That's what they should of done to Hitler much earlier. Manse would need to visit the wall safe. He hated having to consider this. Clearly, Shale knew the importance of guns, but he would never let them dominate his plans. They were in reserve, hidden, and he wanted them to stay like that.

The point was, by concentrating on the tumbling, crinkly auburnness in them Pre-Raphaelite portraits in his drawing room, and the great blues and scarlets of the frocks, and especially the blues, Manse could forget almost totally about the handguns, holsters and bullets nestling behind. At these moments they did not matter. Glorious art took over, deserving and getting complete fucking priority, as it should. Manse would even call it reverence. Then, when the handguns might unfortunately be needed, as, say, down the Valencia soon, he'd carefully lift the Hughes off of its hook without spending gaze time on the tresses and frocks now, and just open up, load the magazine or magazines, strap on a holster or two and arm himself, close the safe, spin the combo out of code, replace the picture, again without no stare period. Manse reckoned he had arranged things so there was two different parts of his life, the art and the guns, and he knew how to keep them nice and separate. Same with women: he tried to keep *them* nice and separate from one another out of consideration for their feelings, though there could be noisy, even public, slip-ups. But such slip-ups never happened as to art and guns which, clearly, not being alive in the ordinary sense, only in the art sense, didn't have the unpredictable side of women, and their clumsiness sometimes, as with Patricia. Also, while the weapons stayed in the safe behind the painting he kept *them* nice and separate from the ammo. That was also in the safe, but properly boxed, so you could almost think the Heckler and Kochs were not guns at all, clearly being unable to shoot unloaded.

Hazel came out from Harpur's house again, but pushing a bicycle, this time. Manse went even lower in the Focus, trying to keep his head right down and not noticeable in case she had decided to have a look at the Focus after all, by bike this time. Once more he wondered whether she'd had a message from her sister. Possibly Hazel would be real nervous and uncertain what to do following the way Harpur talked to her on one of the death spots in the park and so on, and this could explain why she had turned back from the Focus a little while ago. Even if Shale hadn't had the briefing from Ralph, he would of picked out Hazel now and before as a comprehensive school kid. She was

103

not wearing the comp uniform, no, but you could tell she never had deportment lessons like Matilda did, no extra fee. All right, deportment could be tricky with the bike, but just the same to Manse she seemed short of it, probably in the blood from her father. In any case, girls who did deportment would not come from houses where they kept bikes in one of the rooms or the hall, like factory workers in 1920, for God's sake. Maybe at comprehensive schools they did not have many deportment lessons because too much time was took frisking kids for flick knives.

Again he thought she did not even glance at the Focus. Although under it all she might be nervous, she still seemed to possess some of that jauntiness he'd noticed earlier and looked cheerful. This would be another difference from children at the school Matilda and Laurent went to. Them kids always looked like they would be cheeky or sullen to you any minute because they considered you shit. The Harpur girls had never had a chance to be taught to look at other people like this, most probably. Manse pitied Harpur's children and wanted to make up for what she'd missed at least to this one, Hazel. Perhaps Iles, sniffing around in that Assistant Chief way he had, didn't care about girls' deportment, but you could tell from just a few steps when he wore one of his suits he really fancied hisself as a lovely mover, it coming to him by nature, though, not deportment lessons.

Hazel did not ride towards the Focus but in the other direction. It was not exactly a racer – a sports bike. She sat bent over the handlebars, yet relaxed, her hair, also fair like the younger girl's, blowing about as though she felt carefree, even after Chilton Park. He had seen a TV programme about one of them old-type universities with architecture where nearly all students went on bikes, and the girl students rode like that, fast, cheerful, sure of theirselves because they had done all the homework and would be off to play netball or croquet later But they called

104

homework 'prep', meaning preparation. Perhaps Hazel Harpur was preparing for when she went to university.

But now, of course, Manse was into one of the big problems about watching from a car's rear window. Or two big problems. First, if you wanted to tail, you had to get around quick to the driver's seat. Second, if the customer went the wrong way, like Hazel now, you must do a U-turn and hope you caught up. It might seem a doddle to catch up a bike, but not always. A bike could snake through a queue of traffic, leaving you distant and stuck. He had expected that if Hazel came out she would be walking and he could follow far back on foot. That wouldn't suit now. Shale moved swiftly into the driving seat and as soon as there was a chance did a three-point. He could still see the girl and her unworried hair.

Something disturbed him. While he was getting the Focus around, he noticed a red Renault Clio pull out from the kerb ahead and seem to follow Hazel Harpur. It must of been parked in another Residents Only spot nearer to Harpur's house. Shale had not noticed it then. Again sloppy, fucking sloppy. If you ran a watch on somewhere you kept an eye not just on the somewhere for fuck's sake but on anyone else who might have an eye on the somewhere. Shale usually used other people to do surveillance for him, such as the late Denzil, and he knew he had lost some good habits through chiefdom. Big vision could be great, but there was also things close-to that needed work. Yes, so sloppy. Instead of doing a proper scan of other cars in the street he realized he had been taking a mind wallow in the fucking Pre-Raphaelites, and fooling hisself he lived for art, not fucking takings.

It might be only coincidence that the Clio moved. Perhaps the car in a Residents Only spot *belonged* to one of the residents and would of gone that direction anyway, whether the girl had come out with the bicycle or not. But it was the speed of the car that interested Manse – meaning the lack of it. To him it looked like the Clio had tucked itself in behind the bike and would keep it in sight but not overtake. That meant hardly any accelerator. Manse could see two men in the front seats. He knew that if he went in behind the Clio and stayed there his slowness would make him as noticeable as the other car. To stick with the girl, he'd have to risk that, though.

And, definitely, he wanted to stick with the girl. The Clio made that even more important, suppose it *was* tailing Hazel Harpur, and Shale *did* suppose. If not, it might turn off soon, leaving things simpler. Why would them two men follow Hazel like this? Who were they? He had an off-on view of the backs of their heads as other cars overtook first Shale, and came between him and the Clio for a while, then passed the Clio, too, leaving a temporary clear gap. That didn't help him much. Although you might be able to identify someone from the back of his/her head if you already knew him/her well, this view was otherwise more or less fucking dud. Most likely the back of an Alb head would be pretty much the same as the back of a Brit head. Manse thought both men might be dark-haired, which probably would be OK for Albs, but also, obviously, for dark-haired Brits, and there was plenty of them about, think of pictures of the Krays.

The driver seemed squat, big-shouldered, fat-necked, the passenger possibly taller and thinner. Neither wore a hat. Both had on dark jackets, perhaps suits. Some muscle people in the firms did wear dark suits, longing to look civilized for their families' sake or their women's, not just pug-uglies. Albs at the top of firms wore dark suits – and suits bought here, not over in Albania – so they could seem unforeign, like sneaking into the scene. That's what they hoped, the smarmy foreign fuckers. They'd go up to London to get suits made for them, not reach-me-down, in £2000-a-time tailor shops, because suits from Alb probably *looked* like suits from Alb and a laugh – flash-Harry lapels and cloth from old post bags joined up. Alb suits would of made them seem even more foreign. Britain could teach the whole world about suits, but Albania didn't want to learn because it was well known they still believed in the Cold War there and would never copy British suits.

But why would Albs get after Hazel Harpur? Why would anyone? Well, he, Mansel Shale, was a fucking anyone himself, wasn't he, and getting after Hazel Harpur? Did the Clio crew want the same as Manse – to find a lead to Scott Grant, the boyfriend? This gave Shale fret. When you thought about it, he was here to protect the girl, keep her happy, keep her boyfriend alive and uncrippled, keep, above all, Harpur happy. Yes, but suddenly that little scheme seemed a lot tougher. Manse had considered himself right out in front, visioning what Harpur and the girl signified up at Chilton Park, and doing one of his intuits about the boyfriend. Now, he saw that others might of got to all the same visioning and intuiting and got to them faster. Christ, was age starting to drag him?

And them others would not be thinking of protecting this girl, keeping her happy, keeping her boyfriend alive, keeping, above all, Harpur happy. The only people they wanted happy was theirselves. The boyfriend – a target. Why? Was this the follow-up to Chilton Park? People had been killed and injured there. People had been arrested and locked up. But some got clear. Scott Grant, the boyfriend, had got clear? Had the men in the Clio also got clear, and wanted to go on with the fight now? They and Scott were from different firms, warring firms? Or perhaps there was the simpler explanation Manse had already glimpsed: did they think Scott must be a grass and slipped the word to Harpur and his herd, direct or through the girl, that a turf tournament had been timetabled for Morton Cross? Never forgivable, that. Were they stalking him here, via Hazel Harpur, because the area around Scott's parents' house and the local school was still thick with police and no good for a rat hunt? Perhaps they didn't need an identification of him, the way Shale did, because they knew him already. All they wanted was to get to Scott anywhere outside Morton Cross, and the girl could help with that.

Manse tapped himself with one hand over the left tit, a sort of stupid comfort twitch, feeling for the gun he knew was not there. Hadn't he been feeling so prim and sweet because it was not there? Cunt. Oh, God, God, them beautiful Heckler and Kochs, tidy, rectorified, unloaded and, in any case, fucking miles off behind the fucking distinguished diabolical deviousness of the Arthur Hughes. He might have to do something immediate and important here, and had been too dozy and slack to realize it and equip himself. Vision? Intuition? Where the hell had they bolted to? Yes, something immediate and important for the sake of the girl, and the boy, and Harpur, and for the sake of him, Mansel Shale.

After about ten minutes, he could see that Hazel must be making for the central bus station. Of course. Youngsters of her age did crowd there. Shale thought it would be because it was a sort of nothing place – people going and coming, not settled, so nobody around long enough to bother about these kid gangs and fight them for the territory. It was like this area *belonged* to them, because they was the ones who did stay and was there day-after-day and night-after-night. It was like this was their colony. They'd conquered it by sticking around, such as when we had India. He understood how they thought like that. They needed a base. It was a wide stretch of tarmac dotted with long, glass-walled shelters for the passenger queues. They could roam this land, this no man's land. They could skateboard this ground in the parts where a bus or coach was not due yet. Most probably some smoking and pushing went on. Naturally it went on. Kids that age – bound to.

Manse and Ember did not like this as a sales spot, though. It was too open, too obvious, too unignorable even by Iles, too sure to get snarl letters in the local paper every so often about the vile way the city looked to visitors just come in by coach, when all around was teenagers on grass or stronger up to their eyes. Ralphy hated anything that would link him to a social sore. Of course, his fucking club, the Monty, was a social sore, but he thought he'd clean that up soon and get bishops and admirals as members, the hopeful, daft twat.

Hazel Harpur dismounted from the bike and chained it to a lamp post. There was a café at the edge of the bus station and she made for that now on foot. Not far from the café stood a small car park for putting down and picking up and the Clio had stopped there. Shale did the same, though with a few vehicles between him and the other car as cover. Both men stayed in the Clio and, as far as he could make out, both watched Hazel walk towards the café. Shale reckoned they thought the same as he did – that she had come to meet Scott Grant. But God, would they try something here, a busy terminus in the middle of the city? Did them Albs bring full-scale chaos, if they *was* Albs? Again he reached up as if to lift something effective from a shoulder holster and again he could have spat on that fucking smug Arthur Hughes with all them poncy colours.

The café had a balcony from which, in good weather, people due to travel or here to meet someone could sit with a coffee and watch the buses and coaches arrive. Hazel Harpur appeared there now holding a bottle of Pepsi and stared down towards the parking yard. She was speaking into a mobile. She put the bottle down on the ground and then with this free hand gave the finger repeatedly to the Clio, real vigorous and Eurosport and insulting – what you would expect from a girl whose father was Harpur. Occasionally she supported this by sticking her tongue far out like a retch at the two men, which would have interfered with her talk on the mobile. She'd had them marked from the start, had she? Or had the younger girl noticed the Clio and the two men up front and very evident? Shale realized Jill might have missed *him* but seen *them*. Possibly, she came out for that second inspection just now and confirmed, then called the house. And when Hazel came out on *her* first walk, she had not been aware of the Focus at all but wanted to inspect the Clio, *did* inspect the Clio. That lovely relaxed style on her bike was just a show, was it? A senior cop's daughter, and crafty. Well, *two* senior cop's daughters, and crafty. And defiant. Hazel could of stayed in, couldn't she? But maybe she wanted the Clio to make clear what it was up to. She had conned them – made them tail her.

Her finger and her tongue seemed to go very clear and exact towards the Clio, and *only* the Clio. The Focus? She obviously didn't know a thing about it. Manse guessed what the balcony phone call would be, and it wasn't a squeal for help to daddy. She'd be telling Scott Grant not to turn up here this evening after all because a couple of Clio monsters was waiting for him, but, don't worry, love, she'd see them off.

Well, that was her performance. This ended now. Shale found it brilliant. She left the balcony. He waited for her to come back out. She didn't, though. She must of decided to stay in the café. Perhaps she felt scared of the men in the Clio, especially after the way she'd mocked them – *disrespected* them, as the street talk called it these days. Manse hated that kind of language, borrowed most likely from them terrible violent gangs in LA. It struck him that if she did not come out them two might go in and get her. They might not read it the way Shale read it when she was having that cell-phone conversation on the balcony. Maybe they thought Scott was inside with her. His weird wish to protect this copper's daughter fixed on to Manse again. He knew part of it came from the hope to keep things nice with her father for him and Ralph. But there was more. He felt a kind of duty to this child, and especially now she had shown herself so full of fight and poison. Always this search for nobility – as well as for special consideration from big police, and therefore some sheltered trade and good profit.

He looked over at the Clio and saw the two men was still in it. That probably would not last. Shale left the Focus and walked towards the café. They might follow. He felt very, very aware now of being very, very gunless and no longer carried out his useless hand search for a holster and pistol. Maybe he should. It might frighten them two off, the way Michael Corleone and the pastry cook pretend to have guns when guarding the godfather in hospital. Shale kept going. He realized that, in a way, he was trying to match the sudden bit of unexpected bravery from Ralph Ember when he went to help that other young girl – the immigrant whore-by-force in Tirana's car who'd learned some rough slang to thrill clients turned on by words. Manse could not stand the notion that Ralphy might be stauncher than he was. Ralphy Ember? God, never. Panicking? Oh, come on!

Shale's walk into the café had no purpose, and this delighted him. When he watched outside the house, then did the gumshoeing, there'd been a purpose, obviously. He thought Hazel might lead him to the boyfriend. But now he felt certain that would not be so this evening. It was as if he had actually heard her warning the boy off by mobile, though he hadn't of course. Intuition. He trusted his intuition. This stroll to the café had purity to it and goodness because all he wanted to do was help. He would show them two in the Clio that the girl had back-up, and if they tried anything they would have to try it on him, Mansel, or Manse, Shale first.

In a way, not having a gun made things even more pure and good, even more daring. He was doing big risk for her, although there might be no gain. Humaneness – frequently Manse believed in this. That sight of her on the bike with her hair blowing, it really affected him – and not in the dirty, scheming way Iles was affected, but . . . well, because of humaneness. He felt really glad he had come across this word lately. He had known it already, of course, but only realized the other day when reading about the Red Cross in Africa how very right it was for him in many aspects. The hair blowing like that seemed to tell him about this girl's lovely high spirits, and watching her give the Clio so much saucy rubbishing he had felt this even more.

Inside the café he found her at a table with half a dozen friends, all girls, jollying and joking. This heartened Manse a lot. He saw them as like youthfulness – triumphant despite everything. They could not be squashed. They had life, vigour. He quite liked this place. It was cheerful, spacious, pretty clean and the shelves full of sweets, chocolate, drinks in coloured packaging and cartons, giving a true feeling of optimism, in his view. The furniture and counters were mainly Formica. He did not mind this. You would not expect the kind of solid mahogany theme he had in his den room at the rectory. This café was a passing-through area. People came here on their travels – just going for a bus, just come from one and waiting for another – and they wanted a quick bit of refreshment in cheerful, spruce surroundings. You did not expect a bus station caff to look historical. His den room at the rectory had most probably been the clergyman's study, where he did all kinds of serious work, such as the sermons or making notes on the Book of Daniel, and, obviously, it needed a more solid atmosphere than a caff's. Decorum again – what fitted. Manse had a big mahogany desk to go with the room's panelling, plus a leather suite and Salem bookcase. He felt it important to match the sort of flavour the room possessed when owned by the church. He liked to do his accounts in there, the full ones as well as the doctored set for the Agincourt meetings. He had a documents safe in the den, as well as the gun safe behind the Arthur Hughes. The Pre-Raphaelites hung in the drawing room, not the den. They would of been too colourful, in his opinion. He did have a picture in the den, but from what was known as the Dutch School, and less vivid. Now, the point was, surely, the bus station café *needed* vividness, though, so folk weary from journeying could get bucked up. Some would definitely call the bus station café garish. But garishness could work all right sometimes. Think of Las Vegas or a royal wedding – or the *old* kind of royal wedding, not a register office.

Hazel seemed to be doing plenty of talk, perhaps telling them about the cabaret she put on from the balcony just now. Shale did not think she'd give them the whole tale, though – that is, if she understood it. Did she realize she had been tailed because of Scott? She'd probably just say the Clio had a couple of leches in it who'd liked what they saw when she was cycling. Shale bought himself a Fanta and took a table a little way from theirs. He knew it would be wrong to introduce himself to the girl. That would make any future secret watch on her very tricky. Hazel showed them how she had given the finger and they all laughed and hooted. Then two girls stood and Shale guessed they would go out on to the balcony also, and perhaps offer a bit more mockery and rudeness to the Clio. He thought that was all right. Useful. It meant the two men outside must see she had a troupe of pals around her now and could not be approached. They would not try anything.

After a few minutes, the girls came back and said they could spot no Clio, only a silver Ford Focus. They all had a big laugh again because they must of thought Hazel and the finger must of frightened them off. Shale went out to the car park and saw they had it right, and the Clio was gone. He looked about for one or other of the two men but found neither. He sat in the Focus for a while, wondering if Scott might show now, told by mobile that it was all right. This did not happen. The girls came out and Hazel unlocked her bike. They walked together out of the bus station and on to the route taken by her from Arthur Street. Perhaps she had invited them home. Shale watched until they turned a corner, then went back to the rectory.

He didn't have a girl in residence at present and, of course, Denzil, who once lived in a flat at the top of the house, had gone. The children were out at the ice rink for their skating lessons and he would drive over to collect them soon. For now, Manse found the rectory bleak after the bus station café. He went and stood in front of the Pre-Raphaelites. They gave him a kind of companionship. The Pre-Raphaelite artists had organized what they called a Brotherhood. This idea warmed and thrilled him always.

Chapter Six

Mid-evening, Harpur left headquarters and went home. For most of the day, he had sat in as observer while Francis Garland interrogated two men picked up at the Chilton Park ructions. Garland knew about interrogating. He had a delicate but believable way of convincing any prisoner that Francis could put him very much further into the shit than he already was in if he failed to cough intelligently. This kind of persuasion *had* to be delicate because the interviews went on to tape and might be available to the defence at trial. There must be no flagrant pressurizing, or judges grew bug-eyed and niggly. Bye-bye third degree, Hello! Hello! subtlety. Garland seemed young enough to adapt easily. Erogenous Jones had been the supreme interrogator, of course, but Erog was dead from a knife wound delivered on Iles's lawn in Rougemont Place – though not by Iles – a fair while ago now.* Francis might soon get near Erog's standard. What the interrogations confirmed so far was that a range of new firms, besides the Albanians, had been working the Morton Cross area, some of them adopting the Alb tactic of running not just drugs but girls. The names were fairly familiar by now: Tommy the Strong, Bobby Sprale, Adrian Cologne.

When Harpur reached Arthur Street only Jill was in the house, watching boxing on television, but Hazel and several of her friends arrived soon afterwards, probably after

* *In Good Hands.*

one of their regular meet-ups at the central bus station café. The area had become a bit of a haunt for kids of her vintage. Hazel could cycle there in ten minutes: one of the pluses from living inner city, if getting to bus station sessions was a plus. Harpur did wonder. She must have walked her bike back with the girls. Apparently, they'd come here to rehearse scenes from a play they had to perform in Drama class at John Locke. Jill switched off the bout. 'But we've already had some drama, Mr Harpur,' Simone said.

'That right?' he said.

'Hazel on the caff balcony, like Juliet – that's Juliet in *Romeo and Juliet*,' Simone said.

'I'd have guessed,' Harpur said.

'By William Shakespeare,' Simone said.

'Well, yes,' Harpur said.

'He's giving you irony, Simone,' Jill said. 'Because – like – well, most know *Romeo and Juliet* is by William Shakespeare. Although dad is police he's not ignorant on some things. For instance, I've heard him mention literature. And he looked up John Locke in a book and found he wrote about human understanding, which is why they called the school that, because we're human and the school tries to make us understand, although it's a comp. This room used to be full of books. My mother's. *Titus Andronicus*, James Thurber, *La Peste*. Real volumes. We had to chuck them, or most. They got on everyone's nerves.'

'Stupid people, that's all,' Hazel said.

'Who?' Harpur asked.

'In a Clio,' Hazel said.

'Who?' Harpur said.

'Men,' Hazel said.

'You know what they're like, Mr Harpur,' Rose said.

'Who?' Harpur replied.

'Men in a car,' Rose said. 'If they see a girl on a sports bike.'

'What about them?' Harpur said.

116

'Tail,' Simone said.

'That's what they call it,' Rose said.

'What?' Harpur said.

'A girl sitting on a bike saddle. Tail,' Nathalie said.

'So they tail tail,' Rose said. 'Childish.'

'Some men are obsessed by arses,' Simone said. 'This is well known. Women's arses, I mean. Heteros.'

'There's actually a theory about this – like biological, I mean. Some professor. I read it. Or zoological,' Rose said.

'Which is that?' Harpur said.

'Some men, heteros, see the shape of the woman's behind . . . the, well . . . they see the two cheeks . . . as a sort of match for or image of her . . . well, two breasts,' Rose said, 'and therefore . . . well . . . part of womanliness. This comes in certain nudes in sculpture – you can notice things are sort of balanced: buttocks, boobs. Like all chiselled into the same sort of curves. Four . . . As if from a kit. Rodin?'

'This is an eye-opener for me,' Harpur replied. 'The Clio men spotted you in traffic, did they, Haze?'

'Like that,' she said. 'Two.'

'And followed?' Harpur said.

'It happens to all of us,' Rose said, 'especially on bikes.'

'Pathetic,' Simone said.

'Hazel gave them some good slagging, didn't you. Haze?' Rose said.

'*Very* good,' Nathalie said.

'They were waiting outside the caff,' Hazel replied. 'So, I asked them to push off.'

'Meaning she gave them the finger and tongue-poke,' Nathalie said. 'You know that phrase do you, Mr Harpur – "giving the finger"? It's a youth phrase, meaning "Up yours!"' She showed him. 'Or sometimes it can be *two* fingers, like a V but the other way around, not V for Victory. Obviously "Up yours!" has some crudity to it.

What can you do, though, sometimes, blokes being so blokeish? The "yours" in "Up yours!" is –'

'Did you get a number?' Harpur replied.

'Registration?' Hazel said. 'No, it didn't seem . . . well, it was just tailing.'

'Just spotted you and followed you by chance?' Harpur said.

'What else?' Hazel replied.

'*We* thought harassment,' Nathalie said, 'and we would have taken the number but when we went out to the balcony the Clio had gone.'

'You're sure it was only fluke, Hazel?' Harpur said.

'That's how they are, Mr Harpur,' Simone said.

'Who?' Harpur said.

'Men,' Simone said. 'When they've got a car. They think they're prime. They think we're all interested in them because we're too young to drive ourselves.'

'What colour?' Harpur replied.

'What?' Hazel said.

'The car,' Harpur said.

'Red. Why? There's plenty of red Clios about,' Hazel said.

'They can feed "Clio, red" into the computer and come up with a list,' Simone said. 'The police. That's right, isn't it, Mr Harpur?'

'But obviously better with a reg,' Jill said.

'Two men?' Harpur replied.

'They probably look like puked dinners,' Rose said. 'Nobody would go near them. That's why they get their kicks on wheels.'

'But age, build, Haze?' Harpur said.

'Oh, you know what it's like, dad, in the half dark and faces behind a windscreen.'

'Tricky,' Jill said.

'But some idea,' he said. Harpur felt she would not have spoken about any of this if Simone hadn't started it. And now Hazel obviously wanted to stop the questions.

118

'One fattish, one thin, dark clothes,' she said.

'Ages?' Harpur said.

'Thirties? One could be forties,' Hazel said.

'That might be it,' Nathalie said. 'Might.'

'What?' Harpur said.

'Past it,' Nathalie said. 'Clubs, discos – they're too old to pull girls. So they do a cold trawl, a bike chase.'

'It's obvious, when we go out and they're gone,' Simone said.

'What's obvious?' Harpur replied.

'They know they're not going to get anywhere with Haze,' Simone said. 'They can see she's too smart for them – had them spotted when they thought they were being clever. And she told them what she thinks of them – OK, in sign language, but no mistake. So they go looking for someone else. I expect it's their usual night out.'

'White?' Harpur said.

'Yes,' Hazel said.

'Hair?' Harpur said.

'Yes,' Hazel said.

'Light? Dark?' Harpur said.

'Dark,' Hazel said.

'Who else was there?' Harpur said.

'Where?' Hazel replied.

'The café. Scott?' Harpur said.

'No,' Hazel said. Her drawbridge-up voice.

'Oh, Scott's often there, isn't he?' Harpur said.

'Sometimes,' Hazel said.

'Only girls,' Nathalie said. 'It's an all-girls cast for the play.'

'Anything like that, it would be best if you give me a ring,' Harpur said.

'Like what?' Hazel said.

'People hanging about,' Harpur said.

'I've got to deal with it,' Hazel said. 'It's what girls have to deal with, dad. Ask Nathalie, or Simone or Rose – or Denise. And Jill, soon.'

'Yes, I think it would be better if you give me a ring,' Harpur said.

'Most likely it's nothing,' Jill said.

'It's men hounding a girl,' Harpur replied. That previous feeling grew stronger. He sensed now that Jill as well as Hazel knew more than they said. Occasionally, they'd do some conspiring – shut him out of their secrets. Mobile phones allowed a lot of secrets, and spread a lot of secrets, too: ask Prince Charles.

Nathalie said: 'When you were quizzing if it was just fluke they followed her, Mr Harpur – was it because you don't think so? This would be a police way of looking at matters. Police always wonder about things that seem to be obvious, don't they, referred to as "keeping an open mind"?'

'Well, everybody wonders about *some* things,' Jill replied.

'But police wonder more, don't they? They try to see what's underneath something that's simple to everyone else,' Nathalie said. 'This is their training.'

'Wonder what?' Rose said.

'Well, if it wasn't a fluke perhaps that's because they were waiting at the house for Haze to come out,' Nathalie said.

'Why?' Rose said.

'If she'd lead them somewhere,' Nathalie said. 'Did you notice a lurk car, Haze? Or Jill. Were you in Arthur Street earlier, Jill? Anyone sitting in a car – just sitting?'

'Lead them to the bus station?' Rose asked. 'That supposed to be important?'

'If they wanted to see Scott,' Nathalie said.

'Why?' Simone said.

'I don't know, but *if* they did,' Nathalie said. 'Scott's there sometimes with Hazel. Is that what you thought, Mr Harpur? Why you're bothered?'

'So what's the play you have to do?' he replied.

'Scenes from *Look Back in Anger*,' Hazel said. 'It's got whiskers on, but there was a revival somewhere lately.'

'Rose is the star – the Jimmy Porter character. She can do a really ratty voice for the rants.'

'I'm Alison, cowed and loyal and good at ironing,' Hazel said.

'It's very socially aware – the play,' Rose said.

'God, yes,' Simone said. 'Jimmy really had problems. There'd been a war in the 1950s you know, Mr Harpur, when it was written – Suez. That got right up Jimmy's nose owing to Britain's colonial past. Later on the playwright, John Osborne, wrote a real hate letter about England from France.'

'Our problems are different these days, but bad,' Rose said.

'What?' Jill said. 'Getting bothered on bikes?'

'All sorts, all sorts,' Rose said. 'You'll find out when you're older, Jill. It's rough out there.'

'Where?' Jill said.

'Generally,' Rose replied.

Harpur might have stayed in the room with Jill to watch the rehearsal but just as the girls were starting he had one of those pressing phone calls from Jack Lamb. Jack asked for a meeting right away, if possible. And, of course, Harpur would *make* it possible. Harpur always did try to make it possible when Lamb suggested a get-together. Jack Lamb had priority built in. Pity, that: Harpur had wanted to see Hazel do 'cowed'. Acting interested him. He would like to dodge out of his skin himself and become someone else now and then. Although he rarely went to the theatre, when he did he often enjoyed it, despite so much dialogue. On a three-day trip to London, Denise took him to a truly serious piece called *Copenhagen*, about the rights and wrongs of nuclear research in the war, and Harpur considered he'd behaved all right, paying attention throughout and discussing historic moral themes with her afterwards. Some plays really got at things more or less,

121

and this one the girls were doing sounded as if it had been spot on fifty years ago.

But, but . . . there was Jack Lamb, and Jack Lamb today, immediate, not fifty years ago. 'Col,' he said on the phone, 'shall I see you soonest?' It was hardly a question. An instruction. 'In fact, now?'

'Where?'

'Three.'

'OK,' Harpur said. They had a list of rendezvous spots, secure and confidential, or supposed to be secure and confidential, numbered one to six. These included a Second World War concrete defence post on the foreshore, a laundrette, a supermarket car park, the Anglican cathedral. Number One used to be an old anti-aircraft gun site on a hill outside the city, but Jack thought that had become known and they'd dropped it. Three was the concrete defence post, built in 1940 to resist the German invasion that never came. Harpur suspected this might also be known – might even be used by villains for *their* palavers – but Jack liked it best of all the venues, so Harpur did not object. He always let Jack make the conditions. The risks were his entirely, and big. Lamb favoured a military touch to their conferences, if it could be had. Often he turned up in what he considered appropriate uniform from his Army Surplus collection, depending on the chosen place. Lamb had that same impulse as actors – and Harpur – to masquerade occasionally.

'Am I interrupting something at your home, Col?' Jack asked. Harpur's telephone was not in the sitting room, but he'd left the door half open when he came to take the call and Jack must be able to hear something of the first dramatic Rose rant as Jimmy Porter, ripping into Alison/ Hazel on account of her middle-classness and appallingly decent, polite nature. 'Denise is with you?' Jack asked. 'A tiff? Raucous. She really thinks *you're* middle class? Or is Iles there, too? Is she lambasting *him*?'

122

'Vivid exchanges are part of the tapestry of life, aren't they, Jack?'

'Are they?'

'Give and take.'

'I should think you'll be glad to get out of there and come to meet me,' Lamb said.

'Always, Jack.'

Harpur looked into the sitting room before he left. He did not interrupt the show but gave the girls a small wave. Jill came out into the hall to see him off. She was in a younger school class than Hazel and her friends and had no *Look Back in Anger* role.

'Something vital, dad?' she said.

'What?'

'Why you have to go out, like urgent.'

'Not "like urgent". Urgently.'

'Urgently.'

'Not all that urgent. But I need to see someone.'

'Is this your informant, your fink?'

Yes, it was his informant, his fink, and perhaps one of the greatest finks in the world, if greatness and finkery could live together. 'You know I detest that term,' he said.

'Which?'

'Fink.'

'Your grass or informant or whatever, then,' Jill said.

'Information comes from all kinds of sources, Jill.'

'Mr Jack Lamb?'

'I can't discuss with you every phone call I get, love.'

'I met Mr Jack Lamb. He came here once, didn't he? He seemed very nice, I mean, for a fi– For a voice.'

'We depend on such voices, Jill.'

'Who does?'

'The police. The law.'

'But why do they do it?'

'Who?'

'The voices. The finks. Money? They betray people for money?'

'We don't see it as betrayal.'

'But it *is* betrayal, isn't it?'

'They discover what they regard as an evil and feel a duty to get it removed. So they talk to us.'

'For money?'

'Some informants are paid, yes.'

'Mr Jack Lamb? He's got a big house in Chase Woods, hasn't he? It's called Darien, like in some poem. "Silent upon a hill in Darien." And Des Iles's house has a name from poems, too, yes? Idylls. That's Alfred Tennyson. Sometimes I think there's not much difference between low-life people and the legal biggies, like Mr Iles.'

'Because of their house names? Does that make sense?'

'Other things, too.'

'Which?'

'Yes, other things,' Jill said.

'In any case, Mr Jack Lamb is a respected art dealer, not low life,' Harpur said.

'So, it *was* Mr Jack Lamb on the finking phone just now, was it?' Jill said.

'I can't discuss every call I get, Jill.'

'And *does* Mr Jack Lamb get paid for his information?' Jill replied.

No, Mr Jack Lamb did not get paid, or not in money, anyway. His art dealership was brilliantly successful and very unharassed, though. 'They need you in there as audience for the play, Jill,' Harpur replied.

At the blockhouse, Lamb said: 'Tirana, Col. The one they call Tirana.'

'Dead.'

'I know dead. *Called* Tirana.'

'We're working on it.'

'Of course you're working on it,' Lamb replied. 'However –'

'Yes, complicated.'

It was dark outside and darker in the blockhouse. Occasional skinny beams of moonlight penetrated through a loophole before cloud put a stopper on and at these moments Harpur could make out Lamb's bulk against the wall nearest the sea. People who thought of grasses as small, slinky figures would have been surprised by Jack. He weighed about 250 pounds and stood six foot five. Tonight he wore a magnificently cut long grey greatcoat, possibly officer issue in the Polish or French army during the Second World War. Harpur could not make out whether it bore insignia and/or medal ribbons. Jack's green beret, though, was certainly commando British. The desert boots might come from his Rommel ensemble. Jack didn't mind being what he called 'eclectic'.

'I loathe the exploitation of young, penniless, refugee girls, Col.'

'Certainly.'

'That's why I'm talking to you. I'm not your general purpose tale-teller.' It was as if Lamb had been tuned in somehow to Harpur's conversation with Jill about the hygiene of grassing. Harpur first heard Jack's justification for informing an age ago, but he always listened gravely to reruns. Jill's word – 'betrayal' – would be in Lamb's mind, too, of course, and he needed to do his explanations occasionally, or more than occasionally. 'Look, Col, people talk to me and then I might – *might* – talk to you about what they talked to me about. That's how it works. Some of what they talk to me about I would never pass on. I might pay these people who talk to me, but that doesn't mean I want to use *everything* they talk to me about. I sort it out.'

'Choices.'

'True. What I say to myself, Col, is, not *Will this be up Colin Harpur's street?* What I say to myself is, *Do I regard what I hear about as disgusting and evil and do I want it stopped?* If I get an answer *Yes* to that I'll talk to you because you might be able to stop it. This is a cleansing matter, a positive duty matter, Col.'

'So, which people, Jack?' Harpur replied.

'Which people what?'

'Which people talk to you before you might or might not talk to me?' Harpur always put this kind of query to Lamb, knowing it would not be answered, and could not be answered. Informants never identified *their* informants or their informants would stop being their informants. Grassing had its refined procedures, its dainty interdependencies. Harpur asked so that Jack could ignore or reject the question. This enabled Lamb to think he was not just a loose-mouth and blab-all. Harpur did not expect an answer, did not *want* an answer. You looked after the morale of your grass, guided him away from self-contempt, in case self-contempt brought on a guilt-based dry-up. Harpur thought that in retirement he might write a guidebook for young detectives called *Tending Your Grass*.

'My source was there,' Lamb said.

'Morton Cross?'

'The night.'

'When Tirana got it?'

'Very much in the vicinity.'

'He saw something?' Harpur said.

'This could be important, Col.'

'He should be talking to us, not to you.'

'He's the kind who does talk to me. And not to you.'

'Which kind? Does he know it's an offence to withhold evidence?'

'He doesn't withhold it. He tells *me*,' Lamb said.

'Not the same.'

'The same as what?'

'*I* should talk to him.'

'Think of me as a conduit, Col.'

'I still –'

'My source – small-time pusher around the usual spots, the *previous* usual spots, who hears there's an interesting expansion of trade up in that area and decides to have a look-see. You wouldn't have heard of him, even if I told you his name, which I won't, naturally.'

'It might help me gauge the reliability of his information, Jack.'

'That's damn hurtful, Col. An insult. It's not necessary for you to gauge *his* reliability.'

'No?'

'What you've got to gauge is *my* reliability, isn't it, Col? And you gauged that long ago.'

'Well, I –'

'Have I ever given you a dud?'

'You –'

'Have I ever given you a dud?'

'I –'

'If *I* believe him it's because this is my applied judgement. That means *you've* got to believe him because you believe in me,' Lamb replied.

'Jack, I still –'

'He's at Morton Cross on that night and is walking through a couple of the streets where trade seems to be under way, assessing. A girl – very young – comes running towards him, looking really troubled and scared. Well, he's only there to do a commercial reconnoitre and doesn't want any involvement, does he, so he's going to ignore the girl, but she comes across the street to him, still running? She's trying to talk. She's foreign – some English, but not much. He's heard of the Albs infiltrating those parts, obviously, so he thinks maybe Alb, or possibly Turk. Now, he wonders is this some kid whore looking for business? Of course, he's also heard the Albs operate girls up there, as well as pushing substances. He takes her to be one of these sad, shanghaied youngsters.

'Then he notices something unusual, even for a tart. She's got two handfuls of money – paper money, twenties, tens – scrunched up in her fists. She waves one handful at him and is shouting something he doesn't understand at first. Is she saying she wants more like this from him? He's

127

not looking for that. Oh, she's shaggable, he thinks, but his purpose is different. Gradually, though, he picks out some English words among the rest of it. He hears "coach", "please", "bus station", "now", "soon", "pay". She's pulling at his sleeve, but not to drag him into a house or a car or a hedge for bought coitus, but as if she wants something else from him. He realizes he has misunderstood – not misunderstood by thinking she's a tart but misunderstood by thinking she's tarting *now*. She's not. No, slowly, he works it out that she's asking him to take her to the bus station where she can pick up a coach and she'll give him one lot of her cash and buy herself a ticket to somewhere with the rest. She wants escape. Something's happened to give her the chance, and she's scared she'll lose it if she's not quick. He knows some of these kids are conned and forced on to the game – prisoners. And he objects to that, the same as I do myself, the same as you would, Col, or any right thinker and the *Mail* and *Express*. So, he thinks, OK, I'll do it and they go to where he's left his car. Probably it's not all kindness. He could ask her about the scene up there, even though she's not much at English. She's familiar with it from the inside.

'As soon as he starts driving, she perks up and is happy. She knows she's out of it. He can see he's done the right thing. She pushes some money – one whole handful – into his top pocket, but when they reach the station he makes her take it back. He reckons she's going to need it, wherever she goes, and he's got some good to him, this source. Or he *says* he gave it back to her, all of it. You know what sources are like, Col.'

'Of course I do. *You're* a source, Jack. One of mine.'

'You have others, you sod?'

'Minor.'

'Right. Anyway, *my* source had tried to ask her about the money as he drove – where it came from, and so on. She holds up two fingers and he sees she means two men. She's been in a threesome with big payment? Is there a premium for threesomes, Col? You'd probably know. She tells him, "Two from big Jag, one with face rip."'

'Face rip?'

'He thinks she means a scar. Once she has shoved the money into his pocket she's got a hand free, and she puts a finger along his jaw line to show where that face rip was on one of the men.'

'She's doing a bunk with a night's takings before the pimp grabs it?' Harpur said. 'And she needs transport?'

'I wonder if this gets a message to you, Col.'

'What kind?' But, yes, it got one special message to him, and probably the same message as it got to Lamb. However, Jack liked to eke out his stuff and be mysterious, so Harpur would often act defeated. It was another standard ploy to nurse grass ego, grass confidence. Informants always did their revelations unhurriedly, to make them seem more – a spread. 'What are you thinking of, Jack?' he said. Plainly, what Jack would be thinking of was Manse Shale and Ralph Ember.

'The Jaguar. A scarred face. Two men together, apparently with a load of cash on them.'

'It's a puzzler, Jack.'

'Is it?'

No, not a bit. 'We have to ask first, is she telling the truth, and second, is your source reading things right?' Harpur replied.

'This is Mansel Shale and Ralphy, isn't it?' Lamb said. 'Both likely to have plenty in their wallets. There's Ember's famous, throat-close wound mark that stirs the women so much. They stroke it, ladle out the sympathy and admiration. Of course, Ralph hints it happened in some epic gang fight when he took on fearful odds. "You ought to see the other guys" – this sort of thing. I heard that actually he fell on a broken HP sauce bottle in the kitchen at home in Low Pastures when boozed up to ease a panic. And then Shale. He drives the Jag himself these days, since Denzil went under, doesn't he?'

'Shale and Ember? Would they go tarting together? Manse has long-term partnerships at the rectory. Anything up to weeks at a time. And Ralph's got a wife.'

Lamb shifted and did what he usually did at blockhouse meetings. He crouched and gazed seawards through one of the loopholes, as though on watch for Hitler's landing craft and ready to throw them back on his own. During the war, some Polish and Free French army people with greatcoats like Jack's *were* stationed in Britain, and would have helped resist Nazi invaders. Lamb had become Allied Forces in Europe. It was best not to mess up his concentration while he conducted one of these intense sentinel sessions, and Harpur stayed quiet. Lamb grunted – had possibly mind-eyed a pocket battleship out there, masthead swastika aflutter, ready with protective broadsides of 11 inch shells as the troops fought their way ashore.

He stayed in that position when he spoke again: 'The girl says to my source, "Tirana" – asks him if he ever heard of Tirana and he says yes. "He dead," she says. "Dead in car. He love me. He love me so much, but dead." My source, he's not sure he's understanding right what she says, and the love bit he thinks would probably be wishful, anyway. But he does some grief and asks her if it was Tirana who gave her the money, which would make her think he loved her. And she gets ratty and says no, says she has told him already, the Jaguar man and the man with the face rip. My source apologizes and says he just wanted to get things clear. So, was it Jaguar man and face rip man who did Tirana? he asks. No, no, before them, she says. But they both have what she calls "gun bumps". And this time she touches his jacket where a shoulder holster would lie. She's a girl who's very young but who has seen a lot of bad life and most likely a lot of gun bumps, Col.

'My source drops the girl off in the bus station car park to get an intercity coach, says he gives her back the money, then returns to Morton Cross to continue his tour and try to check the Tirana story. It would make a difference to his plans if someone like that had been taken out. There might be more room up there, a trade opening. And when he reaches Morton Cross again he discovers more or less at once that the girl has it right. A street near where he met her has been closed off. Police and police cars everywhere. Also a crowd of spectators kept back behind a barrier. He parks and goes to join them.'

Lamb's lookout stint ended. He could relax from maximum alert and stood straight again. He'd made GB safe.

'Yes, I was down at the BMW with the body when your source joined the crowd, I expect,' Harpur said.

'My source asks people what's up. They're not all too keen on talking but eventually one says that "the king of the Albs" – this was the phrase, Col – one of them says that "the king of the Albs has got his and so he should." My source asks if this means Tirana. "Of course Tirana," he's told. "Didn't I say, king of the Albs?" My source thinks it might not be a wise spot to hang around. He's wary about getting his face remembered given all the circumstances, including his possible plans. He withdraws.'

'I definitely ought to see this source, Jack,' Harpur said. 'It could be entirely in confidence.'

'Except you might want to put him up in court.'

'I –'

'So, you'll ask what's my reading of all this, and why did I call you out tonight,' Lamb replied.

'What's your reading of all this and why did you call me out tonight?'

'I'd say a link between the three aspects.'

'Which three, Jack?'

'Tirana, the girl, Ember and Shale, taking Ember and Shale as a unit.'

'What's it based on, Jack?'

'What?'

'Your idea of a link,' Harpur said.

'It's how I see it.'

131

'But why?'

'Ralphy and Manse are up in Morton Cross for the same reason as my source – to look at what's happening there as a trade situation. Or . . .'

'Or?'

'Well, the "gun bumps", Col. These two are tooled up? It's not usual for them. They love peace, as you know, Col. They've given you peace, you and Iles. But did their patience break? They're frightened by the new competition? Had they decided on a removal job? Were they up there looking for Tirana and arrived too late?'

'And how do they find the girl?' Harpur said.

'Find her? Perhaps they didn't *have* to find her. Maybe she was in the car with Tirana.'

'Was she? Have you got some evidence?'

'He *loves* her, she said. His girl for the night? Only the night gets shortened because he's shot.'

'You think the money's from him? The girl said no.'

'Of course she said no. And she's right. Tirana wouldn't pay. *Droit de seigneur.* And, anyway, it's true love, isn't it? So she thinks. Cash would spoil it. That's why she got angry with my source. The money comes from Ralphy and Manse, as she said. They see Tirana is dead and the girl's alongside him in the car. They get her out of the BMW, pool their tens and twenties and tell her to scarper. There might be two reasons for that. Ralphy Ember can be almost a noble gent sometimes. They call him "Milord Monty", don't they, after the name of his club? A kind of grandeur to him and crooked dignity, even gallantry. Mostly, yes, he's just Panicking Ralphy. But he's capable of the fine gesture. And he's got a daughter around that girl's age. This could touch him, even enough to make him brave. That night, does he suddenly come over humane and persuade Manse to do the same? Ember realizes the girl probably has no papers and will be in a bad spot when your people arrive. And Manse wouldn't care to look

132

cowardly compared to Ralph. Compared to Panicking Ralph! God.

'Second, they might not want to be tied into the Tirana death scene although they didn't do him. Could they *prove* they didn't do him? They have to think how you, and especially how dear Des Iles, would visualize things. The girl had seen them, and would have seen the Jaguar. They'd want her gone, not available as a witness. "Take the money and run, kid." It's a way out from a shit pit life for her. She might really believe Tirana loved her, but he's unavailable now. Everything tells her to vanish. She does run, buys a ticket for the first long distance coach out, maybe London, maybe anywhere. It doesn't really matter where it's going, as long as she can get clear of the regime here. She disappears. She's obviously not on her way to an ideal life, but better than this one.'

'Your source, Jack,' Harpur replied.

'I keep telling you: he wouldn't see you.'

'Small-time pushing around the usual old spots, yes?'

'Very small.'

'Including the bus station, I suppose?' Harpur said.

'Could be the bus station from time to time.'

'He heard about Morton Cross from someone – new territory?'

'As I said.'

'Does he hear about Morton Cross from somebody down at the bus station?'

'Would I know that?' Lamb replied.

'Would you?'

'What's the interest, Col?'

'I have to think about not just the Tirana death but the sequel – Chilton Park,' Harpur said.

'You think someone who was around the bus station could have been in the Park scrap? My source, no. I'm sure. He's not like that. He wouldn't have the connections, or a gun.'

'I'm not thinking about your source.'

133

'Who then?' Lamb said.

'I –'

'Is this someone important to you?' Lamb bent a little and pushed his extensive face close to Harpur's in the dark, trying to read his expression.

'You want us to try to trace the girl, do you?' Harpur replied. 'That's what the meeting is for?'

'When I give information, Col, it's because I'd like something put right.'

'Well, yes –'

'That situation at Morton Cross – intolerable. The kids in slavedom. The violence. If you find the girl, she can be helped, can't she? Her money's going to run out and then what? All she knows about is the game. She's back to where she was – not the same place, the same serfdom, though. You say it's "complicated" on the Tirana inquiries. But she can probably help with those, can't she? The girl saw who did it. She was sitting alongside him.'

'If,' Harpur said.

'Ask Manse. Ask Ember.'

'That can't work.'

'Have a go.'

'You said one reason Manse and Ralph gave her money was so she'd not be here to tell us they were around at the death, Jack. They're going to deny, aren't they? They'll have arranged alibis. That's if they really were there.'

'Of course they were. Mr Jaguar. Mr Rip Face. Mr Rip Face who is also the big-hearted, humane Milord now and then.'

'I do worry about the girl,' Harpur replied, 'if your source has it right. I ought to speak to him.'

'He's got a real aversion.'

'To what?'

'Police.'

'Does he still do the bus station?'

'I'll tell him not to,' Lamb said. 'You're a bit concentrated on that place, aren't you, Col? Why? Double importance?

The girl leaves from there. But some earlier significance, too? What, Col?'

'Perhaps I *will* try Manse or Ralphy,' Harpur replied. 'Not both. Obviously, the second will get a call from the first I see, wising him up. No shock effect possible.'

'Someone at Chilton Park, or *maybe* at Chilton Park is a real worry for you, Col – that so?' Lamb prepared to go. He went to the door of the blockhouse and checked there was nobody around outside. 'I sold Manse Shale a flashy Arthur Hughes a while ago,' he said, over his shoulder. 'Almost certainly genuine. He's into the Pre-Raphaelites. The word thrills him, I think – "Pre-Raphaelite". Saying it right makes him feel educated. If you drop in at the rectory, see if he's still got it, Col, would you? I aim to keep track of stuff I've handled, authentic or fake. It's like wanting a puppy to go to a good home.'

'I'll give you ten minutes before I leave, Jack,' Harpur replied.

Chapter Seven

Ralph Ember hated crowing or anything gaudy like that but he felt satisfaction at the way he went to help that kid in the BMW with Tirana dead. All right, Shale accompanied him, eventually, and got some cash out, eventually, but both *were* eventually, *very* eventually. Manse would never have done either if there'd been no prompt from Ember. Ralph was sure of this. He saw his behaviour as similar to a British officer's leading troops over the top regardless in a First World War no man's land attack. But he would not stretch the comparison, and definitely never speak of it. Ralph always enjoyed the obituaries of daring soldiers in the *Daily Telegraph*, though First War survivors were rare now. Shale had wanted to disappear fast. And, in a way, Ember could see this looked like wisdom. After all, he and Manse visited Morton Cross to do Tirana as a tidy commercial enterprise and, once they'd found him already dead, the requirement ended and they could have very reasonably left. However, perhaps some reasoning was dismally narrow. Certain urges went beyond and above the rational, and Ember considered his wish to save the girl from more trauma showed an almost spiritual side, and one which he longed to develop.

This action had been important to the girl, but much more important to Ember, crucial to Ember. His character and manliness became involved with that abused youngster, depended on that abused youngster. His steps towards the BMW had been steps towards a brilliantly improved, resolute self. How could people think of him as Panicking Ralph, or Ralphy, when he audaciously, quite selflessly, dealt with a perilous situation in this style? Yes, style. Of course, not many would know about it, but, alternatively, and inspiringly, how could he think of *himself* as Panicking Ralph after what happened, although he had sometimes been forced in honesty to admit he did get totally disabling panics.

Noblesse oblige. He recalled that phrase. It meant, roughly, high rank and privilege brought big duties. He thanked God he'd had the resolve to recognize a duty to that pressganged piece BMW'd on the night with a corpse. AlthoughRalph realized he, technically, did not yet possess full *noblesse*, such as a title or true aristocratic background, *noblesse* could also be taken to mean distinction through quality. And, yes, Ralph believed he certainly had distinction, especially when considered against this abducted, corrupted, enslaved, immigrant girl – most likely a '*sans papiers*', as they apparently, touchingly, called themselves in France: 'without papers', without identity.

Whereas, Ember's identity? Established. Acknowledged. Aglow. Didn't he own his club, the Monty, and plan to raise its social rating magnificently very soon, ditching the crooked fucking riff-raff and their noisy slags he had to grant membership at present? Also, Ember was a famed campaigner on environmental and anti-pollution topics, especially rivers and litter, through sharp, positive letters frequently published in the local papers over the names R.W. Ember or Ralph W. Ember, by now familiar to many, and of major weight. Further, he and his family lived in an unmortgaged, three-hundred-plus years old manor house, Low Pastures, with spacious grounds and stables and paddocks for his daughters' riding.

As to French, one of his daughters, Venetia, knew the language, having been to school for a spell at Poitiers, then Bordeaux, and she told Ralph that Low Pastures would be called a '*gentilhommière*' in that country. There had been

French girls at these schools with her who came from *gentilhommières* in, for example, the Auvergne or Bourgogne. Ember loved the word and often enunciated it slowly to himself, *'gentilhommière'*: a gentleman's residence, in the old, full, admirable sense of an English gentleman bound by *noblesse oblige*. You would not expect to find someone like Manse Shale and his ferret eyes and rickety grammar in a *gentilhommière*. If you mentioned that word to Manse, the bewilderment in his face would be comical, though also pitiable. Of course, Manse did scrape around for status and had that one-time rectory. Ralph certainly did not despise the Church, yet a rectory could never add up to a *gentilhommière*. Manse would probably qualify for that new social category mentioned in the Press, a 'chav': someone rich and vulgar. Mansel was the sort who'd admit it and pick up the cliché, 'Better a chav than a chav-not,' as if he'd just thought of it for himself, so as to prove chavs could be witty and frank.

People worked at their image, including Ember. Although Ralph felt warm about the way he spontaneously looked after the girl, he wondered, glancing back, whether he had looked after her *enough*. He must find this conscripted young tart again. Now that his own personal rating – his rating as a *gentilhomme*, fit to live in a *gentilhommière* – yes, now that all this hung on her state and fate, he decided it was morally lacklustre merely to have pulled her out of the car, shed a few measly fucking tens and twenties, and abandoned her. Where could she go? He hadn't troubled to wonder, had he? She'd left, with the money still on show, and walked into the next street, then, presumably the next, and where, finally?

As far as Ralph cared at the time, she could go anywhere because he had performed his little spell of salvaging, and afterwards wanted to forget her – wanted to imagine he had gloriously saved her from something, and that in the future she'd stay safe and free and touchingly grateful. Shale had encouraged that kind of write-off, and this probably influenced Ralph. But he'd been part of the decision himself. And the convenient, callous hand-washing and stupid optimism he now came to see as more suitable to Panicking Ralph, or even Panicking Ralphy, than to a gracious man of honour and officer material, aware *in toto* of his responsibilities. He had tried to buy off his conscience and knew it.

The revelation hit Ember badly. For a second he thought it would put him into one of his authentic Panicking Ralph, or Ralphy, panics. Perhaps despite everything that's who he really was. Oh, God, irony – he finds out he's a *nothing* through trying to be *something*. But he managed to fight off a bumper panic, at least for the moment.

To restore self-belief and escape shame, he decided he must get up to Morton Cross, or near, urgently and trace the girl, check she was all right, and do more than that. He had no sexual feelings for her. Simply, he cared in a principled British way – a way natural to the owner of a *gentilhommière* which went right back in history – simply he cared in a principled British way for this duped, victimized alien. Because he'd seen her, had that slight contact with her, she'd become his responsibility. He asked himself, how *could* he check she was all right, and the answer he gave himself back said she couldn't really be all right. He would tour Morton Cross and see if he could find her among the tarts on the street. And, if he did find her, would that be 'all right' then? No, it would mean she had simply reverted because for her no other livelihood existed or could. A few pounds from him and Manse could not buy her a new career. She was blighted. And, on account of the ruthless pimpery – probably foreign and barbaric – she would not even be able to keep much of the cash. He must change this. His own soul and personal dignity lay invested in her. These amounted to far more than that mere handful of pocket money.

He prepared to go immediately. It might be difficult around Morton Cross, Inton and the Park. Police would still have a big, after-the-event presence there. Usually, they weren't especially down on tarts but tarts had become symptoms of gang war, gang deaths, and these mattered. Such deaths made the Press and troubled the politicians. The police had to respond. Girls parading on offer were sure to be more careful for now. Even before the Chilton Park incident, they must have been fairly discreet when working that district, because the area had a lot of big properties and influential people who would object to street walkers cheapening the scene and possibly making casual use of excellently laid out front gardens, leaving condoms and arse prints on the soil. The fact was, this district lacked altogether a recognized tradition of busy whoredom and kerb cruising. Now, owing to upped police numbers, conditions would be even tougher. Just the same, Ember knew he must look. It might be *his* salvation, as well as the girl's. She could help him finally snuff out and bury Panicking Ralph, or Ralphy. She knew the finality of death.

He thought he would not discuss this quest with his wife. Margaret was probably unaware that some referred to him as Panicking Ralph, or Ralphy. Keep it like that. He intensely needed her to have faith in him and to admire him in his worthwhile Ralph Ember or Ralph W. Ember essence. And without disclosing those demeaning, abominable other names to her, he would not be able to explain the fierce compulsion in him to do a tart tour – the fierce and, he felt, rather illustrious compulsion.

He had no name for the kid to help trace her. He must hope that some of the girls knew she had been in the BMW that night and could point him on to her new work site. It was even possible that Tirana *did* love her and some kind of relationship existed. This would make identification fairly easy, as long as colleagues agreed to talk. Ember put four hundred pounds from the Monty safe in his pockets to ease introductions: fifties, twenties, tens. Although language might be tricky if most of the girls up there were flesh imports, a good glimpse of readies would make them try to understand and help. He took no pistol. It would be inappropriate, in his view. He had a project to aid someone, and through aiding her aid himself. Why should a firearm come into such plans? This girl had probably seen a lot of guns although so young, and she might instantly spot a holster bulge under his jacket and get scared and hostile – might take Ralph to be part of the same brutal scene he wished to free her from.

He told Monty staff he would be gone for a few hours at most and left them to run the club. That was all right. He liked to be at the Monty for the last hour or so before closing at 2 a.m., to make sure things stayed peaceful. Some members might be very full of booze and grandiosity by then and difficult to shift. Oh, God, to be able to ban the fuckers for ever! He should get back in time for doors shut tonight.

Of course, he realized that because of increased police patrols at Morton Cross the girls and the substances trade had possibly shifted ground. Any move would most likely be to the Valencia streets ultimately, where tolerance operated following decades of custom and practice. The story went that Assistant Chief Constable Desmond Iles had a girl down there. Lately, the story also went that one of the new trades people at Morton Cross, Adrian Cologne, had tried to take over running of that girl, and had grown rough with her when she acted awkward. If this were true and Iles found out – which he would, of course – Adrian Cologne might be in line for hard retaliation.

Ralph had certainly heard forecasts from operatives in his firms about transference of these Morton Cross outfits to the Valencia, and had wondered himself. But no news of this invasion reached him so far. Several days after the Chilton Park discord, business might be resuming up there, though in a quieter mode and perhaps more towards the west or south, away from the Park. He thought he'd start his search at the border streets between Morton Cross

141

and Inton, two comparable regions of high suburbia, and, should that produce nothing, he could turn back to the Park.

And as he trekked through the first few Inton avenues and crescents and so on he had a bit of a smile. Always this sort of glossy, bumptious district tickled him. The houses were big – five or six bedrooms, most of them – and their gardens big, too. You could tell that the people who lived here really thought they had achieved something. Yet these smug fuckers probably would not even know what a fucking *gentilhommière* was. Their properties had been constructed of cheapo cement bricks, tinted and antiqued to make them look like the geniune clay-based, oven-baked article. Sad. On the other hand, Low Pastures featured authentic stone walls and Ralph and his adviser on design and decor had decided to keep the stone exposed here and there, as a tribute to its basic beauty and strength. Ralph loved this rawness, this intimacy with the past. As he'd told Margaret, they seemed to place him in a context. He longed to be worthy of that past, this context, which was why he would transform the Monty. Low Pastures dated from a century when Britain secured India and Inton did not exist, except as fields. He drove on slowly. So far he'd seen no girl groups around these streets.

As a matter of fact, Iles lived not far from here in one of these large gimcrack places. You'd think someone like Iles would not be content with such a base. They said Harpur used to get in there a while ago to commingle with Iles's wife when the ACC was away at courses or Association of Chief Police Officer shindigs. The fat, tall hedges helped Harpur slink in and out not too obviously, the shag-happy yob. This furtiveness could not be less like that picture of himself Ralph had as a fearless unit commander heading his men as they burst from their trenches. Iles rumbled the adultery, though, and would occasionally scream the details at Harpur publicly even now, sometimes while in full ceremonial uniform at civic functions. Reports of such behaviour unsettled Ember. If one senior police officer yelled accusations in, say, a cenotaph Remembrance Day service, at another senior police officer about banging his – the first senior officer's – wife on the quiet in the first senior officer's own expensive property, though not of the *gentilhommière* category, plainly, this must embarrass ordinary folk and make them wonder whether suitable people ran law and order here. Often Ralph thought that British standards, as they once were, had begun to slide at such a rate they could never be stopped, let alone fucking reversed.

Now, his instincts did turn out fruitful and he found a trio of corner girls in a short, pricey, very bay-windowed street on the edge of Inton, not quite Morton Cross, and a long way from the Park. He pulled up and lowered the front passenger side window of the Saab. Often his profile affected women. It could be a pest, the way they came after him, but he did not mind tonight. One girl approached at once. The three looked anything between fourteen and eighteen, dressed revelatory, and most likely non-Brit. The one who moved to greet him was dark, very tall, very angular, large-eyed, wide-mouthed. She stuck her head into the car and said: 'Seventy-five long time, dearie, fifty quicky, forty blow. You have that cash?'

Ember translated this as, *Are you only up to window shopping, Mr Poverty-Prick?* 'Yes, plenty,' he said.

The girl gave a backward twitch of her head indicating the other two: 'Me the best. Tight as a mouse's ear. A lot of bounce and emotion.' Ember didn't know an Albanian accent but thought this might be it. Maybe on account of her poor English, she had been given lines to speak and professional jargon: 'dearie', 'long time', 'quicky', 'blow', 'bounce', 'emotion'. And the tight 'mouse's ear', of course. Or perhaps that could be a direct translation from Albanian. They might believe in spelling things out rather coarsely there.

'I'm searching for someone,' he replied.

'Yes, I think so. Me. The best.'

'Another girl,' Ember said. 'I need your help.'

'Another?' She looked insulted and angry.

'A girl not here now but at Morton Cross that night.'

'You got cash?' she replied. 'You will show me cash?'

He thought she smelled really good – not scent but an encouraging, wholesome soap, filling the car. It could be Imperial Leather. They might not have this in her country abroad if it had never owned an empire that produced leather, and she'd probably been won over by the soap and given herself a real sudding. Cleanliness offered a grand plus in a whore of whatever age. Ralph hated ingrained knuckles. There seemed a thorough spruceness to this girl's hair. You would not mind that head on one of your personal pillows if the family were away and you took her home briefly. Or on the back-seat upholstery of even a luxury car. The shakiness of her English made it important to have other favourable factors. He pulled out a couple of fifties and displayed them for her.

She wagged a finger at him, like a mother to her child: 'No good,' she said.

True, forged fifties appeared now and then. Of course, Ralph or someone at the club had checked these, but he did not try to explain that now. She must have been told by the management to refuse them. He put the notes back in his pocket and produced four twenties instead. 'Tirana's girl,' he said.

'Tirana? My city.'

'Ah, you're Albanian. A lovely country, I believe. Mountains. Chrome.'

'Send money home every week.' She touched the twenties but he held on.

'That's very good,' he said. 'We call those "remittance contributions", important factors in some countries' economies. But I mean the businessman they call Tirana, not the town.'

'Ah, businessman.'

'They *called* him Tirana. He was dead in a car. A girl with him. I have to find that girl. There's eighty if you can help me.'

'Me best.' She pointed at his wristwatch. 'One hour. Seventy-five. Eighty is . . . oh, maybe ten more minutes.' She touched the twenties again.

'I have to find that girl.'

'For fucking?'

'No,' he said.

'Not for fucking? Is she a girl not for fucking, never for fucking? She is nun?'

'Yes, she was a girl for fucking, but not tonight. I want to meet her, that's all.'

'Tirana? He had many girls.'

'Yes, but the one with him that night.'

'Eighty is good.'

'Because I'm taking your time,' Ember replied.

'Time? You take it? How take my time?'

'There might be other customers. I'm in the way.'

'To talk about Tirana – we don't like that. Yes, he dead, but we don't like to talk about him.'

'No, I realize that.'

'Dangerous.'

'Yes, but it's not really about Tirana. The girl.'

'You are police?' She did a stare at the dashboard of the Saab, most likely looking for switch-on blue lamps. She had learned the way of things here fast.

'I want to help this girl,' Ember replied.

'Help? Why?'

How did he explain in language she could follow that the one he sought had given him stature, brought him aplomb and goodness, activated his courage? 'Do you know where she's putting out tonight? he said. 'Which street?'

The girl pulled her head back out of the car and turned to speak to the others, perhaps passing on his question or perhaps telling them what a lousy prat she'd got herself stuck with. Ember could hardly hear and knew he wouldn't have understood anyway.

But perhaps she hadn't been speaking to both the others. One of them stepped towards the car now: 'What's she saying, mate? You don't understand, either? Don't fancy her? Too bony? Or you want a bit of Brit?' He put this accent around Leeds or York.

'You're working with them?' Ember replied. 'I thought Albs kept with Albs.'

'Yeah, well things are all over the fucking place lately. Chaos here. Them national barriers, they're all nothing since the trouble. Or you know, do you? You the law?' Now, *she* did a stare at the dashboard, looking for the switch-on blue lamps.

He waved the money. 'No, no. Not police.'

'Eighty's all right,' she replied. He found her easier to give an age to because she talked English, and decided she might be all of seventeen. 'That's a full hour, and everything.' The tall girl had moved away to another car.

'When you say all over the place, you mean after Tirana was killed, and the Chilton Park commotion?' he said.

'Like that. These stupid bloody turf wars.'

He thought of Shale's theory that Harpur's daughter's boyfriend might have been implicated. 'Were you around the Park when it happened?' he said.

'Afternoon. I don't come out till night.'

'Do you hear any names?'

'Names?'

'People who took part.'

'What, you *are* police?'

'No, honestly.'

'Do you think they'd tell us stuff like that?'

'Rumour? Gossip?'

'And if I did know, would I tell someone I've just met? Silence is safer.'

He decided to forget the boyfriend. Ember had not come here to inquire about *him*. Those questions could get in the way of what he really wanted to know. And they only concerned a bit of Shale guesswork and fantasy. 'I'm looking for the girl who was with Tirana,' Ember said.

'Yeah? Oh, that silly, lucky bitch.'

'You know her?'

'You won't find that one. But me, I can do anything you like. What did she have so special, then? Or is it you want to give one to somebody who been getting it from Tirana, like racial – Britannia rules the waves?'

'What do you mean, "silly", "lucky"?'

'Lucky? She's out of it, isn't she?'

'Out of it, how?'

'Remember?' she replied.

'What?'

'Eighty.'

'Right.' He was going to hand her the twenties.

'Not here, moron,' she said, and climbed into the car. 'Drive somewhere. There's eyes about.'

'What eyes?' He did what she said and pulled out from the kerb. 'Police eyes?'

'Pimp eyes. If they see money moving and there's no sex they'll wonder what the pay is for, and they'll guess it's for talking, and they don't like talking, not us talking, the girls.' Ember drove on to a main road. In a while she said: 'Get into this lay-by. It's not busy tonight. Punters are still worried and don't turn up. You're brave.'

This was a word he loved above all and knew he deserved. Sometimes in the *Daily Telegraph* soldier obituaries came a sentence he really dwelt on and felt he might have deserved if he'd been born at a different time and was involved at Tobruk or in the Ardennes: 'As a result of this action he was awarded an immediate bar to his DSO.' 'Brave? I wouldn't say that,' he replied. Perhaps tarts saw the grandeur in him by instinct, and brought out the grandeur in him. They knew a lot of men, obviously, and would be quick on to their qualities. Even if they witnessed one of his most disastrous panics, they would know this was only a blip, not the jonnock Ember. He prized the girl's judgement. Ralph wondered whether he'd make it a hundred. Then she could have at least twenty for herself and her habit.

She smelled quite as good as the first girl, but this *was* scent, and something classy, possibly Red. She'd given her whole body dabs of it, he thought. Whenever she shifted in the car seat he got a waft without even a minor trace of sweat beneath. These girls had decent pride. This one was fair-haired and almost blonde, slight, middle height, over-pale from whatever she was on, gappy teeth, podge nose. He'd been dim to mistake her for foreign: not many blonde Albs. Ralph liked to be kindly and thought she could be called a *jolie laide*. Her short denim skirt only just got a cover on things, but this was standard gear for the game and Ralph would never have remarked on the skimpiness, even if he hadn't wanted to keep things friendly with her so she'd spill.

He pulled up and she said: 'Yes, out of it. Well, she's out of *here*, anyway. She might be at it again somewhere else by now. I mean, what else can she do? A foreign cow, no passport, money that will fade so quick.'

Yes, money that would fade. This was what anguished Ember. He said: 'Money? She had money? How? Punter money?'

'She's running down the street with it by Chilton Park. Handfuls.'

'You saw her?'

'This was on the night,' she replied. 'The night they done Tirana.'

'You saw her?'

'Of course. If you was in that street you couldn't help seeing her. She's wagging this cash around like she robbed a till. More than a hundred. Well, nearly two, I reckoned.'

This girl could count, even at a distance. Most of

the girls could count. As Ralph recalled it there had been £180.

'Escape money,' the girl said.

'To where?'

'You going to follow her? She *must* be special. And Tirana had her around for more than a week, too. What she got?'

'Follow her where?' Ember said.

'Look, she goes to some guy.'

'How do you mean, "goes to some guy"?'

'He's walking in the street and she goes to him. A conversation.'

'Someone she knows?'

'Could be. But I don't think so. He looks surprised.'

'A punter?'

'*She's* waving money at *him*, not *him* at *her*.'

'She wants something from him? What?' Ember said.

'Not just conversation.'

'What?'

'They go around the corner and I can't see no longer. But I think I hear a car start.'

'A punter takes her off in a car, like you and me tonight?' Ember said.

'Also could be. I don't think so. She never comes back. He does. He was like a taxi, if you ask me – shipping her somewhere. Then he's in the crowd where the street's blocked off because of Tirana. I'm there, too. I mean, there wasn't going to be no more tomcats that night, not after the shooting. He asks about Tirana. Someone tells him "king of the Albs", which was right in a way, though he didn't get his head on their stamps.'

'Who was he?'

'The taxi man? Thirties. Nearly bald. Skinny. Jeans and brown leather jacket. New to me.'

'The car?'

'Didn't see it. He parked out of sight both times.'

'The girl?'

'Perhaps she said: "Take me somewhere and I'll pay you." I was too far away to hear.'

'"Take me" where?'

'Like I said, escape. What's to stay for? Her man's dead. Or the man she thinks is her man. Her man for a week. So, her man's dead and she might get bother because of it, police bother, other bother. It could look bad, being in a car with a deceased. Goodbye then. She got money. Enough for a train ticket, coach ticket, even a few fixes at the other end, wherever. Then she works again. Anyway, you won't find her. Not here.'

'What's her name?'

'You're really serious, are you?'

'If she was with Tirana for a while her name must be around,' Ember replied.

'Sometimes Anna. Sometimes Olive. Sometimes Beatrice.'

'But which?'

'We all have a few names, some very fancy. There's a black girl called Honorée, would you believe? She gets trouble from Adrian. Wherever Anna, Olive, Beatrice is she'll be called something else by now.'

'It's vital that I –'

She swung her legs around towards Ralph. His obsession with the other girl obviously still irritated her. This jealousy and the Red buffeted him. 'So, look, do you want something now?' she said. 'You've got fifteen minutes if it's eighty.'

'Raincheck,' he said. He gave her the hundred and began the drive back to her street spot.

'I might not always be where you found us tonight. We could have some changes.'

'That right?'

'Different ground. For a while, anyway.'

'The Valencia?' he said.

'You know, you remind me of someone,' she replied.

'That right?'

'In films.'

'Really?'

She stayed quiet for a minute. 'Do you know who I think it is?'

'Donald Duck?'

'So fucking modest. That big actor. He did El Cid. Moses. Yes, Charlton Heston. You're just like Charlton Heston. When he was younger.'

'I've never heard that before. I'm glad it's when he was younger, though.'

'Definitely. *Ben Hur* on TV every Easter. Great body. Listen, how did you get the mark on your jaw?'

'Some trouble when I was much younger myself.'

'Fighting?'

'I don't seek out fights, but sometimes one has to look after one's self,' he said. Yes, sometimes one had to look after one's self, look *for* one's self – not necessarily in fights, though, but through a missing, foreign, babe tart who had mysteriously given him valour.

And now this Leeds, York, tart put her finger on the scar and traced it down to his chin. 'I shouldn't do this when you're driving. A knife?'

'Some of those fights had weaponry of all sorts.'

'God,' she said. 'What kind of trade are you in?'

'Miscellaneous.'

'I'll look out for you. This a Saab?'

'That's it.'

'I'll remember the reg. Name's Eva, generally,' she said.

'Nice.'

'And you?'

He put her down. 'Cheers, Eva and so on,' he said.

He'd driven about half a mile towards Chilton Park when a spinning blue light came up in his mirror. He pulled over. The police car parked behind and a woman officer walked to his passenger window. He lowered it. The police car was unmarked but had those concealed blue lights the girls looked for in the Saab.

151

'Do you know why I stopped you, sir?' the officer said.

'A rear light on the blink? Sorry. I'll fix it tomorrow.'

'You've been girling, sir.'

'No, I –'

'We watched you do the deal, rejecting one tart, taking another. A flash of money. You go off, then reappear with her. We're trying to stop that kind of thing in this area. Antisocial. You may know there've been some tragedies here lately. We're issuing cautions for a first offence. You won't be charged tonight.' She carried a laptop and glanced at the screen. 'You're Mr Ralph Ember of Low Pastures and the Monty club, yes? We speak to our computer and this is the name it comes up with for your registration number. It's correct?'

'I needed to talk to a girl, that's all.'

'We were behind you to the Easy Lay.'

'To where?'

'Sorry. That's what we call it – the Easy Lay lay-by, sir.'

'I –'

'We've got it right, have we?'

'No, I –'

'The name – Ralph Ember?'

'Ralph W. Ember,' he replied.

'I've heard of you and the Monty, obviously.'

'Yes?'

'Oh, yes. Interesting in its way, I gather.'

'What?'

'The club.'

'It's changing,' he said.

She did a gaze. 'People always mention two things about you, if I may say. One is the resemblance to Charlton Heston when he was younger.'

'I've never heard that before. But I'm glad it's when he was younger.'

'Yes, I can see it, even in this light. No question. Remark-

152

able. *Ben Hur* in those TV reruns. Well, anyone could spot the likeness. And then they speak of your jaw scar.'

'An old rugby accident. Someone's metal boot studs caught me at the bottom of a ruck. All's fair in war and rugby.'

The policewoman leaned in and touched the side of his face. A male sergeant from the police car joined her. She withdrew her hand. The sergeant said: 'Ah, it *is* Mr Ember. The Monty thriving, sir? WPC Brinn has explained, has she? A caution only on this occasion. Oh, very much so, only the caution. Live and let live, up to a point. We wouldn't like to see you trawling here again, though. If you don't mind. It's hazardous. And using a different car won't serve. An incident like this – we ask the computer for the registrations of all vehicles in your name. I'd like to think you could get your relaxation in some other way, sir. You're really a bit brave coming up here after young flesh in view of what's happened, aren't you.'

There was that word again, 'brave'. He fucking loathed it. It meant idiotic. It meant absurd risk. It meant those foolhardy second lieutenants in the Great War capering out of the trenches first and crazily foremost and getting machine-gunned to bits before they'd done five yards. It meant unprofessional. Harpur, Iles – they'd have a report on this stop. Only a caution, but they'd have a report. Iles would giggle himself sick and talk about it all round, and talk about it also when he came on one of his supposed inspection calls with Harpur at the Monty. This kind of reputation could destroy Ralph's mission to lift the club socially. He struggled again to repel a full panic. He could imagine that fucking Iles Adam's apple bobbing up and down when he did his cheery banter: *Ralph, do you think your lay-by activities leave you time to get the Monty up from muck den to respectable?*

'You must have heard we were all over the area here, Mr Ember,' the sergeant said. 'A place like the Monty – a murky, jailbird gang like you've got there, they pick up all the gossip.'

'You're very out of date. The Monty's changing, as a matter of fact,' Ember replied.

'We've got him as just Mr Ralph Ember, sarge. But Mr Ember says it's Ralph W. Ember.'

'Well, yes, I've seen letters over that name in the Press,' the sergeant said. 'Very good. Strong against pollution. That's your topic, isn't it, Mr Ember – pollution?'

'The environment generally,' Ember said.

'Well, I expect you see a lot of it,' the sergeant said. 'I'll amend the records to Ralph W. What's the W? Walter? William? Wayward?'

'Which records?' Ember replied.

'I wouldn't worry about it, Mr Ember. The thing is, no repeat and everything stays more or less confidential.'

'What's that mean?' Ember said.

'What?' the sergeant replied.

'"More or less".'

'Oh, yes, definitely more or less confidential,' the sergeant said. 'And I'm sure you'd be protected. Your person, I mean. You're one who wouldn't expose your wife to a health peril. I'm confident of that. Wife, two children, have I got that right, Mr Ember? Many of these girls up here are unfamiliar to us, you know. Well, naturally. A new area for this kind of activity, isn't it, and new firms – Tirana as was and other Albs, then Bobby Sprale, Adrian Cologne, Tommy the Strong? This girl you were with – one of Adrian's, I think. Calls herself Rita and sometimes Delphine. As I say, new to us, but she's come from somewhere, hasn't she? There might have been a lot of previous intimacies and not always barriered. It's important to be careful. But hark at me! I talk like a sex doctor. The man who runs the Monty doesn't need a chinwag of that kind! Or sometimes Eva.'

'Do you see the resemblance to Chuck Heston, sarge?'

'This sort of duty, we meet all sorts, Mr Ember,' he

replied. 'You'd be shocked at some of the names in the data warehouse. There ought to be a treatment centre, Kerb Crawlers Anonymous.'

'And then in *Earthquake*. Full of boldness, but sensitive, too,' Brinn said.

Things were serene at the Monty when Ember returned. Quite often the club went into these civilized, unpredictable tame spells. He supposed the Athenaeum or Garrick must always be like this. Now, people talked in friendly mode at a few tables and two couples played an amiable game of pool. Ralph took a bottle of Kressmann Armagnac and went to sit and try to recover at a rectangular hinged shelf behind the bar he used as a desk. Sometimes he'd do his accounts and other paperwork here. A heavy metal plate had been bolted to a pillar. It broke the direct line of handgun fire if someone who'd been briefed on Ralph's likely spot entered at the main door and tried to kill him from there. He had arranged for a collage of stuck-on prints from the poet William Blake's collection, *The Marriage of Heaven and Hell*, to make the shield look less worrying and more ornamental and worthwhile. Artificial greenery hung from the bolts, giving a vivid jungle tendril appearance which Ralph thought a feature.

Obviously, though, this bullet-proof screen and the need for it indicated something about the present tone of the Monty and about Ember himself. After that police intervention on the road tonight with their fucking cheek and insults, he felt even more sickened by the sight of the mid-air bulwark. Would he never escape from the degraded nature of the Monty, as the girl, Anna or Olive or Beatrice, might have escaped the degradations of *her* life? He poured and drank. He wished he had someone to talk with about his problems. Occasionally, he used to permit himself to discuss limited areas with Beau Derek, but Beau was knifed to death a while ago on what had to be regarded as a very unsuccessful commercial trip with Ralph to Barney

155

Coss's home in Hampshire, Barney and his women also being dead there.*

Ember loved the taste of Kressmann's and the rapid way it gave good gyp to his bloodstream. Twenty minutes with Kressmann's could neutralize his angsts. This would be less than half a bottle, but more than a quarter. He knew it would take him a little while and a few glasses to get the recollection suppressed of that damn brutal blue lamp dogging him, and the recollection of his failure to get any lead to Anna, Olive, Beatrice, or to spot the intrusive trail car on his way with Eva, Rita, Delphine to Easy Lay lay-by. God, such a sickening, cheap concocted name. Police could be like that, were always like that. They went on courses in how to debase people through crude humour. Clearly, they hadn't accompanied the Saab right into the lay-by. Although it was an unmarked patrol car, Ember would have noticed its arrival. The lay-by had been empty but for him and Eva. This absence of the police pair meant they could not know that only entirely decent, concerned conversation took place, no familiarities of any kind, absolutely no removal of garments, or even interference with garments. Police brought their assumptions. They could be like that, were always like that. They went on other courses in how to make up their minds without evidence. They reasoned that if a man chose a tart and took her to the Easy Lay it must be for sex. Reasoned? Decided. Decided how? Decided according to their previous experience of toms in cars with tarts.

And, Ralph would admit, usually this might be correct. But he, Ralph Ember, or Ralph W. Ember, was not covered by that 'usually'. Ralph Ember, or Ralph W. Ember, did not see himself as a 'usual' kind of person. It would be beyond the WPC and her sergeant to realize that some men followed intense, kindly, constructive impulses, and, yes –

---

* *Naked at the Window.*

since this girl came from abroad – kindly, constructive impulses of an international dimension.

When he felt the armagnac start to take him over, Ralph came out from behind the bar and did some of the security checks and preparations he made almost every night before shut-down. He fancied a bit of normality. It would always console him to tour sectors of his ground. Ralph felt certain George V was heartened as King Emperor when he visited India for the 'Delhi Durbar' in 1911 at the start of his reign. Ralph often thought of British India, because of the age of Low Pastures. He went to close the main Monty door, preventing any more customers entering, though people could leave by using the inside handle. *Yes, leave, leave, leave, now, you fucking soaked limpets and limpettes.* As he pushed the door he was aware of someone standing shadowed in the club car park nearby, a man, short, burly, perhaps wearing a cravat rather than a tie and a broad-brimmed, Stetson-style shiny black hat. This visitor had put himself close against a people carrier – perhaps his own – and was difficult to spot. He must know about such things. He did not move but stood very solid looking at Ember, who was framed by the open door and lit from the bar behind. He realized at once what a beautifully outlined sight and target he must be and wanted to shove the door shut. Company rivalry might not be confined to Chilton Park.

But, *because* he realized at once what a beautifully outlined sight and target he must be, a giant panic grabbed Ember, rushing in to cancel all the happy, soothing armagnac, and bringing twenty seconds of paralysis, plus other routine symptoms. The door remained open. His brain worked all right, though, and came up with something perceptive and obvious: *God, what use a fucking shield if I stroll out from behind it and present myself unarmed?* After those twenty seconds he still didn't shut the door but as a priority got his right hand up to touch the jaw scar, almost as those two women – Eva and Brinn – had touched it earlier. But Ralph didn't caress and reverence the long blemish. His was a standard, ludicrous twitch. Whenever a full panic encompassed him he believed that as part of general break-up his scar had opened and was weeping something obnoxious on to his neck. The scar never did open, naturally, but this involuntary rigmarole always kicked in. Yes, absurd, obsessional, but it did mean the paralysis had begun to pass. He could raise a hand to confirm the scar stayed scar and had not reverted to a wound. This nonsensical, craven action he could regard as an advance. His body worked.

'Excuse the cold call, but I hoped I'd be able to get a word, Mr Ember. I didn't think you'd want me to come in, though.'

Would Ember's voice function? A panic sometimes knotted his throat muscles. 'What word?' he said. Not bad.

'I know you've had a difficult encounter tonight. The police unpleasantness.'

'A mistake.'

'Well, yes.'

'It's their job, I suppose. One has to see it like that.' He had begun to loosen. So, should he slam the door now? He might have, but three long-term, the-night-is-young, piss artists were on their way out. In any case, to cower behind the door would be entire Panicking Ralphy, wouldn't it, a contemptible relapse? 'What word?' he said.

'Of course, I'm familiar with your name, Mr Ember – as a major figure in this city.'

'More folk know Tom Fool than Tom Fool knows,' Ember replied. He thought it stupendous to get this bunkum from his memory in conditions like these.

'And I'm interested in the attention you've been giving the Morton Cross area. Up there tonight, and before that with Manse Shale when Tirana got his. This was remarkable – I mean the cash to the Alb kid. A colleague observed that, but the police pounce tonight I witnessed for myself.

It looked to me as if you kept wonderfully calm during that affront.'

'I see composure as an essential in such circumstances, a sort of duty to selfhood.'

'Few could manage it, though. Afterwards, I had some talk with Eva.'

'You are?' Ember loved this phrasing. No panic touched it, not a fucking trace. He thought it made him sound assured, capable of total, kiss-my-arse insolence to a stranger. That seemed the right way to respond to someone who arrived for a chat in a car park at nearly 2 a.m., and acted uppity by showing straight off he knew plenty plus. Hit back.

'Eva's one of mine,' he replied. 'She said she called herself that with you tonight. She was impressed by the hundred.' He held up one hand. 'And I don't want you to fret about where the extra twenty goes. You obviously intended that for herself. Would I touch it? Never, you can rely on this. She kept the twenty and her usual cut of the eighty.'

But Ember remembered what Eva said about the need for sex if money passed, so a girl could not be accused of selling information. 'She's a useful little piece,' Ember said. 'Clean. We went to Easy Lay.'

'Yes.'

'A hundred seemed right. I really liked her.'

'She felt the same about you – and not just thanks to the money.'

'One thing I've learned in business – reward good service, because good service is rare,' Ember replied.

'And she enjoyed the conversation.'

'I think these girls should be treated as if they're more than . . . more than receptacles. Some preliminary courtesies are simple decency.'

'They don't always get it, Mr Ember – decency from clients.'

'That's so regrettable. Look, I've got things to do here. I don't think –'

'Do you know what I say to myself, Mr Ember?'

'Should I?' Again, Ember really prized the 'Fuck off, Mr Big-gob' quality in this.

'I say, learn from the Albs, Mr Ember. All right, they're new, they're unBritish, some of them probably shouldn't even be here. And they have what could be seen at first as unusual methods – working around suburbia heaven – Morton Cross – for instance, and dealing girls not just substances. Yes, these are abnormal, even freakish, at an initial view. But why? I'm not one to reject good ideas because they're Alb good ideas.'

'You run a firm?' Ember had deduced who he was.

'Cologne,' he replied. 'Adrian Cologne.'

'The name's around, yes.'

'Only one of several, so far.'

'Yes, several.'

'Not a name like Ralph Ember's,' Cologne said, with a very jolly, modest laugh. 'The resonance. Not yet. But they didn't build ICI overnight.'

'I like to think I've contributed to the development and status of this city, and will go on contributing.'

'I can see why you'd want to pay off that young whore in the car with Tirana,' Cologne replied.

'More of that simple decency we've spoken of. I hope I *have* always – and *will* always – uphold such decency.'

'I'm not saying you or Shale popped Tirana and wanted any witness gone. My feeling is, if you'd killed Tirana you'd have killed the girl, too, for silence's sake. That would be only logical. Who wants blabs around? Police would get a translator for her soon enough.'

'Look, I –'

'I see it as clever to send that girl away, all the same. There could have been misunderstandings – maybe deliberate misunderstandings by that scheming major cop – Vials?'

'Iles.'

'I'm still learning the scene.'

'You might be infringing on a girl of his.'

'Oh?'

'Honorée.

'Oh, *her*. She'll learn.'

'Iles is liable to –'

'And Iles's henchman. The thug one. Harpur. If that kid had started blurting a description of you two, it could be trouble. I know Iles has been kindly in some aspects to you and Shale – why I'm here, as a matter of fact – but he would not be able to ignore that kind of information, would he? Not even Iles. All right, you might knock down his case eventually but by then all kinds of damage would have been done to your name. My view is, you and Shale were up there at Morton because you'd heard the trade openings might be brilliant, and you ran into the Tirana situation by accident. In that quick, resolute way I gather you're famed for, Mr Ember, you saw what was best to do and did it. I'm told Shale took much longer in assessing things. Well, that's believable. Who thinks as fast as Ralph Ember?'

The last customers left the club. Ember said: 'Let's go inside briefly, Cologne. It's more civilized.' Ember had decided this visitor might have some thoughts worth a glance. And the bugger *was* knowledgeable to a creepy degree.

Cologne came forward into the Monty and Ralph closed the door. There would be staff around for another half-hour clearing up. Cologne removed the Stetson. On Monty premises, Ralph would generally discourage business conversation about anything other than routine club matters, but he thought that as the bar was virtually empty, and this cold caller actually here, he could allow a brief meeting on other topics. They sat at a corner table and Ralph brought the Kressmann bottle, his own glass and another. He poured. Ember had been right about the cravat – a wide swirl of red, cream, ochre and violet. Cologne had on a brocade waistcoat that picked up some of these colours under a blazer striped red and navy worn open. Several bangles circled both wrists, possibly gold.

Ember liked jokey clothes but found the methodical way Cologne talked strange after all this gloss. He was thick-necked, round-faced, button-nosed, dark-haired, his eyes dark and jumpy, his lips very pale and too thin against the rest of his features. Ember could see why he might go for lurid cravats to get attention away from his mouth. The bangles would also help. They clinked mildly when he moved his arms and gave off a wholesome glint. He looked to Ember like a racecourse tipster needing to stand out among punters. Or maybe a humanities university professor keen to seem picturesque and appear on TV as an expert.

'And I think you're on the ball, Mr Ember – if I may so venture!' He laughed again. More modesty. The laugh said that Mr Ember was never in error. Ralph read the flattery, but this climber, Cologne, wanted to sell something, so smarm would be natural and excusable.

'On the ball, how?' Ember replied.

'The future.'

'In what respect?' Ember said.

'Morton Cross. Your instincts.'

'Which?'

'That this is where our kind of trade will flourish best.'

'*Our* kind?'

'Oh, I know you don't run girls. I didn't myself until lately. That's what I mean – learn from the Albs, earn like the Albs. And then there's the other side of business. All right, that Chilton Park episode – immensely regrettable. Yes, it will set back developments at Morton Cross and around for a while, perhaps even a substantial while. It's awkward there now, hence your grief tonight with the prowl car. These emergency conditions won't continue, though. The police will tire. They have other problems.

162

And then . . . It's obvious, isn't it, that the Valencia is no longer a tolerable area for dealing – too run down and déclassé, even now when seeing some redevelopment? The trade is changing. Professional people want their commodity supplies, but they don't want to go to somewhere like the Valencia for them. It's forbidding. It's frightening.

'Oh, yes, *The Eton Boating Song* is down there and attracts some very select nostrils, but generally speaking the Valencia ambience is negative. That's why I want to bring a girl like Honorée up here. It's true that some trade people from Morton Cross are so nervous now after Chilton Park that they talk of transferring to the Valencia. But I regard this as very rushed and alarmist thinking. Hardly thinking at all. They're panicking. I try to look at long-distance prospects, and I'm sure you do, too. In fact, I'm sure your whole life path is like that or you would hardly be where you are now. You would despise panic judgements.'

Was this bastard on the mock? Ember knew that normally people did not use the word panic or panicking in his hearing, because of the way they might use the word Panicking *out* of his hearing. But perhaps Cologne, a fresh eye, had quickly spotted Ralph's true qualities and ignored the abusive rumours and the filthy nickname, the way Eva did. Cologne got some things grossly wrong, of course. Ralph and Shale had not been at Morton to survey sale possibilities but to see off Tirana, and put an eternal stop on Morton as a competing trade site. But perhaps Cologne did not get *everything* wrong. He might sense Ralph's huge actual worth and solidity behind occasional momentary spells of breakdown. 'Things are extremely volatile,' Ember replied.

'That Chilton Park mess – not ultimately important. Not typical in any way – started by some gun-happy kid working for Tommy the Strong, as I hear it. Virtually an accident. The kid starts firing, so everyone does. I'm going to locate him and make sure he can do nothing similar again.'

'What does that mean? Locate who?' Again Ember recalled Manse Shale's speculation about the Harpur girl's boyfriend, Scott Grant. Ralph had noticed that Cologne got Harpur's name right straight off, though not Iles's. Had Cologne been concentrating on Harpur, trying to make a link from the Park to Harpur?

'We can't risk having people like that around, kid or not,' Cologne said. 'One of the essentials at Morton Cross will be harmony and peace. And that's really why I'm here tonight, Mr Ember. These are your specialities, aren't they, via ACC Iles? That's what my research tells me.'

'Mr Iles and I, we share certain attitudes.'

'Tranquillity on the streets, and especially on the kind of cachet streets we have at Morton Cross?'

'Such tranquillity – yes, Mr Iles and I both seek that. Who sane would not?'

'Exactly. It *is* Iles rather than Harpur who puts tranquillity so high as a requirement, isn't it?'

'Mr Iles, yes. Harpur less so, or even totally against any intelligent, unspoken agreement between trade folk and the police. Harpur's no great mind, you know. He looks at things too simply, because that's all he can manage. His brain's cloudy from too much womanizing.'

'I'm glad it's only Iles.'

'Why?'

The thin lips grew thinner. 'I don't want to make much of it at present. That OK? But let's say some action will be necessary which could affect Harpur – if my information stands up.'

'Affect him?'

'Unfavourably.'

'How?' By removing the boyfriend of Harpur's daughter?

'Could we leave this now?' Cologne drank and the right wrist bracelets rustled charmingly as he raised the glass.

It struck Ember that Cologne had probably never been arrested and handcuffed or he wouldn't like having his wrists under metal like that, even gold. These bangles could indicate big luck or tremendous carefulness. Cologne reeked of talent and threat. On the whole, Ember felt glad he had let him in. Cologne said: 'I'm here to explain that I see a partnership opportunity – you, myself – at Morton Cross in due course, Mr Ember, perhaps also incorporating Mansel Shale. I know you two have an arrangement. I would supply the trade structure already in place up there, suspended for this period of crisis, yes, but ready always to be reactivated, and not entirely dormant, anyway, or you wouldn't have met Eva tonight, would you? And, then in exchange for this, you could bring to this new area – new, that is for you – yes, you could bring the wonderful influence you have with Mr Iles, built so patiently during your glorious, continuing career.'

Might he be correct about the Valencia? Had it started a trade decline, despite the marina-style rebuilding under way there? Was he correct also about the eventual promise of Morton Cross? Ember said: 'Harpur to be affected somehow? That interests me.'

'*Possibly* to be affected. I've got people doing some further research for me, as you'd expect after something like Chilton Park. At this stage, it's uncertain. They've had difficulties keeping their observation unnoticed. Tailing secretly in a car – a very rare skill. But we progress. What is it they say – "Time spent on reconnaissance is never wasted."'

'Reconnaissance where?'

'I don't like to talk about crux matters, though, until I've got things wholly clear.'

Ember felt once more the contrast between Cologne's Mardi Gras outfit and the discipline of his mind. Ember wondered if it had been a mistake to ask again about the impact of things on Harpur. In fact, Ember had asked because Harpur knew how to get rough in response if he considered he'd been messed about, and Ralph had wondered about warning Cologne. But to Cologne the question might sound like concern for Harpur, despite what Ember had said about Harpur's simple, fuck-flustered mind. Perhaps Cologne distrusted Ember, feared leaks, suspected some network that, as a new boy, he did not understand and could not penetrate, yet. So, no details. And, of course, those suspicions would have good basis. Hadn't Shale proposed that he and Ember should whisper advice to the boyfriend – advice to give up the trade and the weaponry? Like Cologne, Shale wanted Scott Grant to do no more gunnery around Morton Cross and Chilton Park, suppose he *had* taken part last time. Cologne proposed a killing. Shale proposed preaching. Cologne might upset Harpur. Shale yearned to please him. Ralph said: 'Look, I must get home now. I'll give your ideas a mull soon. Have you got a business card?'

Chapter Eight

Denise and Harpur never went to bed together in the afternoons at 126 Arthur Street if the children were at home. It would seem wrong, indelicate. Denise and he agreed on this. They had not actually discussed it, but their behaviour showed they both recognized a sort of embargo. Obviously, this did not mean they pretended to the girls there was no sex in their relationship. That would be idiotic. Didn't Hazel and Jill bring them tea in the double bed before breakfast every time Denise stayed? The girls enjoyed seeing Denise and him there, and enjoyed having a chat with them before they got up, like normality. This overnight closeness of Denise and Harpur on the premises seemed to prove love, stability, contentment to the children and gave a happy feeling of family. Harpur knew his daughters found it amazing that a girl as young, beautiful and bright as Denise should want to sleep with their father, and sleep with him regularly, regardless, but these early visits with the tea must reassure them it was true.

The children's reaction might not be the same if Denise and Harpur disappeared upstairs in the afternoon. Hazel and Jill would probably regard that as juvenile and rabbity, not part of a family pattern. Some Saturday afternoons could be all right, though. The girls would go out soon after lunch and not return until evening. They might visit friends' houses. Or, the judo club opened on Saturdays, and often they went there. Most likely, the bus station meet-up was available as well. Occasionally, Harpur had to work a weekend, negativing Saturday. And Denise played lacrosse for the university, the fixtures sometimes Saturdays, but mostly Wednesdays, luckily. Harpur reckoned he and Denise averaged one in three. This Saturday, fine – no lacrosse, and the city as far as he could tell lay quiet for now.

Always, Harpur tried not to admire Denise's body too much. Of course, he *did* admire it, but he wanted to keep his response reasonably controlled. Two reasons. First, he considered that to get outrageously ecstatic about her back, legs, breasts, face, hair, arse and carriage would be a kind of gloating: *I'm nearly twenty years older but look what I can pull.* Pathetic. And simply unwise: he aimed to avoid anything that might emphasize his age, and this would include drooling over Denise's back, legs, breasts, face, hair, arse and carriage because he felt so fortunate. It was Iles who had first pointed out to Harpur the loveliness and sexual zing in some women's backs, as distinct from the more usually reckoned parts. And this would be the back as back – that is, the back *only* – not the back treated as a unit with, or upper storey of, the behind. For a while, Iles had been tremendously moved by the back of a daughter of one of his favourite informants, though nothing much came of this.* Iles had all sorts of perceptions. He certainly amounted to more than continuous mad malice and rage. This girl was a great swimmer and Iles would grow breathless and quivery thinking of her back sluiced feelingly by the water of a pool when she did lengths. For a while, he'd been keen to see her butterfly, especially.

And so, although Harpur did get ecstatic about the total construction of Denise, her back and the tattoo very much included, he schooled himself against getting outrageously ecstatic – or, at least, not *obviously* outrageously ecstatic. His second reason for attempting to keep things moderate was that he would catch himself sometimes storing mem-

* *The Girl with the Long Back.*

ories of Denise brilliantly naked, as if he might lose her any day and should make sure he amassed these recollections as fill-in for her absence. Plainly, the more brilliant she looked naked the more he felt he should hang on to the picture, so that if she did go to someone else eventually he could console himself that he had her when she was at her most perfect. This sad urgency, also, arose from age. It meant he knew he could not rely on a future with her and should therefore file these images away in his brain, the way explorers left pemmican and ship's biscuits in igloos for subsequent journeys. But he did not want to be reminded that he could not rely on a future with her by behaving now as though he knew he could not rely on a future with her.

This Saturday afternoon he gave her some good, moderate admiration. She lay alongside him face down on top of the bedclothes so that he could spend quite a while observing her back. As was usual with Denise, she had lit a cigarette soon after they made love and now and then she took some heavy pulls on that while she got her mind back to work again. There was a kind of ritual to the way she smoked. He approved of rituals when they involved Denise. Rituals equalled continuance and continuity. Harpur himself had never smoked, but he read somewhere lately that nicotine could stave off Alzheimer's and he liked to see Denise inhaling plenty because he dreaded getting forgotten by her and having to live on his memories until he got Alzheimer's.

He said: 'I want to consult you. This is important. People's lives, possibly.'

'Right.' She turned over and sat up. She took one more big drag at the cigarette and then stubbed it out in the dressing-table ashtray the children had bought her. 'I don't regret that coccyx tattoo, you know, Col.'

'No, indeed.'

'You think it's silly and crude, do you? That's why I'll

keep it out of sight now, if you've got something heavy to say. What, real danger?'

'Honestly, I like the tattoo,' Harpur replied.

'Sometimes, I do feel a need to be mature, Col.'

'I know mature people with tattoos.'

'Are they tattoos where *I've* got a tattoo – to flash above low-cuts?'

'Well, I don't go about looking for tattoos on women there.'

'I hope not, but I wouldn't bet on it.'

'I was thinking of men's forearms,' he replied. 'Snakes. Or the words MOTHER ALWAYS in vermilion.'

'Mine is a generational tattoo,' she said.

'That's all right. I'm in favour of your generation.'

'Oh? Do you know a lot from my generation?'

'Obviously, I meant *you* as a product of your generation,' Harpur said.

'*Why* are you in favour?'

'Not just the tattoo. I think there's more to you as a product of your generation than a tattoo.'

'What more? And don't give me all that stuff about my body.'

'Your body does come into it.'

'*Your* body comes into it. Just did.'

'Word-play is definitely one of your strengths, often vulgar,' Harpur replied.

'And?'

'Intelligence. It's why I'm after your advice now.'

'Well, yes. But intelligence is not generational. There are stupid people in my generation.'

'This proves your intelligence.'

'What does?'

'That you can see the difference.'

'You're saying I must be intelligent because I know some people are not?' she asked.

'And your ability to keep on with an argument. This shows youthful energy, tenacity, commitment.'

'You're fed up with it, are you? I can't be shut up? Sorry, Col.'

'I don't want you to shut up. I need guidance.'

'Right,' she said. She picked up the wreckage of the earlier cigarette and eventually got the blackened, squashed-out end to light again.

'Hazel and Jill,' he said.

'You want guidance on them because you think I'm young enough to understand them more easily than you do?' she said.

'Because you're young enough to understand them more easily than I do, and yet mature enough to give a measured view, coccyx tattoo or not,' Harpur replied.

'Right. Do you want me to cover up so you can concentrate?'

'You *have* covered up.'

'What?'

'The coccyx tattoo. By turning over.'

'I meant put on a top,' she replied. 'You know what you're like about breasts.'

'No, what am I like?'

'Interested.'

'In yours.'

'Yeah, yeah.'

'But I can detach myself.'

'Oh?'

'For the moment, I mean. Don't feel hurt.'

'Right.'

'I think they have secrets,' Harpur said.

'Hazel and Jill? Of course they have secrets. They're kids, you're a parent.'

'That's what I mean, you see.'

'What?'

'Insights. You go to it direct. That's probably generational.'

'Right. But you think these are worrying secrets, dangerous secrets?' Denise said.

'Hazel's been followed.'

'That happens. Men follow girls, even underage girls. In fact, some follow underage girls especially.'

'By car, on her bike.'

'It happens, Col.'

'She and her friends treat it like that. Or, at least, her friends do. I'm not sure Hazel does. They come back here and rehearse a play for school, as though everything's fine.'

'What play?'

'About a chap finding true selfhood by shouting at his wife in the 1950s.'

'*Look Back in Anger.*'

'That kind of thing.'

'Kenneth Tynan said he couldn't love anyone who didn't like *Look Back in Anger.*'

'Kenneth Tynan?'

'A critic.'

'Is he the sort I'd *want* to be loved by?'

'He's dead. Do you think these are people looking for Scott?' Denise replied.

'It's possible. She might know it.'

'How?'

'Not sure of that, either. She could have spotted people watching the house, as start point. Or Jill could have and told her.'

'But doesn't it seem roundabout to tail Hazel if they want Scott? It wouldn't be hard to find where he lives, would it?'

'They might think that too obvious. There's a big police contingent around the streets up there, Morton Cross, Inton, the Park. A vehicle in waiting would be noticed.'

She nodded a bit. 'You don't even know Scott was involved.'

'No.'

'So, you broke in, yes? Did you find anything?'

'Nothing.'

'Perhaps it's imagination, Col.'

'Possibly. I suspect it could all start up again. These wars start, stop, start again. And a new factor: I get a tip about some big local dealers seen at Morton Cross, right out of their terrain.'

'Really big?'

'Really big.'

'Not Milord Monty?'

'Where did you come across that name?'

'Some students get into his club now and then. He deals big and biggest, doesn't he?'

'You ought to join the police fast promotion scheme when you finish university,' Harpur replied. It was half joke, half real wish. Denise as cop: that would bring her closer, wouldn't it? 'I considered talking to Ember and one of his pals, but maybe not.'

'Advice?' she said. 'I don't see how I can advise.'

'It's the girls and their reactions.'

'You believe I can read them?'

'Better than I can. That's my problem. Look, then, do you think I can reasonably put restrictions on Hazel and Jill, but especially Hazel?'

'Restrictions?'

'They're out and about, I don't know where. Is that sensible? Will they understand if I clamp down? I don't want them to despise me – see me as alarmist, oppressive. It matters to me what they think. I imagine them looking back on their lives when they're adult. I want to come out of that kind of examination all right, Denise. How would you feel if you were, say, Hazel, and I started to fuss and put limits on where she can go?'

'Col, you have to do what –'

Someone rang the front door bell, two short, one long pushes. 'It's Iles,' Harpur said. He kept his voice low. 'He calls in occasionally if he's got something confidential to say or wants to show off new clothes, especially if he thinks Hazel will be here or around later. He'll calculate,

173

Saturday, no school, so she could be at home. Perhaps he's been out buying summer wear.' The bell rang again, same pattern. Denise and Harpur lay silent.

The bedroom was in the front of the house, curtains closed. After a while a pebble or coin hit the window. Iles yelled: 'Col, are you in there, being conjugal?' A minute later something heavier struck the glass, perhaps a fifty pence piece as against an earlier ten. There could be breakages if he threw stronger, and he would. Iles shouted: 'Did I see the undergrad old Panda parked discreetly down the road? Oh, dear, what'll the neighbours?'

'It might be something worthwhile,' Harpur said. 'I'd better let him in.' He rolled from the bed.

'Shall I come down in a minute?'

'Of course. He knows you're here, and he'll smell the tobacco smoke.'

'Should you put something on, Col?'

But Harpur was already on the stairs. He'd dress later. He didn't want any more street theatre from Iles. What'll the neighbours? There was one along the street who did maximum vigilance. Harpur opened the front door. Iles wore a magnificent beige, two-button, lightweight jacket, obviously made for him, possibly alpaca. Harpur had not seen it before. The shirt was pale blue, perhaps silk, and again almost certainly crafted for him personally and new. He had two buttons open at the neck, but no pendant medallion. It wasn't scarf weather. Iles liked scarves, worn loose and with emphatic tassels. 'I thought I'd just give a ring while passing, in case you were about and idling, Col.'

'That's friendly, sir.' Iles came in and Harpur closed the front door.

'The Panda is relevant to why I'm here.'

'In what way, sir.'

'I always enjoy coming to this kind of area, Col,' Iles reptied. 'An eye-opener.'

'Which kind is that, sir?'

'It's got . . . it's got what I'd call . . . what I'd call a *realness* to it, after Rougemont Place.'

'Well, yes, it *is* quite real,' Harpur said. 'You can feel it under your feet when walking the pavement – the realness – the pavements are made of something real, so one doesn't go through them, or if you touch brickwork on the houses it feels like real br – well, like real brickwork and very real.' He took an overcoat from the hall cupboard and put it on. They went into the sitting room.

'People watch this house, Col. That's what I mean about where the Panda stands now.'

'Oh?'

'Certainly.'

'I don't understand.'

'I've seen other vehicles out there.'

'Yes, well people have to park somewhere and –'

'Lurking cars,' Iles replied.

'Who?'

Iles stared around the sitting room: 'The point is, surely, Col, that although this used to be a very bookish kind of area, with the shelves and volumes and so on, you, personally, are not a bookish person, not in the least,' Iles replied.

'I've read *Scoop* and most of the Bible, plus *Treasure Island* and *Portnoy's Complaint*.'

'And I don't think you should blame yourself in any way for chucking out a very fine, perhaps unique, library built up over the years by Megan. That library was not *you*, Col.'

'What *is* me, sir?'

'It's still a good room, Harpur,' Iles replied.

'I think so.'

'We had a complaint a while back from someone living opposite about fairly flagrant humping here or hereabouts, curtains defiantly open.' Iles pointed to one of the high-backed settees.

175

'Is that what you meant about the house being watched? How is the Panda involved?'

'I thought it shouldn't go any further.'

'What shouldn't, sir?'

'Complaints like that – vindictive. Such a bleat makes too much of what I'd regard as a one-off situation with Denise. Look at the decorous, even prim, way you've put that overcoat on before appearing in front of the windows.'

'Thank you, sir.'

'I see the furniture as being at fault in that earlier incident. It's high-backed yes, but not sufficiently high-backed properly to conceal the rise movement pre thrust. I expect it's a symbolic thing, is it, Col, getting around the various rooms, a kind of assertion of the new nature of rapport between you and her?' His voice began to take on again the volume he'd given it when shouting up to the window from the street. 'And when you were disgustingly in my property, Idylls, in Rougemont Place with my wife were you also trying to assert the nature of a rapport between you and her and –'

'The Panda, sir. It's significant somehow?'

'Significant in that it brings the girl here, doesn't it?'

'But beyond that?'

Iles paced a bit, the alpaca jacket open, but its beautiful tailoring still evident. He said: 'I was going to drop in the other evening, Col – something entirely social, believe me – I didn't even know whether Haze – whether the children would be here – just a casual call, as today's.'

'It's thoughtful, sir. We all appreciate it.'

'I'm a believer in these amities, Col. Part of a pleasant old way of things.'

'True.'

'I'm about to park but notice a Ford Focus near where the Panda is now with someone alone in the back, keeping down, doing the rear-window stuff *à la* Hitchcock, and probably targeting your house. Whoever's in there is not

176

bad at it and only an eye trained in these ploys would have noticed.'

'You always see a lot, sir.'

'I do, Harpur, I do. For instance when you and my wife –'

'Could you get an identity on the watcher in the Focus, sir?'

'It would be dismally slack to spot surveillance of that sort and not take it further, Col.'

'Dismal slackness is hardly a quality anyone would associate with you, sir.'

Iles sat down in one of the red leather easy chairs. He crossed his legs carefully and had a fond glance at his tan slip-ons which were worth plenty of fond glances for their cost. 'Shale,' he said.

'Manse?'

'Those eyes – just right for spying out of a back window.'

'Ferrety.'

'I obviously decided not to interrupt, just observed.'

'This was policing of quite a standard, if I may say, sir.'

'It's policing. It's also friendship, Col.'

'Thank you, sir.'

'I suppose some would expect me to be at least indifferent and possibly vindictive in view of what you and my wife –'

'What's he waiting for, though, sir?' Harpur said.

'Jill comes along and I'd say spots him.'

'She reacts?'

'The child's too clever for that. Your wife must have given them very good brain power, Harpur.'

'Thank you, sir.'

'No, I think Jill spots him but conceals it absolutely, just continues on, as if unaware. But in a while she comes back out and takes another glance, again without seeming to. Smartness on smartness. I think in any case Manse might have been on the floor this time, doing a cower in case detected and possibly eyes down, unable to tell what Jill saw or didn't. She continues and goes out of sight. Mobile phone to Hazel? Shale gets back up and the next thing is, Hazel comes out, has a short walk, returns, then reappears with her bike and pedals off in the opposite direction. Manse wants to tail and has to get to the front seat and turn the car. While he's doing that, a red Clio, two men in it, pulls out ahead and also seems to follow Haze. You'll think I'd been damn remiss there – concentrating on Shale.'

'It's natural, sir, since you would recognize him.'

'Kind, Col. But I'd say, fucking remiss.'

'You're severe with yourself, sir.'

'I am, I am, Col. At Staff College I was sometimes known as Self-Scourging Desmond.'

'You drove behind Shale? There's a convoy of three vehicles? Did you get a number for the Clio?'

'We go to the bus station. They both park near the café. I can't risk that. Shale would recognize me. Perhaps the two in the Clio, also. So, I park in one of the bus bays and soon have to tell a coach company inspector to go fuck himself because I'm staying there, a flourish of warrant card.'

'This would be untypical of you – the coarseness and flourish, sir – but necessary in the circumstances.'

'Speaking of coarseness, I see Hazel come out on to the balcony and give the people in the Clio the "Get stuffed" finger. This is a remarkable girl, Col – as I've always thought.'

'Yes, I know.'

'Know what?'

'In which sense, sir?'

'Do you know she's a remarkable girl or do you know that I've always thought her a remarkable girl?'

'Both,' Harpur said. 'Did you get a number for the Clio?'

'I recall asking you just after Chilton Park about Hazel's boyfriend and the danger he might get pulled into things,' Iles replied. 'I expect you'd considered that anyway but kept quiet about it, in that miserably furtive way of yours. These vehicles – the Clio, Manse's Focus – are they a pointer somehow to involvement? Track Hazel and they get to the boyfriend. This would be their thinking. Is that why you're so concerned about the Clio?'

'You have descriptions of the men?'

'Whether she'd also known about Shale behind the Clio I can't say,' Iles replied.

'Or you behind Shale.'

'I'm rather an accomplished tail, you know, Harpur. I don't make much of it. This is a minor skill, and rarely used as an ACC. But it's there still.'

'Was there a name for you as a tail at Staff College?' Harpur said.

'And did Hazel speak of any of this when she came home?' Iles replied.

'She and her pals treated it very lightly. They soon seemed to forget all that and began to rehearse a play for school.'

'Which play?'

'About someone hating his wife because she's so good-looking and pleasant and doesn't get ratty about the British class system.'

'*Look Back in Anger*? Is Hazel in it?'

'The wife.'

'But could anyone hate Hazel?' Iles said.

'Hardly.'

'True, Col. That's Hazel *per se* as Hazel. But might some hate Hazel because Haze's boyfriend is Scott? I've wondered about that.'

'I'd begun to wonder if you'd wondered about it. And?'

'I'd be inclined to hate anyone who hated Hazel.'

'Yes. And?'

'Well, here's Hazel and some others now, Col!' Iles cried.

179

'These big windows are grand for gazing out as well as in.' Harpur looked and saw Hazel, Jill, Scott Grant and Jill's boyfriend, Darren, on the short front garden path. Hazel let them in with her key and they all came into the sitting room. 'Here's a treat,' Iles cried. 'We were just talking about the school play, *Look Back in Anger.* Sometimes I see myself as akin to one of those post-war stage figures, alienated by a world of banality, degrading compromise and selfishness.'

'A neighbour is out in her porch and told us somebody was shouting up at the front bedroom here not long ago like a maniac,' Darren said.

'It's that kind of area,' Iles replied.

'Is Denise here?' Hazel said. 'I saw her car.'

'Upstairs,' Harpur replied.

'Oh?' Hazel said.

'I don't know why you're dressed like that, dad,' Jill said.

'I wasn't expecting people here,' Harpur said.

'Is that an answer?' Jill replied.

'In the sense that I wouldn't be around with just an overcoat on if I'd known people would turn up,' Harpur said.

'Didn't you know Denise would turn up?' Hazel said.

Jill said: 'We got fed up with the judo club. Too crowded. So we came back to watch the athletics on telly.'

'The neighbour told us this loony was throwing coins up at a bedroom window,' Darren said.

'Streets like this are much more spontaneous than where I live,' Iles said. 'In a street like this, I feel a kind of . . . what would I call it? A kind of . . .'

'Realness?' Harpur said.

'No, no, not realness,' Iles replied. 'That would be non-sensical. Any street is real. What else could it be? In a street like this I feel a kind of cheek-by-jowlness.'

'I didn't know Denise was coming around today,' Hazel said.

180

'Yes, she came around,' Harpur replied.

'I love the conversation here,' Iles said.

'Now, you're police, aren't you, Mr Iles, like Mr Harpur?' Darren said.

'Not exactly like Mr Harpur but, yes, police.'

'I want to ask you something – you or Mr Harpur,' Darren said. 'Scott wouldn't ask, although it's about him. He wouldn't ask because – well, I don't know why he wouldn't. I just know he wouldn't. This is about something his mother said. His mother said she thought somebody had been in their house when they were out and had been searching around. I said she should tell the police but she said no because she doesn't trust the police.'

'There *are* people like that,' Iles said.

'She said it might have *been* the police,' Darren replied.

'Might have been the police what?' Iles asked.

'Searching,' Darren said.

'For?' Iles said.

'She didn't say, just it might have been. That's her view. Nothing was taken from the house. This is what makes her think like that, I suppose. What I wanted to ask you, Mr Iles, and Mr Harpur, do you think she should tell the police? Was I right?'

'Mrs Grant never liked police,' Jill said. 'I don't know why.'

'What do you say, Scott?' Iles asked.

'About?' Scott said. That was how he usually talked to Iles: a snarl, meaning above all, Stay away from Hazel you ACPO jerk. He was as big as Iles, fair hair worn cropped, a bit sharp-nosed and big-chinned, eyes blue and not always friendly or even interested.

Iles said: 'One: Do you think someone did a house search? Two: If so, who? Three: Also, if so, should your parents report it?'

181

'What makes Mrs Grant think someone looked around the house?' Jill said.

'Like a feeling your mother had, wasn't it, Scott?' Darren said. He'd be a couple of years younger than Scott, thin-faced, hair sandy to auburn, as tall as Scott but slighter.

'A feeling's not much,' Jill said. She was getting ready to make tea. They all sat around the room. Denise came in from upstairs, nicely made up and dressed again and carrying Harpur's clothes and shoes.

Iles said: 'Ah, Denise.' They'd met occasionally when he called around to Arthur Street. 'We were just discussing a sort of public–police interconnection matter. Scott's mother thinks their house was searched. Should she make a to-do through us? That's the debate, you see. But, bear in mind as to "us", that Mrs Grant thinks it might be us who did it. If that were so, Mrs Grant would obviously regard it as pointless to bring a complaint to . . . to the same us. Do you remember that scene in the US police film, *The Choirboys*, where an apartment dweller goes next door to protest about the din and threatens to call the police, and the people making the din say, "We *are* the police."?'

Denise said: 'Why does Scott's mother believe the house was searched? What evidence?'

'Exactly,' Jill said. 'Ever hear of persecution mania, Darren?' She left to make the tea. Harpur crossed the room and took his clothes and shoes from Denise. He went into the hall and dressed. Before he'd finished, Iles joined him.

'We take a look at the street, Col. They could have been followed here.'

'I was going to.'

'You went through the Grant house, did you?' Iles replied.

'Jill is right about Mrs Grant. A great deal of suspicion of police there. She might fantasize.'

'Denise knows you broke in, does she?'

'For instance, Mrs Grant is not happy that Scott has

taken up with the daughter of a police officer,' Harpur said.

'*I'm* not happy that he has.'

'That's for a different reason.'

'Is Mrs Grant happy that her son's running armed with a fucking coke, crack and H gang?'

'We don't know that, sir.'

'I'd say it's Tommy the Strong's outfit.'

'Why?'

'Like a feeling,' Iles said. 'Someone's going to zap that boy, if he started Chilton Park, and my information is he might have. Someone like this Adrian Cologne that I hear of could feel vengeful about the Park fracas. I've got Cologne in mind, anyway.'

'Yes?'

'Oh, yes.'

'For what?' Harpur asked.

'Oh, yes, I've got him in mind,' Iles replied. He and Harpur went into Arthur Street and carried out a good survey of the cars. There was no Clio, no Focus. That need not mean much. Cars could be changed. They looked inside every vehicle but didn't find any observers. 'We've got to talk to him, Col. All this evasiveness and pussyfooting – foolish.'

'I think so.'

As they walked back to Harpur's house an elderly, vigilant woman neighbour called from her porch: 'That one you're with – the one in the gold leaf jacket.'

'Him?' Harpur said, pointing with his thumb at Iles.

'Causing a disturbance previously,' she said.

'He does,' Harpur said.

'And it's only a little while ago I heard of indecency in your front room,' she said. 'Now this.'

'I heard of that, too,' Iles said. 'A high-visibility arse.'

'A street like this has to watch its standards,' she said.

'I've told Harpur. It's why I came around today. I felt an urgency. And when he wouldn't open the front door

I refused to give up. Obviously, I glanced in through the front window to see whether anything untoward was under way again, but no. Not in that room.'

Scott and Hazel had left through the back garden to the lane by the time Harpur and Iles returned. The rest were drinking tea and watching athletics on television. Denise said: 'I don't think he liked all that about his mother and the house search.'

'*Alleged* house search,' Iles replied.

'Well, yes,' Denise said.

Hazel came in: 'Scott's gone home on the bus,' she said.

'You saw him get aboard?' Iles asked.

Harpur found it quaint to hear the ACC worry about Scott, and show his worries about Scott to Hazel. But Iles had all sorts of quaintnesses, felt all sorts of unshirkable responsibilities. At Staff College he was probably called Desmond the Dutiful.

Chapter Nine

Manse Shale, waiting in Arthur Street on foot this time, saw Harpur and Iles come out of Harpur's house and start quite an inspection of parked cars, really giving them eyeball. Shale was in a betting shop doorway and out of sight, but them two would come up this far eventually on their car carry-on and, while they both had heads down giving a Mercedes true scrutiny, he left the doorway and went into a back lane at the top of the street.

What was fucking obvious, wasn't it, was they had a tip about the house getting watched from a car lately? That's why this search started now. That's how police always thought. If something happened one way once they expected it to happen that way again, like what they said about generals – always fighting the last war. Maybe that younger kid of Harpur's had seen him in the Focus and reported to her father. Maybe she had seen the Clio, also. Manse had not been able to observe that kid continuous because he had his face down to the floor of the Focus some while, but when he *was* looking at her she did not *seem* to of noticed. This kid was a cop's kid, though, and Manse had realized at the time she might of been doing an act all ignorant and innocent. You could expect kids brought up in a police family to be sly and false, even a kid as young as this – it was in what was known as their genes, like, say, George W. Bush wanting to be President after his father, or, if you was talking about acting, all them Redgraves and Liza Minnelli.

Or perhaps Harpur and Iles knew some other way about the car watch from the street, though Manse could not understand what other way that could be. Information – it leaked around everywhere, no controlling it, although all sort tried, such as the Government with that radio journalist Gilligan who said too much – or said what the Government *thought* was too much – about the Iraq war and so he lost his job, to shut him up.

It annoyed Shale that these two, Harpur and Iles, could imagine he was so stupid he would do the same kind of watch here as before, that is by car. Didn't they understand Mansel Shale had sense and experience? He believed in always being ahead, and this meant always changing the way you done things. His car was not even in this street, nor the next. He wanted it right out of the picture. He had parked and walked. He reckoned he would stay much less obvious like that. A car could always be a give-away, especially a parked car with someone in it. All right, he had realized this on his last visit and tried to hide things a bit by getting into the back. But, of course, police knew that trick. Most probably they made it up theirselves. Even a cop's *kid* might know it, them genes again.

Obviously, it was not only the people in Harpur's house Manse had to worry about. Them two Clio people could be here. They might not be in the Clio but they could be here in a different vehicle or like hisself on foot. The thought of that pair troubled him and at the rectory he had unhooked the Arthur Hughes painting and taken one of the 9 mm pistols from the safe, loaded it fully and strapped it on in a shoulder holster before closing up and putting the Hughes back.

From the end of the lane, Manse could go on watching, just squinting down the street, keeping his head half back. Iles and Harpur came as far as double yellows opposite the betting shop and then turned around. They had done every vehicle, both sides. They found nothing, not even the Clio people. When Iles and Harpur came near his house on the way back, some oldish woman from a porch near started yelling at them. Manse could not hear all the words, but it was rage. She kept pointing to Harpur's house upstairs and downstairs. She seemed to speak about a disturbance and indecency. Iles wore some sort of custard colour jacket and a ponce pale blue shirt. He had a conversation with her, all fucking charm and lies, most probably, although Shale thought Iles spoke of 'a high-visibility arse'. What this concerned he could not tell.

Shale had grown sure the boy, Scott, was in Harpur's house. Manse could not do a non-stop watch on Arthur Street. He had a company to look after. But a few minutes after he'd walked into the street this afternoon, he'd seen four youngsters enter 126, Harpur's two daughters and two lads, one, well-built, about seventeen or eighteen, the other a couple of years less and slighter. These would be the two boyfriends. Manse had calculated he'd get a good chance of confronting the older boy when he left to go home. Shale felt triumphant. In his view, it remained vital to get a talk with him in private, tell him to get out of whatever firm he was in, most likely Tommy the Strong's, and hope Scott would tell Hazel Harpur, or even Harpur himself, that he was quitting because of wisdom from Mansel Shale, who knew the commercial scene here so well.

The original plan had been Ember and Manse would do this kindly chat together, to help their firms along via Harpur and possibly Iles. But Ember didn't seem so determined on it as Manse, and had not been available for discussions lately at all. Shale had even heard a rumour Ember was picked up by police for kerb crawling and banging a tart in Easy Lay lay-by, not far from Morton Cross and Inton. God, Manse hated that kind of behaviour. But it would be like Ember. He'd go after it anywhere, although married. Iles, the same. This sort of cock compulsion was equal for louts like Ralph and for police, even very senior police. Cocks got active regardless. Iles's girl was ethnic, called Honorée, and a tale said she might be run these days by one of them new commercial intruders who dealt girls as well as the commodities, Adrian Cologne. A tale also said Cologne had given her some beatings for being too choosy. Iles might turn a bit fresh about that. Shale preferred getting a woman into the rectory on a decently planned and settled basis for really considerable spells. He particularly liked having someone there for Christmas and New Year and other bank holidays. He believed times of celebration should be shared for a while.

Harpur and Iles seemed to have finished their chat with the neighbour and moved on towards 126, the woman screaming after them still, about 'standards', but they ignored her now. Shale's attention was pulled away from that scene. He heard a door of one of the back gardens behind him open and then close. Then there was the sound of running footsteps, a minor sort of sound. He thought two people, both in trainers coming towards him. He did not want to be seen skulking here at the end of the lane or somebody might think a burglar casing the street and dial 999. He crossed the road to the betting shop doorway again. That would be all right. Iles and Harpur were facing the other direction and had almost reached Harpur's front garden.

Shale stood as if reading some notices in the betting shop window and watched a reflection of the end of the lane. Hazel Harpur appeared with the older boy. When they reached the street, they paused and looked down towards the house, part concealing themselves, as Shale had earlier. Iles and Harpur were back inside by now. Hazel and Scott came out into Arthur Street and began to walk away together. They moved quickly, but didn't run now. Perhaps they thought that would be noticeable.

They turned into the main road. Shale followed. When he went around the corner he saw they had reached a bus stop and waited there. He found another doorway and paused. After a few minutes a double decker bus with a Morton Cross destination sign on it pulled in. Hazel and Scott kissed. Scott stepped aboard the bus, glanced at her and gave a wave. Hazel waved, too. The bus moved off. Hazel came back towards Arthur Street. Shale stayed in the doorway, facing the shop. Once the girl had passed he went to get his car, near here, in a side street. He reached it quickly and after a mile on the main road was able to slot in behind the bus.

Manse thought he must have had great luck. It should be possible to get to Scott when he left the bus near his home. Perhaps they could talk in Shale's car. He did not understand what might have happened at Harpur's house. The two had looked as though they wanted to escape, and saw a chance when Harpur and Iles were out examining the cars. Escape what? Why? Did their scour of the street show they knew Scott had got himself into something dangerous? Was the crafty, swift back yard exit a way of dodging questions when the two officers returned? To Shale, that seemed a likely. There could be no question any longer about the boy's involvement in the trade.

The bus stopped not far from Chilton Park and Scott jumped off and began to walk. Shale parked and left the car. The boy walked pretty fast and Shale had to more or less trot to gain on him. He considered calling out, but this might scare the boy. If he disappeared into one of the houses, that would be the collapse of this operation. He wanted to get alongside Scott and say something at once that would make him feel all right, not scared. Of course, Shale realized the boy would possibly recognize him, on account of his prominence in city commerce. That might be all right, or it might frighten Scott more. Manse must play it careful. He thought he would catch up on him and say something like, 'This is a friendly call, believe me. I got to speak to you about your safety. I seen you with that girl,

189

Hazel Harpur, and I know you don't want to upset her by getting hurt or worse. Let's have a discuss, all right?' He would keep his voice very gentle.

And then ahead, and approaching Scott Grant, Shale saw a black VW Polo, at least two men in it, and the two up front recognizable at once from the Clio and the bus station, the same fat-necked one driving, the skinny one in the passenger seat, the same or similar dark suits. Jesus, someone must be as eager as eager to get this boy wiped out if they would try it here in Morton Cross, heavy with police heavies. They must of abandoned Arthur Street and the bus station as no use and decided, after all, that Scott had to come and go from his parents' house and better be done there.

Manse yelled: 'Scott! Scott!' and began to run. The boy turned his head and Shale shouted again: 'The VW.' He pulled his Heckler and Koch from its holster. The boy looked back up the road. The Polo had almost reached him. This was a classy street, big front gardens behind knee-high brick walls. Scott did a dive over one of these and disappeared, like familiar with gun-fight dodges. But the VW was about to pull in. They'd leave the car and find him. Then, though, the skinny one stared along the street and seemed to see Shale, and seemed to see the pistol. Shale stopped and two-handed, feet apart, aimed at the car.

And the sight of him must of truly terrified them. He would look like a professional, like a police marksman. They might of heard of that deadeye, Vic Calinicos, and 'holes are where the heart is'. The VW engine roared and the car raced past Shale. He followed it with the pistol but did not shoot. Then he stood for a few minutes, the gun down at his side and inconspicuous, he hoped. He thought the VW might go round the block and try again when them two got their fucking frail nerves in order again. The

190

Polo seemed to have gone, though. He put the pistol back in the holster and walked to where Scott had rolled over the wall. He still lay there, tucked in hard, his hands over his head, helmeting. He looked up. 'Please,' he said.

'This is a friendly call, believe me,' Shale said. 'I need to speak to you about safety. I seen you with that girl, Hazel Harpur, and I know you don't want to upset her by getting hurt or worse. Let's have a discuss, all right?' He was breathless but kept his voice very gentle.

'Discuss what?'

'They'll come again for you,' Shale said. 'They think you're upsetting their game.'

'What game?'

'You've heard of someone called Adrian Cologne? He'll send more people for you, no question.'

'Cologne?'

'You're working for Tommy the Strong, are you?'

Scott stood. It was a Saturday afternoon and daylight. There'd been nobody around when the VW did its approach and when Shale produced the gun. But now he saw a woman had come from the house at the top of this garden and was standing near french windows. Scott smiled at her and gave the same sort of wave as when he and Hazel parted. 'You know her?' Shale asked.

'My mother. I live here.'

'Listen, Scott, chuck that sort of life,' Shale said.

'Which?'

'Cologne's got you marked.'

'Look, mate, what's it all about?'

'You know what it's about. And don't give me the fucking mate stuff.'

The woman said: 'What is it, Scott?'

'Some crazy muddle,' he said and walked up the garden to the house.

'They'll come for you,' Shale called.

191

'Who is it?' the woman asked. 'What's he saying?'

'He's rather confused, if you know what I mean,' Scott replied.

'Is he the police?' the woman said. 'They're all over the damn place with their antics.'

Chapter Ten

Ralph Ember had terrific ambitions for himself, his family and his club, the Monty in Shield Terrace. Occasionally, though, such as now, some hellish setback would come. And often these setbacks centred on the Monty, as a matter of fact. This fucking murdered crook he found in the club car park at 2 a.m. would definitely rate as a snag, and Ralph had one of his panics, naturally, on first noticing him. But after about twenty minutes, even a bit less, he achieved recovery. He reached it by concentrating on all the strengths and glories of his and his family's position, and their brilliant future. And, once this recovery arrived, Ralph began to plan how he would counter the admittedly considerable drawback of what he'd just come across, and then go on to chase his good objectives again. There had been a previous time when a body was left in the Monty yard for disposal by Ember. Ralph had dealt with that all right. He could do it again.

Avoid, avoid permanent collapse. Avoid, avoid despair. If Ralph had a gospel, this must be it. He wanted that principle to guide his life – all his life, every aspect of it. One of the reasons he hated the *Godfather* films was their message that once somebody went lawless there could be no return to virtue, only a continuing slide into evil. That's what happens to Michael Corleone in the films. But Ralph knew he must resist such a cave-in merely because some sod had dumped this defaced villain here. As a boy he'd often heard his mother brand despair as the unforgivable sin since it denied the Lord's power to save. Although he would not have liked his mother to be present for the discovery of this shot hoodlum on Monty ground, her lesson stuck. All right, Ember did not think much about the Lord these days, but Ember had his own personal reasons for finding despair unforgivable. The end of *Godfather 2* showed Michael Corleone seated alone near a lake and looking worn, hard, beaky and degenerate now after all his terrible brutalities. Brown, fallen leaves blow past him, to signify galloping spiritual decay. But Ember considered that his own looks had, on the contrary, improved with time. That definite resemblance to the young Charlton Heston brought even more idolatrous, excited comments from women than previously, quite a few presentable and very, very up for it, even a woman police officer. He believed that, despite some connection with wickedness, a man – a man such as himself – a man could eventually return to full legality and cleanness. This fucking deado – who put him here? Iles? Shale? That was not the main question, though. How to get rid? Only this really mattered.

As Ralph saw things, once this immediate problem had been handled, he could continue his move into full respect-ability by carefully using the profits of certain criminal episodes in his life to secure recognized worth and great-ness. You bought your way to honesty. This, surely, would chime with church teaching – the making of good from bad, recalling the conversion of Saul of Tarsus. In Ember's opinion, several of the most distinguished, titled families in Britain and abroad had reached their position by this method. Consider the tainted ancestors of many earls and so on in the House of Lords. What was it Lord Kinnock called them – before he could get the robes on and become one himself? Brigands. And remember that record-breaking crook, Joe Kennedy: ambassador, father of JFK, Robert and Edward, and patriarch of an unquestionably top, current US dynasty. Ember despised the formula, box-office moralizing of *Godfather 1* and *2*, and possibly *3*, though he'd never been able to get through that sequel.

Ember would triumph, he and the family. He knew it. Despite this unfortunate fucking blip in the Monty car park now, tonight, the club, under his care, was sure to gain a new, brilliantly worthwhile character. As to the family, his two daughters attended their select private school which seemed reasonably safe, despite the deplorable Chilton Park agitation so close. He regretted – resented – that the school had chucked Latin and Greek, and taught Classical Studies in English now, but knew this to be a general, feeble and disgusting trend. Ember had protested to the head, in vain. At least Michael Corleone in *Godfather* prized his children. Ember would admit this. Then, looking at his own development, Ralph – seeking intellectual challenge – had begun that mature student degree at the local university. For the present, he'd suspended this because of business demands. However, he did mean to resume.

Above all he intended improving the status and membership quality of the Monty. Simply, he wanted to get a renown for it so nobody would even think of dumping a mutilated corpse on club land. It would be too much at variance with the new eminence of the Monty, inappropriate. As well as *Godfather*, Ember also detested those greasy failure tales he'd met on his university foundation course, such as the Icarus legend about a boy who tries to fly, goes too near the sun and falls because of melted wings; and that novel, *The Great Gatsby*, which suggests the so-called 'American dream' of success can only be founded on crookedness: this must be where *Godfather 1* and *2* got their smug pessimism from. Ember thought everyone should, as it were, fly for ever upwards. He thought everyone should have fine dreams. *He* did.

Admittedly, these dreams could sometimes spatter into pieces. Certainly, after this very bad find on the premises – all right, not inside the building itself, but definitely on

195

the premises – yes, after this very bad find on the premises, Ember did begin to fear he would never get his club up to the same distinction as, say, the Athenaeum in London, or even the Garrick or Boodle's. That had always been one of Ember's major aims, and this terrible encounter, solo, in the middle of the night could only be a harsh upset, he would not dispute it – if he allowed it to be. Such an event might in an almost heartbreaking way undo so much of his constant, devoted, fruitful work: through good, constant patrols of the lavatories and odd corners by staff, Ember believed he prevented pretty well all drugs use or dealing in the club; and he could almost always make sure that no violence at all – or, at the worst, only limited, non-knife, non-firearm, quickly squashed violence – yes, he could make sure no violence started in the numerous Monty celebration junkets for acquittals, wakes, long-stretch releases, paroles, christenings, overturned guilty verdicts on Appeal, weddings, bail wins or victorious gang turf battles, however big and spun-out the party.

But then came this bloody sick discovery, this bloody sick situation, which Ember could not possibly have guarded against. Nobody could have. Sometimes – in spite of his mother and his own inner light – he did feel himself dropping towards what he'd admit could only be termed despair and, of course, panic. After shifting this fucking wreck he'd have to burn all the clothes he wore for it, and shoes. It seemed clear to Ralph that this kind of crisis would hardly ever happen, if at all, in major London clubs.

During visits to the capital, Ember had several times been over to get the authentic atmosphere of the Garrick in Garrick Street, the Athenaeum in Pall Mall and Boodle's in St James's Street. It could only be from outside, of course, just to absorb the look of the places, admire the architecture and tall doors, and observe comings and goings. He did not actually belong to any of these London clubs, and the tall doors had doormen. He knew he probably never *would* belong to any of these clubs, nor the Reform or the Carlton or White's. Ember had heard it took six years for a membership application at the Garrick to be processed and anyone wanting to get in had to be recommended by one or more current members. The long waiting list proved that to belong to the Garrick gave what was termed 'social cachet'. He didn't know a member in the Athenaeum, Boodle's or the Garrick, nor the Reform or the Carlton or White's, and he couldn't just approach on the pavement a member coming from one of these clubs and ask him for sponsorship. This would not be the way matters were handled at all. It would seem pushy.

Just the same, he liked the idea of both the Garrick and the street being called after a famed British actor from centuries ago, David Garrick, giving his memory double respect. As a result of this long connection with the theatre, Ember understood that many present Garrick members came from the arts, meaning not just the stage, but literary and media figures, such as Lord Bragg, and the BBC's interviewer, Jeremy Paxman, apparently let in at a second attempt. Ember's club definitely had nobody like this, yet. If Jeremy Paxman applied to the Monty, Ember would undoubtedly try to see he did not get blackballed again. Ember had sent out information about his club to local media and arts people, such as editors at the evening paper, the museum's pictures curator and television executives and presenters, but without take-up. If you had an address like the Athenaeum's – Pall Mall – it would probably put you ahead of a club in Shield Terrace. Not long ago he had seen in one of the papers an announcement about a dinner held at the Athenaeum to celebrate the 'Immortal Memory' of the Scottish poet, Robbie Burns. One of the main guests made a speech in which he 'Addressed the Haggis'. And another proposed a toast to 'The Lassies'. Then a woman replied on behalf of 'The Lassies'. Ember wondered whether he'd ever be able to get something like this going in the Monty. Not many present members would have heard of Robbie Burns. Although Ralph knew where to send for a haggis, he couldn't think of anyone who would agree to talk to it playfully but properly, not even when pissed. And some of the women who came to the Monty would get awkward and foul-mouthed if anyone called them lassies.

The Athenaeum possibly included some people from the arts, like the Garrick, and they obviously knew about Burns, but mainly the Athenaeums was major civil servants, academics, bishops and business leaders. Boodle's, from right back in the eighteenth century, would feature many very upper class names, some titled, on their list, and Ember, pacing back and forth to keep warm opposite the entrance for a couple of hours each time one February, had twice watched members wearing what were obviously first class shoes, off most likely individual lasts, going in and leaving.

So far, nobody with a title belonged to the Monty, but for a long while it had been one of Ember's dearest aims to make the social rating and general quality of membership and facilities equal to those of any top, renowned London establishment. He believed that when this happened he, personally, would move up socially and morally with the club. He, also personally, would reach legality and distinction. He would not sit sad among fucking dead leaves symbolizing his fall, thank you. Somewhere he had come across a line by some thinker or writer: 'Behind every great fortune is a great crime.' Although this sounded something like *The Great Gatsby*'s sermon, Ember thought the quotation slightly different and felt bucked. It gave a fruition promise to crime.

The Monty had a fine mahogany bar and panelling and genuine brass fittings which Ember made sure truly shone always. These fittings said one thing – class. He felt pretty sure there would be plenty of mahogany in the Athenaeum, not Formica. Naturally, people joked about the metal shield fixed to a pillar and protecting Ralph from gunfire: 'Shield Terrace, so get Ralph a shield.' Ember would have bet that none of those London clubs needed such a defensive screen, and he hoped to dispense with the Monty's once he changed its tone. The Monty's membership had no particular flavour as, for instance, the Garrick's did. Ember recognized that the Monty could be said to be more general.

At just after 2 a.m., on one of his usual closing-time inspection rounds, it really troubled him to find this much-shot male – no question, male – this much-shot, dead male near the emergency exit door in the club's car park. It not only troubled him. It brought that tumble into dejection and near-despair and made Ember ask himself whether his ambitions for the club were on track. Occasionally, he did almost fold beneath such doubts. Although the Garrick, Athenaeum and Boodle's might provide private car parks, Ember would give big odds that nobody from any of those clubs – management or membership – had come across a naked, dead pimp there lately: naked or even properly clothed, most probably.

Of course, Ember knew him instantly, despite the absence of Adrian Cologne's customary, vivid, stupidly expensive, loutish clothes, and regardless of the deep damage to his head and face. A club security light shone over the emergency door and gave the body some gleam. Ember considered himself very strong on security and safety – the security and safety of anyone at or around the club, plus his own. Adrian Cologne's security and safety were beyond Ember's care now. But he didn't feel he had failed in his responsibilities because he suspected that Cologne had almost definitely been killed elsewhere, probably shot a few more times from close range after death, stripped, then brought here and left. This would be out of venom, tactics or playfulness.

Despite his concerns for security, Ember could not risk closed circuit television at the Monty, so there'd be no film of Adrian's arrival. It would have anguished some members to know their movements into, and particularly out of, the club had been filmed and timed and dated. They'd regard that as surveillance: this kind of record might provide prosecution evidence or blackmail material. Ember had read about Nixon and those fucking crazy, suicidal White House tapes in the 1970s.

And Ember himself did not want that kind of burdensome, unhelpfully exact data, in case police approached him, say to crack an alibi of some member or members. Ember needed to stay non-involved. He considered discretion an essential habit in a club proprietor, and especially a club proprietor of a club like the Monty, as it currently was, whatever the future. Ember would like to kick out for ever many of his present members – probably nearly all – but while they remained on his books he must give them strong loyalty, which might include silence about their times of arrival and/or departure at/from the Monty. Of course, he realized that he might finish up like Adrian in the car park if he, Ember, did *not* give loyalty and silence, when relevant, which might be often. The nicely collaged shield could look after him in only one spot, and even there someone really skilled and set on doing him – maybe contracted – would probably be able to shoot around it.

This thought had come to him, of course, the night Adrian Cologne turned up at the Monty to suggest a kind of partnership with Ralph. Well, no chance of that now. When Ember looked back to this meeting, he realized how sensitive and respectful Cologne had been: he would not presume to enter the Monty for a business discussion with Ember, because he must have known how Ralph usually forbade any talk of that sort in the club. It had been up to Ember to ignore his own rule and take Cologne to the bar. There was something grimly circular now about this earlier encounter in the Monty yard and tonight this one.

Ember longed to wipe out for ever the very possibility of this kind of dark pattern. That would be accomplished by

lifting the Monty towards a more glittering nature mod-
elled on the Athenaeum's. That was the club he really
admired – full of considerable industrialists, scholars and
administrators. As well as Burns Night, other meetings at
the Athenaeum were often reported in the big London
newspapers, naming the guest speaker and the important
topic discussed, usually politics or economics, especially
the Third World and Scotland. Ember aimed to get the
Monty similar coverage to the Athenaeum's one day.
Because eminent people arranged appearances a long way
ahead he'd already prepared a list of celebrities he'd invite
to give talks: Clinton, obviously; a Nobel prizewinner, such
as the poet Seamus Heaney; Nelson Mandela; Brad Pitt.
Yes, Ember found it was the Athenaeum above all he
wanted as model for the new Monty. The Garrick might be
all right, but bohemian, and you never knew where that
could end up. And he considered the name Boodle's sort of
deliberately unserious, oafish, with flippant rhymes, like
doodle, noodle and caboodle. He wondered whether he
would actually rename the club, 'The New Monty', taking
a lead from 'New Labour'.

Pondering this body, Ember could see very well why
Cologne might have been taken out. Given his line, all
sorts of people would want to target him. Some of his girls
could have parents who objected fiercely to the work he
expected from their daughters. Well, *most* parents would, if
they knew about it, unless on the game themselves, which
could happen, in a dynastic way. Or there were those
pimps from abroad who might see Adrian Cologne as
stealing their method of work – girls as well as the commodities – and decide to finish him, as someone, or more
than one, had finished Tirana. Wars inter-firm would per-
sist, unless a proper understanding with, say, ACC Iles
could be achieved. Adrian Cologne's foul, pricey garments
and slabs of jewellery would cause very rough envy
among immigrant pimps. He wore those farcical cravats
but to some these might have appeared ducal or Left Bank.

Without a cravat, or anything else, now he looked fairly ordinary, except for the injuries.

Almost always when the club shut, Ember did this good, final, all-clear tour himself. That job he would not delegate and often he'd be there after all the staff left. Ember had enemies. Naturally he had enemies. Anybody who made £600,000 a year from drugs wholesaling, plus Monty profits, must stir jealousy, just as in his minor, decorative, sleazy way, Adrian Cologne did. Although Ember wore very conventional, subdued, though fine, made-to-measure suits bought in London, and absolutely no jewellery beyond a fairly ordinary watch, he realized he could not avoid being noticed. The £600,000 might be too damn easy for others to estimate. Some said more. Some said a Big One, a million. Not so, but the idea circulated and ideas could be dangerous. And then the Monty takings in addition. Because of such factors, Ember knew he stood out, with the Heston resemblance additional and liable to rile some.

Ember accepted the risks that came with wealth and systematically did what he could to guard against them, meaning more than just the shield: on his early morning rounds he always looked for incendiary stuff, or people lurking before a break-in, or a booby bomb under his car. Dumping a controversial, abused body on Ralph's territory could be another way of getting at him. Perhaps some rival in the commerce hoped Ember would be tried for the murder, jailed, and in that way pulled out of the substances scene for a decade or so. After all, one of Ember's decades equalled £6 million at the current state of earnings. Ember felt life and trade grew more and more competitive, and were laced with menace, such as shot Adrian, on bollock-naked, small-hours show like this, not far from where properly licensed and insured cars had stood, many this year's top-of-the-range, including four wheel drive jobs.

It puzzled him that Adrian should have been placed so

near the security light, as if meant to be found. Others leaving the club might have seen him, might in fact have seen him delivered there, but few of the Monty's present members would report this sort of thing to Ember or the law, for fear of getting dragged in. They would notice, as Ember did, the nearness to the light and deduce they were intended to have a stare and then pass the word. So, a trap? So, obviously – very fucking obviously – don't fall for it. So, no mention.

Besides, many Monty members had no regard for pusher-pimps – Cologne or any other. Some said pimps hurt the Monty's image, and Ember had to agree with this, though he considered the image very unsatisfactory, anyway, at present, pimps or not. People would feel unanxious about leaving Adrian's corpse on the ground in a car park or anywhere else.

This death perhaps indicated all kinds of shifts in the local commercial scene and made Ember worry that, unless he began transforming the club upwards socially very soon, he might have some of these recently arrived Albanian pimps as well as Brit new wave people applying for Monty membership. Although Ember would never regard himself as at all a Little Englander or racist, he foresaw difficulty if such Alb applications came in. Yes, pimps were looked down on, and foreign pimps would probably be exceptionally unwelcome. The Membership Committee might reject them and this could cause resentment, leading to more brutalities.

Another factor. Another fucking *vital* factor: any corpse on Monty ground would have been a pain to Ember, but in an important way Cologne rated as special, special even among pimps. One of the girls who possibly worked to him now was the black kid called Honorée and mentioned that evening up at Morton Cross by Eva, Delphine, Rita.

The main point about Honorée – and this main point could not be more damn main – the main point was that for quite a time now she ran a business liaison with

Assistant Chief Constable (Operations), Desmond Iles. This had become pretty well known. Some said the relationship amounted to an affair, although, naturally, Honorée saw many other clients as well as Iles. The ACC could be an out-and-out hun, of course, but there was also something democratic about him. A tale that went around not long ago said she gave the Assistant Chief crabs. He stayed with her just the same. To Ember it seemed notable that when Iles was at some official occasion, possibly chatting sweetly and shaking hands with the Lord Lieutenant, the Pope or even the Queen, these busy travelling lice might be getting themselves dug in and comfy under his superior blue uniform trousers. Ember wondered if there could be some sort of parable in this, on whited sepulchre lines.

What perturbed him, though, was the rumour that Honorée now worked for Adrian, and that he had turned savage with her lately, and so invited retaliation, revenge, wipe-out by one of her admirer regulars: i.e. Iles. Pimps often grew savage. A girl might offend somehow. It would be either skimming from customer payments; or refusing certain customers on account of gut, breath, grime, disease or age; or not getting enough customers; or drawing the line at some perv extras. It had to be likely that these days Honorée would turn down approaches she didn't fancy. When you were dealing regularly with an Assistant Chief (Operations), sometimes, apparently, in a hire car on waste ground in the Valencia Esplanade district – well, when a girl had that kind of polished client, she might grow picky.

This could be serious, if, for instance, she declined a friend or friends of Adrian, or distinguished villains he lined up for her, ready to pay big from heavy loot wads. For that kind of hoity-toityness a whore could get ferociously knocked about. Girls were generally beaten with a broomstick on the soles of their feet by the pimp, so as not to disfigure them and reduce drawing power. The girl

204

would be held down on a table by an apprentice pimp, or tied down, with her feet over the edge. The soles of the feet were uncrucial body areas for tarts. They did not have to walk much, just stood and waited and talked bill-of-fare, then generally went in cars.

As he stood near Cologne, Ember naturally felt the Panicking Ralph, or even Panicking Ralphy, symptoms trying to capture him. Adrian dead with bullet wounds on Monty soil, plus – oh, God, yes, *plus* – his possible link to Iles via Honorée, brought bad stress, and as soon as he recognized Cologne, Ember had felt that well-known rectangle of fright-sweat take up station across his shoulders. Also, his legs did not want to try anything reliable for the moment and he leaned against the emergency door doing breathing exercises. He touched his jaw scar again, in case it was weeping something sticky and beigish down his neck and on to his shirt. During that foundation year at university when he started his mature student degree they were asked to read a novel by Anthony Trollope called *Can You Forgive Her?* in which one of the characters – George Something – had a face scar that at stress moments seemed to get very lively and dangerous. Ember had sympathized.

So, one devilish possibility had to be that the body did not, in fact, come to Ember from a business rival looking to get him Botany Bayed, but from one of Honorée's very best and glossiest chums. Adrian, annihilated and fly-tipped here, was the kind of mischievous little trick Iles could pull if Honorée really had been one of Adrian's and the pimp had turned on her. That way he'd qualify for some Iles-type justice. As he would see it, a girl called Honorée deserved to be honoured.

Also, there were deeper considerations, weren't there? How about the hint given by Cologne to Ralph that he intended getting rid of Harpur's daughter's boyfriend Scott Grant, because he'd initiated the Chilton Park shoot-out and might cause more bother. Had Iles decided he'd do something on Harpur's behalf, and the girl's? Iles might be capable of that. In a way, of course, this would be strange. Everyone knew that Iles had an interest in Hazel Harpur. It did not matter that the ACC was married and also visited Honorée from time to time. He liked a roam. God, though, the influence of girls! Iles could have dropped Adrian off knowing that Ember must feel compelled to make him disappear efficiently, fast and in secret because of his mission to get the Monty up to a brilliantly elite rating alongside the Athenaeum. Media publicity featuring a bare, pulped pimp on club land would inevitably knock that fine purpose. So, divert the clear-up task to good old Ralph. Ember could become one of Iles's hellbent Operations.

And Ralph's panic came because he wondered what would happen if he failed to shift Adrian to somewhere that gave no possible traces, and, instead, notified police headquarters about him, as would be the normal drill for most people who found a murdered body. In that case, Iles might do everything he could to fix the death on Ember. Iles's everythings were a lot. You did not become ACC (Operations) without a flair for craft and tireless hunting. Iles would know others might see a motive link from Adrian via Honorée to him, or even via the boy, Scott Grant: Ralph might not be the only one who'd heard that threat.

And/or there could be trade results. At present a very sensible, constructive arrangement still more or less functioned between Iles and Ember and Mansel Shale, in the wholesale drugs enterprise, though several factors had weakened this lately. As long as Ember and Manse kept violence off the streets, Iles did not get difficult about the dealing. He believed there would always be drugs and thought it pointless, absurd, to fight the supply. National policy was gradually catching up on his view. But if Ember failed to cart Adrian off somewhere and immediately, this brilliant alliance with the Assistant Chief might end.

Ember would be persecuted, even charged. Mansel Shale could slip into monopoly, a monopoly of £1,200,000 a year, untaxable. Plainly, Ember must stop this or he would never be able to buy legality, respectability, purity. In *Godfather 1*, Michael Corleone promises that the family will be legitimate in five years. Instead, the slide gets faster. Ember must resist that. Of course, it could be Manse himself who, for some reasons of his own, did Adrian, and then arranged that Ember should have the corpse. There had been that suggested cooperation between Manse and Ember, hadn't there, to look after Scott Grant? Perhaps Manse had done Adrian as his part of the joint venture, and now he bequeathed Ralph the body to do *his* share of the project. Or, of course, Manse might hope Ember would get caught for the killing and put away, leading to that blessed state of Manse monopoly.

Ember bent closer to the corpse, wanting to see whether Adrian clutched a letter in one of his fists, such as, *Get rid of him, Ralph, there's a dear.* This would be the kind of fruity insolence Iles was capable of, wouldn't it? Wouldn't it? They reckoned that, way back, Iles might have seen off two lads found not guilty of killing an undercover cop, a verdict Iles disliked and decided should be adjusted. Ember wouldn't have been surprised to read: *Destroy this note after reading, Ralphy. Do not retain for your archive at Harvard.*

Ember found no message and went back into the deserted club. He took off his suit and put on a pair of dungarees kept in the office cupboard for maintenance tasks. Yes, burn tomorrow. Although some panic fragments remained, he could cope with the change of clothes, his fingers more or less capable on the buttons, and his balance OK for standing one-legged while getting into the dungaree trousers. He knew he would reach normality again in a while. This was why he detested the nickname Panicking Ralph, or much worse, Panicking Ralphy. These spasms did come, yes, but they never lasted, not long enough to justify the slur. As the sweat and the leg weakness and the jaw scar delusions faded, he brought his Saab around without lights on to Adrian and opened the boot. Luckily, it was lined with a big plastic tray. That could go into the incinerator, too. He felt ashamed of incinerating plastic because of the pollution factor. Burning this tray and the clothes would produce considerable smoke, and could be regarded as hypocritical. But normally when he was arguing in print for more cleanliness and care he did not have the sort of sharp problem created by Adrian Cologne.

In the future, as soon as he began to raise the Monty to a more refined category, one of the first club events Ember would discontinue was the kind of après-funeral shindig that took place there today. Yes, he knew the proverb saying nobody should speak ill of the dead, but this did not necessarily mean you had to open your club to Adrian Cologne's relatives, associates, girls and minder-muscle. Ember was amazed that Adrian actually *had* relatives, or, at least, relatives who would want to admit, even demonstrate, they *were* relatives, through attending his funeral and follow-up. All right, all right, possibly people went back to the Athenaeum after the funeral of a member or relative of a member in London, but the member or relative would most likely be some sort of genuine dignitary, known at All Souls College, Oxford, or the Inns of Court, or Whitehall, not a pimp. And if he *was* an Athenaeum pimp it would be for undoubtedly well-dressed girls who could ask really bumper payments on the best West End street corners, such as in Shepherd Market. Also, his relatives would not look how Adrian's relatives looked. Occasionally, Ember wondered whether it was harsh and snobby to make these judgements on some people and their appearance. They could not help their obvious baseness. No, they fucking couldn't. That was the point, wasn't it? One of Cologne's cousins lived locally and had Monty membership, or Ralph would not have felt obliged to let them all into the club post funeral. It might have been the cousin who told Cologne about Morton Cross possibilities and brought him to the city.

Assistant Chief Iles and his sidekick, Detective Chief Superintendent Colin Harpur, turned up late in the afternoon, when things had started to get a bit relaxed. Ember expected their visit. Iles wore uniform, Harpur a kind of suit. Iles loved this type of invasion, and not just for free drinks. Without needing to ask, Ember mixed the ACC a port and lemon – 'the old whore's refresher', as Iles called it – and a gin and cider in a half-pint glass for Harpur. Iles would regularly come into such functions mainly to terrorize – to terrorize Ember, club members and guests. Iles glared about and set a vicious, high-rank shadow over everything. His face said he'd make sure half the people here would be locked up by New Year. Protocol would forbid Iles to attend the actual funeral of rubbish like Adrian, however much he might have longed to chortle there at the wipe-out, but he could come to the Monty knees-up on some pretext.

Ember had heard Honorée also missed the funeral, and she did not appear here now, so his guess at one of the reasons for Adrian's death might be spot on. If she was his and he'd been rough she wouldn't want to join in any service or subsequent send-off. Ember did not have to go to the funeral himself, since Cologne had not been a member. Occasionally, Ralph would attend members' obsequies, especially natural causes deaths, which definitely happened from time to time. If there was a proprietor of the Athenaeum he'd get along to important funerals, suppose, say, Winston Churchill had been a member. But when you'd tried to lose a body in the sea for ever, and it got washed up regardless only a week later and still identifiable, you dodged out of any further unnecessary links.

Iles said in a big, empty voice: 'Ralphy, a sombre interlude.'

'True,' Ember replied. He had to wonder whether Iles blamed him for not making sure Adrian really vanished. But Ember did avoid another breakdown panic. This he regarded as a triumph – a triumph over self, the hardest kind.

'Harpur and I thought we must look in with commiserations,' Iles said.

'Thank you, Mr Iles,' Ember said.

'We know you grieve for folk who go in such coarse circumstances, Ralph,' Iles said.

'Yes,' Ember said. 'These are hard lessons on the uncertainty of life.'

'I'm afraid we're altogether baffled by this one, Ralph,' Iles replied. 'How he got into the sea, why, where he was killed and by whom, and the reasons for what seem to Harpur and me some deliberate bullet mutilations after death, but before coastal rock damage. Our inquiries – a blank. Did he fall from a ship? Was he dropped from a plane?'

He was saying, was he, that, after all, he wouldn't penalize Ember for the poor disposal? Was he? Or he was saying, was he, that Harpur and he genuinely had no ideas on Adrian's death and the trips for the body that followed? Possible? Yes, just about.

'These questions raised by Mr Iles are considerable puzzlers,' Harpur said.

'Indeed so,' Ember replied.

Iles still eyed the grief mob. The bulk of the people here would have despised Adrian, but they wanted to be part of a folk occasion. Ember could see Unhinged Humphrey and some friends behaving quite delicately so far. Although Unhinged was another who would never get membership in The New Monty, of course, Ember experienced a kind of pride in him now. But Iles said: 'Do you think you'll be able to control this bag of slipshod, rampant derelicts once they've got into full drinking pace, Ralph? Might you need some CS knock-out gas or horseback police?'

'They have to sedate their sorrows,' Ember said. 'I can sympathize with that. Adrian was fairly new to the city, yet had become incredibly dear to such a range of acquaintances. They loved his verve and bangles, coupled with an unexpectedly tender streak. He contributed to many charities such as the People's Dispensary for Sick Animals, though without any public fanfare. I gather he'd talk very movingly about the eating of dogs in Formosa.'

Iles said: 'Pardon me, Ralph, I appreciate how much you cherish the Monty, and have grand visions for its new role, but, I must tell you, I don't think I've ever known a place able to attract so many of life's wastrels, old lags and muggers at one time.'

'How are Honorée's feet now, Mr Iles?' Ember replied.

'It was Col who suggested the visit,' Iles said. 'He worries about safety when there's a huge and dubious rabble like this, and liquored up. Harpur *is* a worrier, you know – pedantic about regulations. Fire doors. Sprinklers. All that. I admire him for this rigour – and for much else, oh, indeed, yes. I've told him I, too, see potential trouble, but that Ralph W. Ember probably knows damn well how to run a death drink-up. Harpur still insisted on the call.'

'A formality,' Harpur said.

'Could you show us, for instance, the emergency exit, Ralph?' Iles said. 'This might be important if, say, a fracas occurred later on, followed by a stampede of low life piss artists. Strangely, the lower the low life – and, you'll agree, it couldn't be lower than this lot – the lower the low lives, the more people possessed of those low lives seem keen to hang on to them.'

'Mr Iles always fears fracas,' Harpur said.

'Ralph and Manse Shale have ensured at least until very recently that we don't have fracas on the streets,' Iles replied. 'And one is grateful. One is *very* grateful to you, Ralph. Very.'

'Thank you, Mr Iles,' Ember said.

'That understanding between us must certainly continue,' Iles said. '*Will* certainly continue.'

'Thank you, Mr Iles,' Ember said. So, everything stayed OK, yes? Yes? Could it actually be that Iles knew nothing about the end of Adrian and his arrival in the yard? Would it be soft-headed lunacy to assume for once something good, or at least neutral, in Iles? Perhaps Adrian had *not* run Honorée. Some girls worked solo. Perhaps Iles had not wanted to protect Scott Grant and, through him, Hazel Harpur and Harpur himself.

Ember led them through the crowd to the emergency door. People stood back for Iles, cowering a bit, even though most had already reached a juiced, 'Ta-ta-then-Adrian' state. Ember pushed at the release bar on the emergency door which opened beautifully. Wearing dungarees, he personally oiled the mechanism every fortnight while observing his basic maintenance programme. He must get new ones. The three of them went out into the car park.

'And a fine night light above the doors,' Iles said.

This might be a routine comment about club equipment, or it might be the insignia'd yob boasting he could confidentially pass Ember a bare dead body even in the brightest section of the car park. Did Iles ever go in for routine comments? Was he here to thank him, but also to indicate that Ember would be for ever vulnerable, whatever safeguards he put in place? But this would amount to normality again, thank God. 'The light is to aid members in the wholly unlikely event that my club had to be evacuated,' Ember replied, 'but also to illuminate the car park through all hours of darkness so that no intruders, prowlers, vandals or any other contemptibly lawless elements can use the ground for villainy.'

'Which kind of villainy, Ralph?' Iles said.

'So many shapes to villainy, I fear,' Ember replied.

Iles said: '"Contemptibly lawless elements". They're

always about, aren't they, Ralph, and always we must resist them, and resist again?'

'Indeed,' Ember replied.

'But, no, I shouldn't think they'd have much chance for their outrageous schemes here, these "contemptibly law-less elements",' Iles said.

'Thank you,' Ember said.

Iles and Harpur didn't seem to want to go back into the club but moved towards their car on the other side of the yard. Ember strolled with them. Get rid, get rid, get rid. Harpur drove. Ember waved, then returned to the club. More people had arrived. In a way, he'd admit it was inspiring: community solidarity reached even someone as depraved as Adrian, and the Monty was the natural stage for its display. Ember again felt pride. Perhaps, after all, the Monty had something those London clubs could not equal. It was as if the Monty had taken the role of a church or mosque. It had its faithful.

In the crowd, Ember saw Mansel Shale at a table just under the defence shield with Lowri, one of his proven live-ins. Ember joined them and signalled to the barman to bring over the Kressmann Armagnac bottle and three glasses. Lowri was a nice Welsh piece. Shale would let her move into the rectory with him and settle like a full part-ner, often for up to four weeks. Manse possessed quite a considerate side. Ember had heard people speak very unsarcastically of this. In so many ways, Ember could regard him as a colleague. Ralph poured.

Shale seemed to sense Ember's thought: 'An occasion, regardless, Ralph,' he said. 'The Monty – like a hub. A club but a hub.' He liked this and said it again. 'A club but a hub.'

'Thanks, Manse.'

'He was a whoremaster, wasn't he?' Lowri asked. Ember loved her accent. She gave the 'h' sound in 'whoremaster' a beautiful shake. You could see why male voice choirs from Wales came over so strong. Apparently, one of the great things about Lowri was she really appreciated the Pre-Raphaelite paintings Manse had hanging at his place and could make sane comments about them full of checkable knowledge. That thrilled Shale. Most probably, he thought it showed she must have taste, and therefore wanted to fuck him. The paintings were originals, not prints. They cost. Art collecting did cost, and could be a reason Shale would want and work for monopoly. Apparently, Shale bought some of the paintings from Jack Lamb, a local dealer, so they might not be fakes. Shale had told Ember that 'reference to bed or on the Chinese carpets' Lowri would 'do it always and all ways'. Ember thought it wrong to disclose sexual matters like that, but he could believe it of Lowri. Her eyes seemed very wide apart and tan-coloured, although you could not always tell everything from their eyes.

'Yes, a rough profession, Adrian's,' Shale replied. 'Why I say it's not the death in itself. We all got to admit – except maybe his woman and so on, through loyalty, which is understandable – we all got to admit it's hard to get upset over Adrian as Adrian in what would be known as his personal entity. You know that phrase at all, Ralph, "personal entity"? But as I see it, even a turd like Adrian is still part of the fabric.'

'Which?' Lowri asked.

'Which what?' Shale said.

'Which fabric?' Lowri said.

'Oh, yes, the fabric,' Shale said. 'Part of that. As we all are, like willy-nilly. And yet, the methodology.'

'Methodology of what, Manse?' Lowri asked.

'The bullets. The stripping. The sea burial,' Shale said. 'The *try* at sea burial. There's a methodology in it.'

'This is such a mystery, yes,' Ember replied.

'A mystery,' Shale said. 'That sod might of gone after a young kid and killed him, you know, Ralph.'

'That right?'

'Not at all helpful.'

'True.'

'I like the committing to the deep,' Shale replied.

'But not deep *enough*,' Lowri said.

Ember could see why Shale might get fed up with her after four weeks. A while ago, Shale had taken the trouble to explain to Ember that the four weeks maximum had nothing to do with her cycle. 'Ralph, I don't even ask where she is in her monthlies when I invite her. God, that would be such an insult, not just to Lowri or any of the others, but to womankind, like all they was for was shagging. It's just that four weeks seems as much as I want to cohabit these days with Lowri. It can vary with others. Where I live used to be a rectory, as you know, Ralph, and I feel I got to show it some respect. More than a certain duration with girls there would get some guilt going in me. In any case, Lowri's cycle is not so important because, as mentioned, she likes it all ways. This is a plus, as well as her genuine fondness for art. Did I see you with Mr Iles and Harpur?'

'They said a mystery,' Ember said.

'How?' Shale said.

'How what?' Ember replied.

'How did they say it?' Shale said.

'In what sense, Manse?' Ember said. 'An "m" first, then going through to the "y".'

'Like, what's known as tone or sometimes timbre. Did you believe it?' Shale said;

'What?'

'Did you believe it when they said a mystery?'

'Well, it *is* a mystery, isn't it?' Ember said.

'But did you believe it when *they* said it was a mystery for *them*? Iles can do the irony side. He's teasing sometimes, looking for disclosures. You familiar with irony, Ralph? It's around often.'

'And then before he was in the sea where was he?' Ember replied.

'This is part of the mystery,' Shale said.

215

'And where killed? What happened to his clothes?' Ember said.

'These are major questions,' Shale said.

'Clothes will burn,' Lowri said.

'Well, I suppose that's right,' Ember said.

'He hears things,' Shale said.

'Who?' Ember said.

'Harpur,' Shale said. 'He stands there and Iles talks, but Harpur hears things.'

'What sort of things?' Ember said.

'The background,' Shale said. 'Which one of them said it?'

'What?' Ember asked.

'That it was a mystery,' Shale said.

'Iles,' Ember said.

'Harpur don't tell him everything,' Shale said. 'That's police in the top jobs.'

'What kind of thing?' Ember said.

'The methodology,' Shale replied. 'Into the yard?'

'They wanted to see the exit door,' Ember said.

'Ah.'

'What's that mean, Manse?' Lowri asked.

'What?' Shale replied.

'In case of overcrowding,' Ember said.

'Ah,' Shale said.

'They were glad to note there was a light out there,' Ember said.

'There's a light out there, is there?' Shale said.

'Well, there would be, wouldn't there, for convenience?' Lowri said.

'I'm fussy about that kind of thing,' Ember said.

'I suppose Iles strutted about under it like he was Shirley Bassey. But that got to be to your credit, Ralph,' Shale said. 'That kind of care is why the Monty got its role as what might be called "a focal point" of the community – I don't know if you heard that term before, Ralph, "focal point". You can be proud of it.'

'A responsibility,' Ember said.

'Well, it is, it is,' Shale said. 'You're like a kind of flag troops clustered around in battle and rallied. Troops used to do that if they got a flag. They rallied – even if the flag was tattered because of the shelling.'

This recalled Ember's no man's land picture of himself and he liked the new version of that, except for 'tattered'. Someone with skin like Shale's should not make round-about comments. 'I'd be upset if anything besmirched what I see as the Monty's symbolic quality,' Ember said.

'What sort of thing *could* besmirch it?' Lowri asked.

'I can understand your feelings on that, Ralph,' Shale replied. 'A symbol can say so much, as long as it's . . . well, symbolic.'

When Ember went over to see Adrian's family and so on near the pool tables, he gave some true commiseration in a carefully gentle voice, and he hoped they could hear it, what with all the sup-up bellowing and coin-slot, hulla-baloo music. He would never let on in the smallest amount even that he considered Adrian horse shit, and thought most of those connected with him looked like sweepings. He could see that some of the women in this crew spotted his Charlton Heston aspect, but he did not want anything like that tonight with this kind, some oldish and more than oldish, one most likely Adrian's mother. Ralph spoke with unbroken tenderness and told the barman to serve the group free with anything they wanted, including cham-pagne, non-vintage. Although this could lead to untidy vomiting later and possibly fights, he felt that as host he must provide this gesture. It was what he meant when he spoke to Shale about responsibility.

Chapter Eleven

In the car, Iles said: 'That fucker, Ralphy, thinks I did Adrian.'

Harpur felt he did not want to take on this kind of conversation. One of the things about Iles was he sometimes refused to leave difficult topics understood but not discussed. He could slide into surplus bluntness. He loved confrontation. Harpur said: 'Ember was always one for ideas. He writes those letters to the Press on environmental subjects – Ralph W. Ember. Did you trace the Clio and the two men in it back to Adrian Cologne and assume their job was to hunt Hazel as a route to hunting Scott? This would be large-minded of you, sir, though by no means untypical. You could have decided not to bother about Cologne, leaving Scott in continuing danger of slaughter.'

'And then, Honorée's feet,' Iles replied.

'Yes, he did refer to those, in a caring way.'

'He thinks a pimp-style sole beating?' Iles said.

'Probably.'

'And assumes this set me off? The avenger?'

'Like that, yes.'

'What about you, Col?'

'What?'

'You agree with him?'

'In which direction, sir?'

'Adrian. The death etcetera.'

'It's a puzzler.' Harpur would believe anything of Iles, apart from taking backhanders. Most other people who

218

knew him to any depth would believe almost anything of Iles. 'I don't suppose you'd like it if Cologne conscripted her and then turned cruel.'

'No.'

'*Are* her feet bad?'

'A lovely kid, Honorée,' Iles replied.

'These days I can't work out which girl is with which overlord,' Harpur replied. 'And it's not just me. The Vice people lose track. Kaleidoscopic tart scene. We get these infusions.'

'Yes, infusions,' Iles said.

'East Europe, plus further.'

'True. And yet I'm still with Honorée, more or less as constant, Harpur.'

'It's an impressive relationship, sir.'

'This is a girl who must operate on her own, despite everything. I mean the syndicates.'

'Remarkable.'

'You'll ask why a girl with so much character picks this kind of life.'

'No, I don't think I'd ask that, sir. A few bad decisions, a few bad bits of luck, can dig a pit for anyone.'

'You're exceptionally humane, Col.'

'Thank you, sir.'

'Except, of course, Harpur, when messing up someone else's marriage by –'

'I had to wonder when you said you wanted to see the emergency exit door,' Harpur replied.

'Wonder what?'

'About the whole picture,' Harpur said.

'Which picture?'

'Adrian. The death etcetera.'

'I didn't say *I* wanted to see the emergency door. I said *you* wanted to see it because you were keen on all the Health and Safety regs – to your undoubted credit as an officer.'

'I know you said I wanted to see it and that it was to my

credit as an officer, but I'd never said I wanted to see it, so I thought you must want to see it for some special reason but didn't want to let on to Ember that you wanted to see it because if you said you wanted to see it it could be a give-away somehow.'

'Wonder what?' Iles replied.

'In which regard, sir?'

'You said mention of the emergency door made you wonder.'

'I'd had a whisper about the emergency door. This would be pre your request to see it.' There had been another meeting at 3 with Jack Lamb, this time wearing an RAF tunic, the single wing of an air gunner on show. Jack knew a lot of people who used the Monty.

'What whisper?' Iles said.

'This whisper concerned a body out there one night, just folded over underneath the light. You mentioned the light.'

'Who whispered that?'

'A source,' Harpur said.

'Well, yes, I thought it would be a source, didn't I? If you get a whisper the whisper has to come from a whisperer. That whisperer would in these circumstances be a fucking source, wouldn't he/she?'

'Right,' Harpur replied.

'What kind of body?'

'Dead. Naked. Male. About Adrian's age.'

'Somebody saw a dead, naked male body and said nothing to us about it, for God's sake?'

'They don't, do they, sir?'

'Who?'

'We're not dealing with your usual citizenry.'

'Whom *are* we dealing with, Col?'

'People who go to Ralphy Ember's place. This is not the Athenaeum. The culture is different. And, of course, it's untrue they said nothing about it. They did say something to someone who passed it on again.'

'Passed it on to whom?' Iles replied.

'My source who –'

'But *you* didn't pass this on to *me*.'

'You know how it is with stuff from sources, sir.'

'What?'

'Sensitive – how it's got to be handled.'

'*You* handle it by keeping quiet about it,' Iles said.

'Up to this point.'

'Because you thought I might have put Adrian there? What about the source and the source's source?'

'What, sir?' Harpur replied.

'Did *they* say they thought it must be me who put him there?'

'I wondered if Honorée had been abused somehow. Or whether you'd had thoughts about Scott and the need to look after him for us. This would be magnificently selfless of you, sir.'

'And did your source and the source's source wonder if Honorée had been abused?' Iles replied. 'Is everyone in this city talking about my love life? I'm an Assistant Chief Constable, for God's sake. I'd like some fucking deference.' Usually, when Iles said 'Assistant' in 'Assistant Chief Constable' he lingered on the 's' sounds to make the word seem footling and contemptible: *only* an Assistant because of the slimy, sinister, sick, sadistic system scheming specifically against him. But now he spoke clipped and made the whole title resonate with status. 'Oh, you'll say, if I wanted deference I shouldn't be hooked up with a hooker. But that's narrowness, Col. That's offensively negative, Harpur.'

'The point is, even if she had been working alone, someone like Adrian might have got at her,' Harpur replied. 'Or *because* she worked alone. This is competition. This could be seen as defiance. Adrian might hate freelancers. She's a very lovely girl.'

221

'Thanks, Col. She'll appreciate that. I'm going to mention you to her as someone quite worthwhile. I might have already.'

'Her attractiveness would in fact make Adrian even more determined to run and profit from her. She can charge big, a face and body like that and no implants.'

'How do you know, Harpur?'

'What?'

'No implants.'

'You think there might be?' Harpur replied.

'Your certainty on this – where does it come from?'

'I've met her once or twice, if you recall.'

'Oh?'

'You were present, sir,' Harpur said. 'And, implants – one can spot them, usually.'

'You being a detective,' Iles said. 'This is certainly a girl who doesn't need to be cheap.'

'I don't think you'd go to anyone like that, sir.'

'Thanks, Harpur. And yet if I was short of funds suddenly, I think she'd take me free.'

'This is a fine woman, sir.'

'Or at a damn good discount.'

'A proof of real feelings, sir.'

'That's what I need, Col.'

'What?'

'Someone with real feelings for me.'

'We all want that, sir.'

'I've met people who find it difficult.'

'What?'

'To have real feelings for me. I don't mean villains, which is to be expected. But others.'

'Which sort, sir?'

'Yes, she's really rare, Harpur,' Iles replied.

'Maybe Adrian would want a slice of her earnings. It's what I meant about competition. He'd be up against a lot of that – the East European camp. Incidentally, we think an overseas girl was in the BMW with Tirana when he

222

died. Francis is trying to trace her. She seems to have left the city.'

'Honorée – someday *she* might leave the city. My God, Col, where am I then?'

'I thought that if Adrian Cologne had been harsh with her you're not the sort to ignore it. You'd act on her behalf. Chivalric. Yes, I see you as chivalric. Likewise possibly over Scott, even though you stupidly fancy your elderly chances with Hazel and might have been almost glad to see him gone. If you'd been born in a different century, I think you'd probably be a stone effigy in a cathedral now, helmet, breastplate, sword, commemorating some grand deeds.'

'Which?'

'Which what?'

'Which cathedral? Not some fucking backwater place with a pissed organist?'

'And, in your calculating way, you'd know Ember would have to cope with the disposal. He'd do it because of his damn magnificent and idiotic ideas for the club. We all love Ralph, obviously, but as I said the Monty's not the Athenaeum – meaning the Monty has a way to go yet.'

'"Magnificent" is, indeed, the right word for Ralph W. Ember. And "idiotic".'

'I thought you were really gentle with him, despite the feet inquiry.'

'Why not be gentle?' Iles asked.

'Of course, Ember or Manse Shale might have known Cologne menaced Scott Grant and one of them, or even both, could have done Adrian. He/they would hope I'd guess he/they had and feel so grateful I'd give them a bit of quid pro quoism.'

'Would they really, after so much time, fucking well imagine you had any power, Harpur?'

They drove a while. Then Harpur said: 'It would be an audacious thing to dump the body under the light, and later insist on going back to the spot with Ralphy, to let him see there's a pleasant bond between the two of you. I could associate that sort of dauntlessness with you, sir. This was what set me wondering.'

'Thanks, Harpur. So, you still think I did him, regardless of the theory about Shale or Ralphy?'

Harpur couldn't tell whether Iles wanted him to believe it or not. The chivalry reference and general fawning rigmarole would have got to him, as Harpur had known it would, and mention of the possible grand self-denial and generosity if he'd saved Scott for Hazel. Harpur drew up at Iles's house, Idylls. 'I won't come in, sir.'

'Wise, Col. Sarah finds you and the memory of you and her rather comical these days.'

'That so?'

'Oh, yes. I'd hate to see someone wearing such a suit hurt by a woman's uncontrollable laughter.'

'Thank you, sir. These various developments are obviously going to change the girl scene overall, aren't they?' Harpur replied.

'In what respect, Col?'

'Well, you can hardly carry on farcically stalking and bothering Hazel if you've done something so noble for her.'

'If.'

'Nobility is natural to you.'

'Some would agree with that,' Iles said.

'Many.'

'Name them.'

'Oh, yes, many,' Harpur replied.

C